LANDER RIDGE

DIANE J. REED

Bandits Ranch Books

Copyright © 2019 by Diane J. Reed

All rights reserved.

No part of this book may be reproduced in any form or by any electronic or mechanical means, including information storage and retrieval systems, without written permission from the author, except for the use of brief quotations in a book review.

Cover design by Najla Qamber at Najla Qamber Designs, www.najlaqamberdesigns.com

I

Nicky Box stood in a flimsy, floral dress on the edge of a cliff overlooking the sunrise on the French Riviera, freezing her butt off.

She was used to it.

Only crazy people, like those in the fashion industry, booked modeling shoots for summer resort wear at daybreak in March, when the temperature could dip below thirty-five degrees. The brisk wind spun Nicky's long, black hair into knots and chilled her to the bone. It didn't help matters that she hadn't eaten solid food in two weeks in preparation for the shoot, surviving on protein shakes while putting herself through grueling workouts to keep her BMI below eighteen, like most top models. Goosebumps fanned her entire frame, and she resisted the urge to huddle her arms against her waist to keep warm. As Nicky gazed out over the Mediterranean Sea, she wondered if they'd photoshop out the slightly blue hue that had begun to surface on her skin. Nevertheless, she lifted her chin and forced her lips to stop trembling long enough to curl into a serene smile, as though she were a high-society woman about to indulge in the vacation of everyone's dreams. Nicky's large brown eyes, sensuous lips, and smooth caramel skin were the stuff of magazine legend—and dozens of lucrative fashion campaigns that had skyrocketed her to modeling stardom.

"Exquisite! You're stunning, darling!" cooed the photographer, angling his camera to capture her extraordinary features against the infinite blue sky above Cannes. "Throw that nose up in the air, baby! Everyone wants you and can *never* have you!"

That's for damn sure, Nicky thought, trying not to shiver while appearing unflappably pleasant. *No one can have me because I'm not real…*

Nicky knew that in a matter of weeks, the photo editors of *Trend & Style Magazine* would reduce her chilly morning in Cannes to a two-dimensional layout of paper images designed to make millions of readers go mad with desire for the unobtainable—

Because it didn't exist.

She didn't exist.

It was all a glossy mirage designed to sell luxury items.

Nicky never came from an aristocratic family that jet-setted around the world in private airplanes. She was a poor orphan from Colorado who happened to have exceptional bone structure and a five-foot, ten-inch frame that designers loved to hang their threads on. And who now made a living playing everyone but herself.

As Nicky stepped away from the cliff toward the palatial

estate that the magazine had rented for the photo shoot, she turned to give the photographer various smiles and pouts from her repertoire. Out of the corner of her eye, she caught a glimpse of the small fleet of assistants who huddled in thick parkas beside portable lights, envying their warmth as they tapped their toes to the latest Eurodance song blaring from a nearby boombox. When the melody died down, Nicky overheard the hair stylist talking to the fashion director.

"Is this model Latinx, Middle Eastern, or African American? I need to prepare the girl's hair who's going to pose with her in the next series of shots. Do you want stick straight, wavy, or a maybe a cute afro with bows? I think they're supposed to look like mother and daughter."

"Nicky's what's known in the industry as generically ethnic," the fashion director replied with a knowing smile. "That's why she's a superstar—she can be anything. People project onto her whatever they want. That chick is pure gold."

Nicky winced at their words. With the right hair and makeup, she could even look Caribbean or Tibetan. She had every identity and no identity. Yet the irony remained that although most of her bookings came from American fashion magazines, no one had ever asked her to be who she really was.

Ute.

Born into a Southwestern tribe of the first Americans.

At twenty-three-years old, Nicky had been climbing the ranks of the fashion industry ever since she was discovered at eighteen, right after graduating from the Wilson Ranch for Wayward Boys and Girls in Bandits Hollow, Colorado. All alone in the world with no parents to guide her, she had to be tough to hack it in the modeling industry, like she'd learned at the infamous Wilson Ranch, where "incorrigible" orphans who'd been in trouble with the law were treated like prison inmates. For Nicky, modeling had been her ticket out.

As well as her fast track to everywhere—and nowhere—at the same time. Though she posed in the world's finest clothes and her face appeared alongside scores of glamorous products, she'd been virtually homeless for five solid years, surfing international hotels for one modeling gig after another, while no one knew the real Nicky Box at all.

It didn't make good copy that her parents had died in a tragic carbon monoxide poisoning accident in their home when she was fifteen, and afterwards she'd become a chronic delinquent in the foster system due to her anger. Rage didn't sell pretty magazines, nor did the abuse she suffered after she was sent to the Wilson Ranch that had marked her soul with scars and left her heart tangled in a labyrinth of self-doubt. It had seemed easier at eighteen to run away from Colorado and play other people with sleeker lives than to try and fix what had become broken inside her. But now, in the frigid French Riviera air, doing her umpteenth photo shoot designed to make people she didn't know salivate for clothes she would never wear, Nicky wondered if pretending to be a soulless mannequin was really the long-term answer.

After all, if you don't have your soul, what's left?

Nicky glanced at the little girl who sat under a heavy blanket on a nearby bench beside her mother, waiting for her turn to be photographed. She recognized the girl's glassy stare.

She didn't want to be here in the freezing cold, either.

"Come on, sweetie!" called the fashion director to the little girl. "It's your turn for photos!"

As the girl stood up from the bench, wearing exactly the same outfit as Nicky, her hands clenched into fists to stop her trembling from the crisp wind. She scampered over to the hair stylist, who quickly brushed her dark hair stick straight like Nicky's, then gave her a soft shove to head for the photographer.

"Hi," Nicky said warmly as the girl approached. She kneeled down and deliberately looked her in the eye so the girl wouldn't feel invisible. "I'm Nicky. What's your name?"

"Genevieve," the girl replied, teeth chattering.

"What a lovely name. Where are you from, Genevieve?" Nicky asked kindly.

"I-I'm from Cincinnati."

"Wow, all the way from Ohio?" Nicky said. "That's quite a distance—you must be a very popular model. I'm from Colorado, by the way. Are you cold, sweetie? Here, let me wrap an arm around you till the photographer tells us what to do."

Nicky stood to her feet and embraced her, blocking the direction of the wind, while Genevieve smiled and snuggled against her waist. She noticed a turquoise pendant that hung by a slim piece of leather around Nicky's neck. "That's pretty," Genevieve remarked, pointing at the deep-blue stone.

Nicky's face flushed that her secret pendant had slipped out. She always wore it beneath her high fashion outfits as a small reminder of who she really was. The pendant had been given to her when she was ten by her Ute grandmother, Tavachi. She'd told her the stone was Lander

Blue, the most precious turquoise in the world—rarer than diamonds. Only a hundred pounds had ever been discovered back in the early 1970s, with a deep-blue color that rivaled the sky and a spidery black matrix. "I'm giving this to you so you'll always remember how much I love you and how precious you are," her grandmother had declared, clutching her close in a warm, soft embrace. Little did Nicky know that within a few short years, her grandmother would pass away of natural causes, and she would never see her parents again.

"Thank you," Nicky replied to Genevieve, gazing at the pendant. "This was my grandmother's. She gave it to me as an heirloom. She told me everything has spirit, and this stone would guide me."

"Guide you?" Genevieve asked, cinching her arms tighter around Nicky's waist to offset the cold.

Nicky held up the pendant so Genevieve could see it better. "My people call this stone *sakwakar*. In our view of the world, it represents the middle of the earth, between water and sky. The sacred center where all the colors pull together to make this vibrant, living blue. It's where the wolf reigns."

Genevieve touched the stone shyly, snapping back her fingers as if it must be powerful. "The wolf?"

"The guardian of our children and families." Nicky's lips curved into a smile while she tucked the turquoise pendant beneath her dress again so no one could see. "You know how grandmas are—she told me someday I'd meet a wolf who'd be my guardian, too. I think she was hinting at boyfriends."

Genevieve giggled, covering her mouth. She was only about nine or ten, the same age Nicky had been when she'd received the pendant, and the thought of boyfriends made her blush.

"What do you mean by *your* people?" Genevieve asked.

Nicky cringed for a moment. When she was little, and her parents had taken her from their home in Bandits Hollow to the Ute reservation for the annual spring Bear Dance, they used to laugh at members of the tribe who didn't know the right dance steps, calling them exactly what she'd become now: Paper Indians. People who were so caught up in their cell phones and material culture that they didn't have a clue about the old ways, and you'd never guess they had Native American heritage. They were simply Indians on paper. Nicky turned and gazed with longing at a mountain range far off in the distance. She pointed to the jagged peaks covered in snow.

"My people are from the Shining Mountains. Like the Southern Alps over there, only in the Rockies of Colorado," she said. "They're Ute, the Mountain People." She hoisted Genevieve up in her arms so she could see the peaks and cuddled her close. "Let's dance for a minute to keep warm, okay?" She swayed her hips to the Eurodance beat from the boombox. "Hopefully, the photographer will get his act together soon."

"Genevieve! What on earth are you doing?" shrieked her mother from the nearby bench. She threw off her blanket and stood up, then stormed over to Nicky and her daughter. "Dancing around in a thousand-dollar summer dress from Prada is *not* anyone's idea of professionalism! You're supposed to look posh," she insisted, ripping Genevieve out of Nicky's arms. She set the girl on the ground and swiftly pressed out the wrinkles on her dress with her hands. "Remember," she hissed, wagging a finger in Genevieve's face, "you're not a special snowflake. This is work, young lady, for which we are handsomely paid. There are dozens of girls they can get for a shoot like this, so you'd better be the best."

"Pardon me, Madame," said the photographer in a clipped tone that sounded accustomed to dismissing stage-mother types. He brushed the woman aside and told her to go back to the bench, then stood in front of Nicky and Genevieve. "Our next series of shots is beside that tree along the cliff. I want you to look like you're telling your daughter a story. You know, like an old fairy tale—something full of wonder and magic."

Nicky nodded and glared at Genevieve's overbearing mother on the bench to keep her distance, then took the girl by the hand and walked over to the pine tree growing out of a rock near the cliff. It was ancient and gnarled, and it reminded Nicky of the trees her grandmother used to tell her about near Pikes Peak. Long before the reservation era, her people used to make pilgrimages to *Tava*, their name for the peak and the most sacred of all mountains where the sunrise always strikes first. Along the way, they sculpted special trees they'd chosen, returning each year to bend and twist the trunks and branches into various shapes by tying them with yucca ropes. It took generations to contour the trees into definable forms, each one selected for a sacred purpose: medicine, ceremonies, legends— even prophecies. Nicky ran her hand along a deep vertical line that had cut into the old pine tree, recognizing its source.

"Once upon a time," she said to Genevieve in a soothing fairy-tale tone, noticing that the girl seemed a bit rattled after her mother's outburst, "my people used to send their prayers into their sacred trees. See this scar?"

Genevieve nodded at the long line in the bark.

"That means this tree was struck by lightning," Nicky told her. "It shows it has a very strong spirit because it survived. Such trees are considered special." She glanced over at Genevieve's mother, who was leaning forward on the bench with her fists clenched, as if ready at any second to give her daughter a pounding. Nicky rolled her eyes and cupped the little girl's cheeks. "You're special too, Genevieve," she whispered protectively. "And strong. Strong as this tree and brave enough to be who you really are."

Nicky reached over to stroke the rough bark on a branch as tenderly as if it were her grandmother's arm. "My grandma told me these old trees will always listen to you. No trouble is too great—you can leave your hopes and dreams with them, and they'll be carried from the tops of their branches by the wind to the Creator." She brushed the girl's hair from her eyes. "Forever after, that tree will be your friend—like the *sakwakar* stone. Whenever I've had a bad time in my life," she said, recalling the Wilson Ranch for Wayward Boys and Girls, "I prayed at a sacred old tree near my school. And sometimes," she lowered her voice and leaned in close to Genevieve, "I even heard the tree's spirit whisper to me. Its soft voice on the breeze told me I was strong. A warrior who could get through anything, no matter how hard times were. And one day, it promised, I would find home. My *real* home."

Genevieve shot a glance at her mother's disgruntled face like the woman was her prison guard. "Did you?" she asked with a hint of desperation in her voice, leaning her ear against the tree to see if she could hear it. "Did you ever find your *real* home? I mean, not where everyone tells you where to go or who to be." She turned her face from her mother as though accustomed to preventing her from reading her lips. "But where you really *belong?*"

Shivers traveled up Nicky's spine—and not from the cold wind this time.

Swallowing hard, she mustered the courage to tell Genevieve the truth. "Not yet," Nicky admitted, gazing at the glitzy French Riviera coastline with its shimmering casinos, bars, and discotheques that always made her feel more foreign and alone. "But the tree gave me the faith that someday I will."

At that moment, they heard an owl call overhead, a long series of hoots that echoed through the air as though the owl were greeting the sunrise. Nicky thought it was odd not to be a songbird or some rooster at that early hour, when she saw a dark, wide-winged silhouette pass ominously over the tree. But when she looked up, she couldn't spy the owl anywhere, and she startled when the photographer asked for more poses. She'd been so caught up in talking to Genevieve that she'd forgotten all about the man clicking his camera.

"Great storytelling shots, ladies!" enthused the photographer, taking advantage of the lapse in their conversation. "But we need to change gears with a few different poses now."

"Can I climb the tree, please?" Genevieve begged with a sparkle in her eye. She cast a cautious glance at her mother as if such behavior might be against the law—with dire consequences.

Nicky shifted her gaze to the woman on the bench a few yards away, looking like she was ready to spring.

"Oh, what the hell," Nicky smiled, giving the photographer a wink. "You're a little girl, for crying out loud—you should be allowed to play. We'll be quick about it, okay?"

Nicky gave Genevieve a lift and helped her scamper up the tree branches, then reached up and hung on a branch herself, dangling her legs. The two of them giggled like school girls as Nicky swung her feet back and forth, while the photographer snapped pictures with a huge grin on his face.

"Brilliant!" cried the photographer, clicking like mad while Genevieve shimmied down to the branch where Nicky was and dangled her legs as well. "So fresh and original! The editor-in-chief is going to love these photos!"

"How dare you!" shouted Genevieve's mother, her cheeks swelling to an angry red, despite the cold. She bolted from the bench and ignored the fashion assistants who barked at her to stay back. "Oh my God, do you see that rip?" she said as soon as she reached Genevieve, pointing to a tear on her daughter's dress. "We can't possibly pay for this!" She glared at Nicky and jammed her finger into her chest. "This is all your fault. You let her climb the tree, so you'd better reimburse the designer in full for that dress, or I promise I'll sue!"

Nicky sighed and dropped from the branch to her feet. Clenching her fist, it took everything she had not to bloody the woman's nose, like she'd learned to do with expert precision to the mean girls at the Wilson Ranch. Drawing a deep breath, she silently counted to ten to resist the urge to deck her that would surely end in a lawsuit.

"Believe me," Nicky enunciated in a measured tone, "I am more than happy to pay for that dress so your daughter can be allowed to be a little girl for a change. To be free to be who she really is."

The woman's mouth dropped as though she'd been slapped.

"What are you saying?" she demanded. "That I'm a bad mother? We have bills to pay, Miss High-and-Mighty Top Model. Unlike you." To Nicky's surprise, the woman gave her a push, baiting for a fight.

"Mommy, watch out!" Genevieve yelped. She leaped down from the branch, but it was no use. Nicky had already stumbled back from the force of the woman's shove, her high heels twisting on the rocky terrain. Struggling to regain her balance, she reached forward to grab a large boulder, when the stones began to slide beneath her feet. Gripping the boulder with all her might, Nicky's fingers started to slip, and she felt the sharp pain on her chest as her body fell on the loose gravel and skittered toward the cliff's abrupt edge.

Genevieve's mother gasped when she realized what was happening. She quickly dropped to her knees and grabbed for Nicky's elbow, only to feel Nicky's arm slide through her hands—

All at once, Nicky found herself hurtling into the early morning air, caught in the great expanse of blue sky above the Mediterranean Sea. Suspended in a wide limbo of blue…

And as her body descended toward the churning ocean waves below, all Nicky could hear was the sound of everyone's screams.

2

A shock of water enveloped Nicky's body, oddly warmer than the cliffside air, giving her a peculiar relief from the chill. Nevertheless, she panicked and swam with all her strength toward the wavy rays of light that sliced through the water's surface. But she was in the ocean far too deep to come close. Kicking her legs desperately to reach air, she soon spied her turquoise pendant a few feet above her.

Dammit, Nicky thought, paddling furiously, if I'm going to drown, I might as well have my grandma's pendant while I sink to my watery grave.

Just as she managed to defy the odds and break through to the surface, she stretched her hand out toward the stone. The moment she barely touched it with her fingers, she heard the call of that strange owl again. Suddenly, a man appeared in a deep swath of blue before her. He was tall and Native American with long black hair, like hers, wearing a dark coat and deerskin pants with old-fashioned boots. For the life of her, Nicky couldn't tell if the blue that surrounded him was the sea or the sky. Or if she was even still alive…

Yet she recognized that man.

Everyone from Bandits Hollow knew about Iron Feather, a famous part-Apache, part-Ute outlaw who robbed trains and stagecoaches in the nineteenth century in order to help his people return home. Over the years, he'd secretly smuggled dozens of Native American children from their captivity in government-run, Indian Boarding Schools, where they'd been stripped of their languages and identities. Then he escorted them on clandestine pathways back to their families on reservations.

Mysteriously, Iron Feather now held Nicky's turquoise pendant in his palms in a protective stance, as if guarding it for safekeeping. He began to sing a song in a language she didn't understand. When he was finished, his obsidian eyes arrested hers.

"Take care of the children, *pia-muguan*," he said, invoking a familiar Ute term of endearment that her grandmother had once used. Yet the gravity behind his tone made his urging no mere suggestion. It was more like a commission—

His dark eyes bored into hers.

"Take care of the children and the trees. They are your family now. Your home—*káni*," he insisted in Ute.

Iron Feather held up the turquoise pendant.

"The wolf will help you. As your grandmother promised."

Iron Feather's image began to slowly dissolve into the deep blue. Confused, Nicky reached for him, but his form became as watery as the waves.

"Be careful, *pia-muguan*." She heard his voice like it was

echoing down a long tunnel. "The wolf's heart is as dark as it is light. But you are strong. Strong enough for him."

Iron Feather paused. All Nicky could see in at that moment was the thin outline of his form. His rolling voice washed over her and faded into the water.

"You are strong enough for his love."

Nicky blinked several times—but he was gone. Gradually, she thought she detected a rhythmic drumming in the distance. As it grew closer, it sounded like the choppy noise of a motor boat approaching. The ocean waves began to swell and grow erratic. They rocked her body back and forth with such force that the momentum tossed her over.

Then Nicky blacked out.

3

"Tavinika Box?" A man announced in a sharp tone. He added a cough to make sure Nicky was awake.

Nicky's eyes fluttered open.

She hadn't heard that name in over a decade—

Her *real* name.

Only her grandmother and her parents had ever called her Tavinika, which meant "sunshine" in Ute. Nicky glanced around at the pale, sterile walls of her hospital room, suddenly remembering where she was.

Denver, Colorado.

She'd woken up in a French emergency room a couple of days prior, her skin scraped all to hell down her arms and legs from the cliff fall, but luckily nothing was broken. Shortly thereafter, she lobbied to be cleared to fly back to the states. Her doctors reluctantly agreed, but only if she immediately transferred to an American hospital to remain under observation for a few days, since she'd passed out in the water before the rescue boat had reached her.

Nicky stared at the portly man before her in a navy suit with a round face and equally round glasses. When she spied his briefcase, it confirmed her hunch that he hadn't exactly dropped by during visiting hours for social reasons.

"Are you Tavinika Box?" he pressed.

"Y-Yes," answered Nicky, still surprised to hear that name from his lips. "How do you know my…tribal name?"

"It's my job," he answered flatly. "I'm a private investigator."

Nicky's pulse raced as the man reached into his suit pocket for a business card and tossed it onto the bed. She'd already done her time in the juvenile corrections system for pickpocketing years ago. Why would some private investigator want to catch up with her now?

"I'm Walter Booth," he explained. "I was hired by the Wilson Ranch School Board to find you."

"The Wilson Ranch?" Nicky repeated in shock, drawing her bed sheets up to her chin. Damn—it had been years since her shadow had darkened that godforsaken place, yet the mere mention of it could still get to her.

"What does the school want from *me*?" she asked. "Please don't tell me it's a donation, because they're not getting a goddamn cent. I hate that place."

"Really?" Walter sniffed. "Because it's yours."

"What?" Nicky said, aghast.

"You heard me." Walter sat down on a chair beside the bed and pulled a few documents from his briefcase. "Your grandfather was recently diagnosed with the early stages of dementia. The school charter specifically states that, should he ever experience ill health that incapacitates his ability to manage the school's affairs, his next of kin must take over full directorship of the school."

Walter handed Nicky an official-looking document. At the top of the page on a management flow chart were the words *Thorne Wilson* as the director of the school. Beneath his name as his next of kin was Nicky's mother, designated as *daughter*, with the word *deceased* and the date of her passing below. Underneath her mother's name were the words *Tavinika Box, granddaughter*.

Nicky sucked air as her fingers began to shake. She suddenly felt as though she'd been sucker punched in the gut, and her stomach lurched like she might throw up. She dropped the document onto the bed as if it were on fire.

"G-Granddaughter?" she gasped. "Of Thorne Wilson, the embodiment of Satan? This has to be some kind of joke—"

Walter merely blinked.

"Indeed, you are legally Thorne Wilson's granddaughter. One of the richest cattle ranchers in the West, and the new director of the Wilson Ranch for Wayward Boys and Girls. County records show you're the product of a former liaison between Tavachi Cloud and Thorne Wilson. By all accounts from elderly residents in Bandits Hollow, your grandmother eventually dumped Thorne Wilson after she became pregnant because he was, well—"

"An asshole? A completely evil man who loves to hurt kids in the name of discipline and only opened that horrible school for a tax write off? I have *his* blood in my veins?"

"I'm afraid so," Walter confirmed. "And given that Thorne

Wilson is no longer deemed mentally competent to run the school, that job now goes to you. Please sign here, Ms. Box."

Walter held out a pen.

"To hell I will!" Nicky exclaimed. "Why would I *ever* take on that wretched excuse for a school?"

"Unless you have pulmonary edema from your near-drowning incident, as the doctors originally feared, and you happen to die here, Ms. Box, you *are* legally responsible for making all future decisions for the school."

"Great!" Nicky snapped, seizing his pen. She signed her name as the new director on the bottom line and handed the pen and paper back to him. "Now tell them to burn it the ground."

"I can do as you wish," Walter said in a crisp tone, neatly filing the document back into his briefcase. "But where will the children go? They have no other homes, Ms. Box. As you recall, they're all orphans."

A chill scurried down Nicky's neck. "W-What about the foster system?" she spit out, in spite of the knot that tightened in her throat. She knew damn well from her own experience how flawed the system really was. The chances of finding good homes were a crapshoot, and the atmosphere in juvenile hall was far worse. Walter sighed while Nicky stubbornly stared at her bed sheets. She could practically hear his eye roll.

"Ms. Box, I'm fully aware of Thorne Wilson's heinous reputation," Walter conceded. "And that the only reason he contracted with the state to open the school decades ago was for beneficial tax purposes. With his powerful political connections, the school was beyond scrutiny, though Child

Protective Services certainly tried their best. But you and I both know that the foster system is hardly the answer."

He held up a sheet detailing the names and addresses of all the foster homes she'd been kicked out of. Walter's eyes regarded hers with no-nonsense clarity. "I have a hunch you were relieved each time you acted out so badly that they moved you to the next place."

Tears moistened the edges of Nicky's eyes at those painful memories.

Crap, she thought. As a private investigator, Walter had sure done his homework—and he'd nailed it.

Nicky swallowed hard, studying her bedsheets again. After five long years of climbing to the top of the fashion world, she hadn't gotten a single phone call or get well card from anyone in the industry. The nasty scrapes on her arms and legs made her unbookable for several months, and as far as she knew, everyone had already forgotten her. The only person who'd sent her a crayon-written note was Genevieve, the little girl she'd modeled with on the French Riviera. It was tucked inside an envelope from their mutual agent, along with a bill for the two ruined Prada dresses. Genevieve's note had said, "Hope you feel better soon. I'll never forget the tree."

The tree…

Nicky glanced up at Walter Booth. There was a particular sacred tree on a ridge at the Wilson Ranch that she always went to when she was in pain. She swore its quiet, ancient strength had helped her persevere.

Its whispers had bolstered her soul…

That tree was the only friend she'd had in the whole world, and the reason Nicky felt she'd survived.

Nicky thought about the school, and the teens there who surely feel as lost as she once did. What if she *did* take on the directorship of the school? What if this was a unique opportunity to become the tree of strength for those kids—and to make a difference in their lives?

"By the way, you don't have to know anything about education to run the school," Walter said, as if he'd read her thoughts. "Unlike your grandfather, you can change things and hire the best minds in Colorado to consult with you on what's right for the students. These children have nowhere else to go, Ms. Box. With the school's endowment, you could initiate a whole new era of—"

"Hope?" Nicky finished his sentence.

Moisture swelled in her eyes again. Oh, what she would have given to have genuine hope back in those days. Despite attempting to will her emotions back, a tear slipped down her cheek.

Nicky gazed around her empty hospital room, at the lack of flowers and cards. At the lack of a *life*—

She knew in that moment that modeling held nothing for her anymore. All at once, Iron Feather's words came back to her:

Take care of the children and the trees. They are your family now. Your home—káni.

Goosebumps spread over her skin, but they weren't from fear. They were from the adrenaline of wondering how she could possibly meet this type of challenge.

Maybe I can do this, she thought, mulling over Walter's advice to hire top education professionals.

Maybe I can really do this—

Nicky's eyes met Walter's.

"There's a cabin beside the school that was used by a prior ranch foreman," Walter informed her. "The documents stipulate that future school directors are allowed to live there. And there's a small stipend—"

"I don't want a dime from Thorne Wilson," Nicky hissed, cutting him off. "If I run this school, it's going to be in spite of him, not because of him. And I'm going to give those kids the best damn education money can buy. Whatever relationship my grandma had with that man, I know for a fact she lived the rest of her days with her people and never accepted a cent from him, because she hardly lived in the lap of luxury." Nicky glared at Walter. "And it's in Tavachi Cloud's brave spirit that I will totally revamp that school, so it becomes a place where children are loved and told every single day that they are precious."

Nicky clutched the place on her chest where her grandmother's turquoise pendant used to hang, deeply feeling its loss to the Mediterranean Sea. But she knew nothing could ever take away her grandmother's words that had filled her heart.

Nicky folded her arms. "Mr. Booth, please inform the Wilson Ranch School Board to have the director's quarters made ready for habitation in exactly one week," she insisted with a new-found authority she didn't know she had. "Because they're about to get a new school director. And believe me, *everything* is going to change."

4

Lander Iron Feather stood with a spyglass propped against a window, surveying the Rocky Mountain landscape like a military general preparing for his next conquest. He was in the infamous Owl's Nest, perched atop the main mansion at the Iron Feather Brothers Ranch, a large glass conservatory with a 360-degree view that overlooked the vast land holdings he shared with his brothers Dillon and Barrett. Here, Lander specialized in forging the kinds of deals that inevitably landed him in *The Wall Street Journal* and *Fortune Magazine*. Though still in his twenties, he was already renowned for being one of the most cutthroat ranchers in the West.

And the craziest—

No one would have ever guessed he could bank millions in stud fees for taking a chance on an obscure Thoroughbred stallion that the racing world had overlooked, which had produced winner after winner over the last several years. Or that he would uncover large gold deposits on a remote section of the ranch, which he removed using state-of-the-art, environmental mining techniques. Or that the prices of his USDA prime beef, supreme-grade alfalfa, and extraordinary collection of American art would skyrocket within a few short years, making the entire world stand up and take notice that Lander Iron Feather was a financial genius. His brilliant business strategies were legendary, and his rivals couldn't help wondering if he also possessed the secret to entrepreneurial voodoo.

Lander was possessed all right—

With an obsession for ruthless competition.

Every moment he lived and breathed beyond his graduation from the Wilson Ranch for Wayward Boys and Girls five years ago, he'd been plotting to ruin the owner Thorne Wilson by running him into the ground. As next-door neighbors, their massive ranches were separated by thin barbed wires, and the two of them were constantly neck and neck in a battle to be the top ranchers in the West.

Lander wasn't about to stop until he'd wiped the name of Thorne Wilson from the face of the earth.

This was the same man who'd thought nothing of abusing Lander and his brothers at his so-called school, all so he could receive a generous tax write off. The hours Lander had spent in solitary confinement as a teen for acting out after his parents passed away in a car crash lingered inside him like a dark tattoo on his soul. He and his brothers had endured cruel taunts, severe belt thrashes, even bullwhippings from staff. Yet with every lash and wound, Lander vowed he'd shut down the school by bankrupting Thorne Wilson, if it's the last thing he ever did.

Dressed in torn jeans, scuffed cowboy boots, and a dusty shirt from cutting cattle that morning, Lander brushed back his long blonde hair that fell past his broad, work-toughened shoulders and squinted at the spyglass, ignoring the small group of businessmen seated nearby at a boardroom table. The men were deliberating over an offer they were about to make on Lander's prize Thoroughbred stallion, Danáskés. While they talked, Lander examined the miles of fences that surrounded the ranch for signs of breaks in the barbed wire. Cattle rustling had become a huge problem lately, and Lander had lost ten head over the last two months—the equivalent of thirty-thousand dollars—to thieves who'd probably rebranded his livestock and shuttled them to quick-sale barns in nearby states.

If there's one thing Lander hated most, it was to *ever* lose.

Not even his security cameras had caught the thieves in action, and now Lander was prepared to patrol the whole damn ranch at midnight himself, carrying his favorite rifle astride his stallion Danáskés.

"Excuse me, Mr. Iron Feather?" said a man in a custom-made suit at the boardroom table, interrupting Lander's vigil. "I believe we have a lucrative offer for your stallion that's going to make you quite happy—and even richer."

"Spit it out," Lander replied, adjusting the lens of his spyglass. "I'm listening."

The man twisted his hands nervously beneath the table where Lander couldn't see. Everyone in the business world knew Lander was so off-the-charts brilliant that he never bothered to wear a suit while making multi-million dollar deals, because he couldn't care less what other people thought of him. Nor did he ever trouble himself to sit at a table. Lander called all the shots, and business people were given precisely fifteen-minutes to make their offers, at which point he turned from his window and either accepted their terms or sent them packing—sometimes using his fists to make a point, depending on his mood.

Crazy went with Lander Iron Feather territory.

Lander trained his spyglass on another spot at the window, checking out a high ridge that came between his and Thorne Wilson's property. It was his favorite place on the ranch with a spectacular view of the Rockies, an area his brothers had nicknamed "Lander Ridge" due to his habit of spending the night there in a tipi whenever he had big deals to consider. Rumors circulated that he chanted and consulted with spirits before making any major business decisions, which didn't exactly soften his eccentric reputation. All at once, Lander detected subtle movement on the ridge. He fiddled with the focus of his spyglass.

There, on the ridge beneath a grove of pine trees, he spied a beautiful woman walking alone in the shadows.

A strange tingling arose in Lander's palm and began to work up his arm.

Lander shook his head, surprised.

Just to be sure, he dipped his hand into his jeans pocket and rolled two smooth wolf bones, one colored dark and one bleached white, between his fingers.

They were small, cylindrical bones fashioned from the forearm of a wolf that his ancestor Iron Feather had left his descendants in a faded, turquoise-colored pouch—the ones Lander consulted before business deals. The old bones came from the legendary hand game, or *náyu-kwa-pu*—an ancient form of Native American gambling that taught their youth how to be intuitive and to take risks, using traditions that predated recorded history. Those who were able to guess which color bones their opponents held, using what some called psychic hunches, always won the hand game. Whenever Lander wanted to know if a business risk was worthwhile, he did extensive research and then spent time in isolation in his tipi on the ridge to ask the bones. If he experienced a tingling up his hand and arm when he touched the bones, it meant he would win. But a peculiar icy feeling on his fingertips meant he would lose.

Why was he feeling that warm tingling now?

Lander had already consulted the bones regarding the businessmen in the Owl's Nest, and he was prepared to give them his answer shortly.

Could the tingling sensation mean he would win against the cattle rustlers, too?

Lander returned his gaze to the spyglass.

The woman walking on the ridge was exceptionally tall with shiny black hair that fell to her waist, a lot like his mother who'd been full-blood Apache. She approached a barbed-wire fence and paused before glancing left and right, as if to gauge whether anyone might be watching. Then she dipped down to her hands and knees and began to crawl beneath the thin fence that separated his property from Thorne Wilson's. Sinking to her stomach, she wriggled underneath the sharp prongs using her elbows for momentum. When she managed not to get hooked by the metal barbs and reached the other side, she stood to her feet and smiled like a clever snake.

"Well I'll be damned," Lander muttered. "Who the hell would have the guts to sneak onto my property to rustle cattle in broad daylight? And of all things, it's a woman." He raised his spyglass to see if he could catch a glimpse of a stock trailer beyond the trees, but there was none in sight. "I'll bet she parked a quarter of a mile down the hill on Lost Lake Road. Our cattle are so tame, she could probably herd them there with a stick."

"Want me to lasso her, boss?" offered one of Lander's ranch hands who stood dutifully beside the door of the Owl's Nest like a bouncer. "I can hold her till your brother Barrett comes and makes an arrest."

Lander thought about it for a moment, envisioning the satisfaction of watching his police officer brother snag the intruder, then put her in handcuffs and escort her to his cruiser. At that moment, a shaft of sunlight broke through the trees, caressing the woman's high cheekbones, full lips, and smooth skin with a warm, soft glow. She was standing with her arms folded on the ridge, staring at an old, gnarled ponderosa.

Lander's breath caught in his throat—

Though dressed in a simple khaki shirt and jeans, the woman was without a doubt the most gorgeous creature he'd ever seen. Tall, slim, and elegantly proportioned as though her refined features had been designed by an artist, she had an intense dignity to her gaze that conveyed she was on some kind of mission. Lander was blown away by her fierce beauty, and given his frequent appearances in tabloids with scores of glamorous women that the media claimed he wooed, that was saying a *lot*.

Strangely, the tingling sensation skittered up his arm again.

As well as a few other places Lander didn't expect to pay attention to in that moment. He'd certainly met beautiful women before who made such sensations threaten to take over all rational thought, but he could already tell this woman was different—

Something about her extraordinary face, sharpened by her air of conviction and come-hell-or-high-water focus, threatened to take over a man's…

Soul.

Lander could have sworn the tingling spread straight to his heart—where it burned with a fire against his will, as though he were in jeopardy of getting swept up in this woman's determination, too. Confused, he removed the spyglass from the window and rubbed his eyes, issuing a short cough to try to collect himself.

"No need to wrangle the trespasser," Lander finally replied to his ranch hand. "With all the cattle left to cut this afternoon, you've got enough on your plate. Leave it to me—I'll deal with her myself."

"I *bet* you will," the ranch hand retorted, craning his neck to glance at the ridge. "Why is it I get the feeling your cattle rustler is a looker? Watch out—she might be a wild one."

"Let's hope." Lander's usual smirk stretched into his familiar megawatt smile, the one that always broke hearts and made him famous in the press. Nevertheless, he felt unnerved by those tingling sensations that refused to stop nagging him.

"Uh, Mr. Iron Feather?" broke in one of the businessmen

who sat at the boardroom table. "We'd like an answer for our offer on your stallion."

Lander whipped around, startled that the men were still there.

"Then what the hell's your offer?" he demanded, annoyed. "If you're going to deal—deal! You have exactly thirty seconds to propose your terms, or we're through. I've got work to do."

The businessman stood to his feet, proudly holding up a document with newly-inked signatures. "We, The Dallas Flat Racing Conglomerate, composed of top industry leaders and financiers throughout Texas," he gestured with a smile at the other men at the table, "are offering you the sum of ten-million dollars for your stallion registered as New Moon, also known in the Ute language as Danáskés."

Lander leveled a gaze at the man, feeling the old wolf bones in his pocket suddenly turn cold. He slapped his palms down, making the entire table shake. "Let me make sure I completely understand you," he clarified in a low voice, leaning forward. His dark brown eyes seared into the man like a predator. "You're willing to part with *ten-million dollars* for the only living Thoroughbred that's sired the most international winners since the legendary Man o' War?"

The man fidgeted a little. He glanced at the other men, who gave him nods of approval. "Yes," he beamed with pride. "We can have the money wired to your account by this afternoon."

Without warning, Lander yanked a concealed pistol from his belt under his shirt and fired at the man standing at the other end of the table. The bullet grazed the stray hair at his temple and made the window behind him explode into shards of glass. Instantly, the other businessmen ducked for cover, while the man standing remained stock still, his fingers trembling violently on the document.

Lander's ranch hand rolled his eyes and sighed—

Yet another day of work for Lander Iron Feather.

"Want me to place a call to the Bandits Hollow Mercantile again for more glass?" the ranch hand asked in a weary tone.

Lander nodded slowly. "Have them send the bill to the Dallas Flat Racing Conglomerate."

He glared at the businessman across from him, who still managed to stand on his feet, though his body was shaking wildly. "Get the hell off my land," Lander growled from the bottom of his throat. "If you had any sense at all, you would have offered *twice* that amount." He motioned for his ranch hand to open the Owl's Nest door. "Now you and your fandangled conglomerate get gone from my ranch in a real hurry. Or believe me, my next shot will hit its mark."

5

Lander knew every hill and valley on the Iron Feather Brothers Ranch like the back of his hand. He expertly rode Danáskés downwind through a thick forest to avoid detection, having covered his horse's hooves with buckskin in the old Apache way so they wouldn't make a sound. As a descendent of the notorious outlaw and tracker Iron Feather, such strategies were in his blood. When he and Danáskés closed in on the ridge, Lander steered his stallion to a high knoll hidden in the woods where he could quietly check on the woman's activity. Since the time he'd left the Owl's Nest, she'd meandered a quarter of a mile from the fence line to another old tree.

One that Lander knew well—

It was a sacred tree, originally formed hundreds of years ago by fusing two saplings together with yucca rope. Over time, generations of Utes had carefully curled a couple of the branches around the giant fused trunk like loving arms.

The two trees had become one, locked in an eternal embrace...

When Lander was a boy, his father had told him this was a prophecy tree, and he showed his son the old ligature marks from the yucca ropes. Lander's father was half Ute and half white, and though he was as blonde as Lander, he often described the traditions his own father had taught him whenever they went hunting. Most of the sacred trees they'd found pointed to game trails or fresh creeks with their carefully angled branches, creating a natural map for the Utes' annual pilgrimages to Pikes Peak. But this time, Lander and his father had stumbled across a more unusual tree—

One that told a story not of long ago, but of things yet to come.

Lander's father tapped a large burl at chest height on the prophecy tree, then patted his own heart. "This burl," he said, "was initiated during a ceremony when my father's people buried something inside, now only known by the heart of the tree. When you touch the burl, you touch the tree's heart."

Ever since then, this old tree had always been Lander's favorite, because it reminded him of his parents' guidance and love. Whenever he fell into despair at the Wilson Ranch, years after Thorne Wilson had acquired the parcel that he and his father used to hunt on, Lander gained comfort by laying his hand on the burl and remembering his childhood. There, he allowed his pain to empty into the tree's core, where his father promised the tree would take on his sorrow and deliver his hopes to the Creator. Lander couldn't quite explain it, but he always felt stronger near the tree, and he swore its ancient presence whispered to him that he had the courage to endure.

Now, the land belonged to Lander, scooped up in a secret deal after Thorne Wilson had sold it to a lumber company. At the time, Lander had paid double the market value, claiming he was simply expanding his pasture land. But deep inside he knew the truth—

He was saving the sacred trees on the ridge.

From his distance on the knoll, Lander watched in silence as the woman stepped closer to the tree that held so many memories for him. She paused for a moment and closed her eyes, tilting her head slightly with her ear up as though listening carefully to the breeze. Then her eyes fluttered open and she reached out a hand, taking another step to touch the burl on the nearly four-hundred-year-old pine, as indicated by the smoothness of the grain on its rich, red bark.

"Thataway, honey," Lander whispered, his lips creasing into a smile. "Just a few more steps, and you're all *mine*."

Lander leaned forward in his saddle, eagerly waiting for the inevitable.

Like clockwork, as soon as the woman took another stride, she was instantly snared by a giant net that had been camouflaged under a layer of pine needles and dirt. Within seconds, the net hoisted her six feet in air, where she dangled from the old ponderosa by a high branch.

Her scream echoed across the ridge like a wild animal.

Lander cued his stallion to bolt from the knoll, dashing down to the tree in a full-blown gallop. When he brought Danáskés to a sliding stop, he dismounted and dropped the reins for his horse to ground tie. Stepping forward, he stood before the woman and folded his arms.

"Well I must say," he gloated, admiring the effectiveness of his trap, "you've got to be the prettiest goddamned rustler I've ever seen."

"What? I'm not a rustler!" The woman wriggled fiercely, only to drive her hands and feet further through the net's thick, nylon mesh at awkward angles. "Get me out of here!" she demanded at a high pitch.

Lander rocked back on his heels and laughed.

He didn't lift a finger.

"This isn't funny!" She squirmed in protest, her face plastered against the mesh that smushed her features and made the nylon cords press painfully into her cheeks.

In spite of the odd indentations to her skin, she was still breathtakingly beautiful, with her bee-stung lips, huge brown eyes, and long curtain of black hair that dangled through the gaps in the mesh. Lander studied the ground for a moment, his jaw slicing back and forth. He was trying not to betray how mind-bogglingly attractive she was, despite the fact that she had one foot stuck over her head and an arm pinned awkwardly beneath her perfectly shaped butt, making her resemble a jigsaw puzzle that had been shaken into a bag.

"It sure is a damn shame I have to notify my brother to arrest you," Lander taunted after regaining his usual, arrogant air. He dug into his pocket and held up a cell phone. "You seem far too lovely to be a criminal. But then, I guess that's the most effective kind." He snapped her picture for good measure, only making her madder. "I'm forwarding this photo to the police department so they'll come and arrest you faster. You'd be amazed at how the sight of a pretty woman can motivate law men."

"Arrest me? Why would anyone arrest *me*?" she challenged,

trying to arrange her long limbs into more comfortable positions, which only forced them into worse angles.

Lander made no effort to hide his smirk. "Well, despite how fetching you are—pardon the pun, since you're *fetched* inside my net—I don't take kindly to people trespassing on my property in order to steal my prize cattle."

"What are you—crazy?" she hissed, balling her hands into fists. No matter how hard she punched at the net, it simply gripped her tighter.

"You'd hardly be the first to say that," Lander replied. He stepped tantalizingly close to the net and traced his finger along a thick nylon cord until it brushed against her pillowy lips. The woman's eyes widened in surprise. Without warning, Lander leaned forward and seized her for a kiss. His lips worked over hers, long and slow, as though he had all the time in the world to relish this rare delicacy. All the while, he kept a steady hand on the net so her writhing wouldn't make it swing back and forth. Ignoring her furious, muffled protests, he smiled like a bandit when he broke away.

"One thing's for certain—I *am* crazy enough to steal a kiss from a beautiful woman. When the chance strikes, of course."

"That was totally uncalled for!" she screeched. "*You're* the one breaking any decent sense of propriety here. First, you illegally nab me in a net, and then take advantage of me like an opportunistic asshole—"

"Opportunistic asshole…"

Lander tapped his chin, pleased with the moniker.

"I've been called a hell of lot of things in my day—womanizer, reckless gambler, egomaniac. But I don't believe anyone's ever pegged me quite so…*accurately*…Miss—"

"Box. Nicky Box. And I'm *not* a cattle rustler. I have absolutely no intention of messing with your stupid herd. Besides, this isn't your property anyway. I'll have you know I went to the Wilson Ranch for Wayward Boys and Girls five years ago, and I know every inch of these grounds. It belongs to Thorne Wilson. Now get me down from here immediately!"

"Wait," Lander's eyes narrowed. "You *went* to the Wilson Ranch?"

The woman released a heavy breath as though trying to dispel a difficult memory. "Unfortunately, it's true. I used to come to this ridge all the time when I was a teen to visit the trees. My family's Ute, and I guess you could say this tree gave me solace."

"Then you must have skedaddled the second you graduated," Lander pointed out, estimating her age as close to his own. "Or you'd know I bought this parcel the instant it became available." He shot a glance at the grove of old ponderosas on the ridge. "My fence line now splits that stand of trees in half."

"You *own* this property?" Nicky said, taken aback. "Wow, I-I guess that makes us neighbors."

"What do you mean *neighbors*, if you're just visiting the trees you remembered from school? I'm surprised Thorne Wilson hasn't pumped buckshot into your butt for trespassing by now. He's not exactly known to be civil—"

"Because I told you, I'm *not* trespassing!" she huffed. "I was checking out the ridge for a legitimate project I'm setting up with the forest service and the school to catalog the old trees so they can be preserved. I never expected to see a new barbed-wire fence here. Besides, you haven't even bothered to tell me who *you* are—"

"Iron Feather," he cut in. "Lander Iron Feather."

Nicky's eyes stretched to twice their usual size. She rolled over awkwardly in the net to get a better look at him. "Y-You're one of the Iron Feather brothers?" She scanned Lander up and down as though startled he owned anything at all, much less property next to Thorne Wilson's ranch.

Lander tilted his head, amused. "You look surprised. Were you expecting me to be incarcerated by now, like everyone else at the Wilson Ranch?" He gave her a wink. "The boy voted most likely to do federal time."

Nicky blushed—that's *exactly* what she'd been thinking. And Lander's rugged, rebel good looks, with his rock-hard body in torn jeans and a faded shirt and his mountain-man long hair that framed his rough-cut features only cemented that impression. "Uh, well, it's just that everybody called you and your brothers the biggest badasses ever to go to that school," she backpedaled quickly. "I had no idea one day you might, um—"

"Own one of the biggest ranches in Colorado?" Lander sniffed. "Too bad they never allowed the boys' section and the girls' section to fraternize back then." He stepped closer to her face again, making her tremble slightly when she felt his warm breath against her cheek. "I certainly would have remembered *you*, Nicky Box."

Flustered, Nicky attempted to pull away, but it was no use —her motion only made the net bump her face even more seductively close to his. "N-Now that we're on a first name basis," she stammered a little, unable to deny his drool-worthy, chiseled features that put the dandified male models she used to work with to shame, "and it's pretty obvious I don't intend to steal your cattle, can you finally get me down from here?"

Lander licked his lips, allowing them to curl into a wolfish smile.

It was one of *those* smiles—the kind that sends sparks up and down a woman's body, lingering in places they didn't belong where they spread and took on a life of their own. It was the smile of man who knows exactly what he wants and fully intends to take it—regardless if she was dangling precariously from a tree limb.

"I'll let you down," Lander whispered, "when you give me another kiss."

Despite his low volume, it wasn't a request—it was a demand.

Anger darkened Nicky's eyes, and she pulled her face away, gritting her teeth. "If my hands were any freer," she promised, pawing at the net, "I would have slapped you by now."

"I'd like that," Lander replied, bemused. "Here," he pressed his cheek against the nylon mesh. "Give it a shot."

Fuming, Nicky batted at him, swinging both her hands, only to get her fingers snarled in the nylon cords. Breathless, she sank dejectedly into the net. "Seriously? You're going to be a total lech and expect another kiss from me?"

"Let's see, opportunistic asshole and total lech…you just keep nailing the bull's eye, don't you, Nicky?" Lander looped his thumbs into his jeans pockets, appearing more pleased with her predicament by the second.

Seething, Nicky couldn't help noticing how he looked even more impossibly handsome with that infernal smirk on his face. Taller than her with wide, ranch-toned shoulders and a muscled physique that filled out his jeans and shirt far too well for any woman's blood pressure, Lander was as hot as hell—heavy emphasis on *hell*. This man is the devil incarnate, she thought, fighting the butterflies that flitted in her stomach. Obviously, he's been sent by some dark force to torment me...

But it was the way Lander's eyes smoldered as he absorbed her face that left Nicky really unsettled. If she didn't know better, she'd swear he was...

Smitten.

And already laying plans for what he'd like to do to her body—

Because he certainly appeared entitled to another kiss.

Not in a self-satisfied, possessive way, like all of the other alpha-billionaire types who'd courted her in glamorous international cities, only to behave as if she were their property. Yet another trophy to show off at sparkling events to pad their egos.

No, the penetrating way Lander gazed at her said he wanted to taste every inch of her, body and soul. Plumb to her depths to see what mysteries might lie hidden there...

And then do it again and again, until he'd discovered all of her secrets and laid them bare.

The fire in Lander's eyes caused every vulnerable place on Nicky's body to hum and throb, making her wince.

"You may not be a cattle rustler," Lander contended in a low tone as the heat of his gaze lingered on her skin, making her more uncomfortable by the second. "But if I didn't give you permission to be here, and neither did Thorne Wilson, you're *still* trespassing."

Despite his intense focus, he pulled out his cell phone and texted a quick message, which Nicky prayed was to halt the police from arriving to make an arrest. Then to her surprise, Lander gently lifted a strand of tangled hair from her face, slowly skimming her smooth forehead with the heat of his fingertips. He paused to relish her silky lock in his palm as though it were something precious. Gently, he tucked the strand behind Nicky's ear and spooled his finger along her ear's inner folds, back and forth with a languid rhythm, his warm, moist breath delicately caressing her skin until he felt her quiver. Then he pressed his calloused hand to rest on her cheek, softly cupping her face and running his gaze hungrily down her curves as though he fully intended one day to embrace her body—and a whole lot more. For the life of her, Nicky couldn't fight the sensation that his palm felt like…

Home.

Nicky had been around plenty of sexy continental men, all of whom now seemed like bungling fools compared to Lander Iron Feather. Never in her life had she felt like a man had magically slipped under her skin with such a simple gesture, making her feel like she'd somehow been stripped naked down to her very soul while she wasn't looking. Tingling sensations seeped between her thighs, rippling past her navel until her nipples rushed forward and pressed against her shirt, eager against her better judgement for more of Lander's touch. Nicky squeezed her eyes shut, overwhelmed by her body's reaction, yet unable to deny the way Lander's raw male closeness and complex scent was a downright heady combination. He smelled like fresh hay in the afternoon sun and vintage leather, mixed with a touch of whiskey and…

Desire.

Nicky opened her eyes, reeling, and she caught another peek at his jaw-droppingly handsome face and rugged physique. All at once, crazy thoughts swirled through her brain, imagining how it might feel to have wild sex with this hot stranger inside a net suspended from a tree. Aghast, she shook her head, trying to regain her focus on the topic at hand. Gulping a quick a breath, she cleared her throat.

"Y-You're right," she confessed, struggling to respond to Lander's accusation of trespassing, "Thorne Wilson *doesn't* know I'm here. And he probably wouldn't remember me even if he did."

Nicky glanced away from Lander and pointed toward Thorne Wilson's big white mansion on a hill about a half a mile from the fence line. "That's because he's living on the top floor of his house with round-the-clock caretakers. He's in the early stages of dementia, and his staff don't want him to get hurt. I'm his granddaughter, by the way. And the new director of the school, since he can't run it anymore."

"You're…Thorne Wilson's…granddaughter?"

Lander blinked several times in disbelief. He leaned forward and took his time to scrutinize her face, trying to find any resemblance to the man whatsoever. He shook his head, appearing to come up short. "As in, you're actually *related* to him?"

"Yep," Nicky replied, a bit unnerved by his reaction, and still hardly able to believe it herself.

A cold hardness began to suffuse Lander's gaze, the polar opposite of his attention earlier. His eyes narrowed on Nicky as though she'd become Satan personified.

Nicky studied his face, shocked by the change in expression. Every muscle in Lander's body flexed tight, like a trap ready to spring.

Without another word, Lander turned on his heels and marched over to his horse, where he untied and grabbed a rifle from the back of his saddle. When he returned, he set the rifle butt on the ground and pulled out a large hunting knife with an obsidian blade from a leather sheath on his belt. In one swift motion, he sliced open the net, sending Nicky tumbling to the ground.

"Get the hell off my land," Lander demanded, tucking the knife into his belt. He picked up the rifle and pointed it at her. "And don't ever mention Thorne Wilson or his goddamned school to me again."

6

Nicky stood at a podium before an outdoor assembly of Wilson Ranch students, gazing up at the tree-lined ridge only a quarter of a mile away that had once given her comfort. This time, however, the sight of it made her cringe. Lander Iron Feather had totally humiliated her that morning, using the limb of an old, sacred tree to capture her in his net. And now all Nicky could think about was the dozen ways she'd like to kill him.

Slowly—

Painfully…

And with extreme prejudice.

So he could never get under her skin and then literally dump her on her ass again.

Doesn't that egotistical jerk understand that I've returned to improve the school? she thought, her molars still grinding over the incident, not to mention that her butt ached from a painful bruise.

It didn't help that it was April Fool's Day—and Nicky certainly felt like a fool. Welcome to the world of the Iron Feather brothers, she thought, shaking her head. Everyone in Bandits Hollow knew that tangling with the likes of them was asking for trouble—in triplicate.

Clearing her throat, Nicky threw back her shoulders, reminding herself that she was a leader now to the hundred students who sat on wooden benches and stared back at her in the small amphitheater—fifty boys on the right, fifty girls on the left. Nicky was their new director, a former alum who was uniquely qualified to understand the obstacles they faced, and it was her job to give them....

Hope.

Courage.

Just like the sacred tree used to whisper to her.

Along with a whole new life.

Tears threatened the corners of Nicky's eyes as she gazed out at the beautiful young faces in front of her. These teens may have endured problems in the past, but one thing she new for certain is that they had their whole lives ahead of them—and she couldn't wait to become a positive part of it. Her fingers skimmed the place on her neck where her grandmother's turquoise pendant used to sit. Oh, what she would give for her grandmother to see her now, ready to do everything in her power to instill the same confidence in these young people that her grandmother had instilled in her. Drawing a deep breath, she scanned the audience and gave them a smile.

"Good afternoon," Nicky announced into the microphone, waiting for them to fall quiet as the late-afternoon sun dipped over the tree tops, creating a warm glow in the amphitheater. "My name is Tavinika Box. As some of you may have heard, I'm the new director of the Wilson Ranch for Wayward Boys and Girls. But the truth is…"

She paused for a moment, allowing her silence to grab their attention.

"I…am…a pickpocket."

Low murmurs stirred through the crowd, followed by giggles.

"You heard me right. Like you, I was once an orphan and a juvenile delinquent at the Wilson Ranch," Nicky explained. "I lost my parents after a carbon monoxide poisoning accident in our home due to a faulty water heater. I was only fifteen and happened to be sleeping at a friend's house at the time. Unfortunately, my grandmother had already passed, and my next of kin were too scattered across the country to provide a stable home for—shall we say—a less-than-law-abiding teen. Little did I know that my grandfather was none other than…"

She took another deep breath, her heart racing at her confession.

"Thorne Wilson."

Gasps erupted from the students, setting off a chain reaction of more murmurs.

"I didn't know that then," Nicky said. "And I don't think Thorne Wilson did either. It took a private investigator and a recent DNA test to confirm that fact. So, after getting into scrapes with the law and bouncing from one foster home to the next, I was finally sent to the Wilson Ranch to be, well…reformed."

Nicky smirked, giving them a small shrug.

"Only I didn't exactly change my ways."

More giggles rippled through the amphitheater as expectant faces waited to hear the rest of her story.

"Nope," she confided with a tinge of pride. "I learned how to become the best damn pickpocket this side of the Mississippi, right here at the Wilson Ranch." When Nicky saw the students' surprised reactions, she rolled her eyes. "Aw, come on! How many of you have gained mad skills since coming here? You know, fighting, stealing, lying, a little forgery to boot. Be honest—give me a show of hands."

A few sheepish hands turned up, accompanied by nervous laughter.

Nicky nodded matter-of-factly. "I think what I was trying to do through pickpocketing was even the score," she admitted. "Life had stolen the people I loved most, and in my anger, I wanted to take something back. But one thing I learned along the way is that you can't steal love, no matter how hard you try. It's something you have to find inside your own heart. And the irony is that the more you find, the more you can give away—and the more love fills you up all over again. But first, you have to love yourself. And that's exactly what I'm here today to guide you to do. For starters, this school is no longer going to be a place for wayward boys and girls at all. Your heart knows exactly where you want to go, and so do I—to a place of love. You're not wayward—you're simply finding your way home. So I'm renaming this place the Sun Mountain School, where each morning, like the Utes who cared for this land, we take our inspiration from the strength and brightness of *Tava*, also known as Pikes Peak, where the sunrise always shines first. Sun Mountain was the place of creation for the Utes, over fourteen-thousand feet and so high in the sky they could never lose their way. Like this magnificent mountain beacon, I want our school to be a compass so our hearts will always find home."

Nicky paused, allowing her words to sink in.

"And along with our new name, there are going to be a lot of changes around here. Before you get too excited, the boys' and girls' dorms will still be separated."

Groans issued from the crowd, and Nicky gave the students an amused wink.

"But as of today, the Sun Mountain School is going to give you the best education possible. We've created a whole new robotics and computer program, updated the track and sports field, and hired new staff of all-star teachers who are the best in their fields. I've also purchased state-of-the-art computers to bring us up to technology standards, and I've brought in a renowned school psychologist to bring us up to *state-of-the-heart* standards. Because here at the Sun Mountain School, my goal is to make us all warriors of the heart. Never again will there be severe punishments or emotional abuse. We're starting over at the Sun Mountain School, and I want you to know that I believe in you, and that you're the best and brightest Colorado has to offer. I know from the bottom of my heart that you deserve a shining future."

Nicky gazed at the old trees on the ridge like they were her biggest supporters and held her chin up.

"See those trees over there?" she said, pointing her finger. "For hundreds of years, my people, the Ute tribe, selected special ponderosas on that ridge to become their sacred trees, the repositories of their highest hopes and dreams."

Nicky leaned down and clutched a pine sapling with its roots covered in burlap at her feet. She lifted it up and held it high for all to see.

"Tomorrow, a group of us will plant this young tree on the ridge to launch a new era for the Sun Mountain School. After a brief ceremony, we'll mold this pine's branches in the traditional way with yucca ropes to signify for generations to come that a new beginning—and a brand new story—has started here. As the sapling grows, we'll gather around it in a circle each year and send it our highest hopes and dreams, which the wind will carry from its branches to the Creator."

Nicky glanced up at the clear blue sky above her, as blue as her grandmother's pendant, which she dearly missed like her right arm. At that moment, an owl called in the distance, its sound echoing from the nearby ridge—just like that day when she'd fallen into the ocean. The owl hooted again and the echo passed over them like an invisible cloak, reverberating within the amphitheater. The sound gave Nicky chills.

"If-if you want," she stammered, unnerved by the odd coincidence, "you can sign up to be part of our new club that collaborates with the forest service to catalog the old trees in our area. The sign-up tables are right over there." Nicky motioned to several tables under an overhang, manned by staff. "Along with your core academics, you can also sign up for robotics, art, sports, music, and other electives. So please rise to your feet," she encouraged enthusiastically, "and head to the tables to choose your new future. Are there any questions?"

"Yeah," a lanky teen boy with ragged, dark hair piped up. He stood to his feet and crossed his arms, slanting a defiant gaze at Nicky. "Have you met him? I mean, since you got the DNA test. Bet he welcomed you with open arms."

Heat rushed to Nicky's cheeks.

Damn—she'd forgotten how quick the kids were here, able to suss out a person's vulnerabilities in a nano-second. *Of course* she was anxious about meeting Thorne Wilson. He was the man who'd considered her a throwaway orphan, who her own grandmother had dumped because of his caustic ways. Approaching him would be like shaking hands with a vampire, wouldn't it? Nicky figured it wouldn't do much good to lie—this boy could probably smell deceit a mile away.

"No," she admitted, her throat clenching tight. "To be honest, I haven't worked up the nerve. With his disability, I'm not even sure if Thorne Wilson understands I'm here. As far as he's concerned, I'm simply some distant relative who's been appointed to run the school—"

"Were you *really* a top model once?" gushed a red-haired girl, cutting into to the conversation. She craned her neck to get a better glimpse of Nicky's acclaimed features. "I saw a magazine in the supermarket with a woman on the cover who looked just like you."

Nicky blushed again—that photo had been taken three months ago, before she'd quit the business. "Yes, I'm afraid that rumor's true. But modeling's a funny thing—you're never paid to be yourself. Believe it or not, you can lose sight of who you are. I'm really happy to be here now."

Nicky scanned the seats that were quickly emptying in the amphitheater. Most of the teens had filed into lines at the sign-up tables, eager to check out the new classes, which made her proud. She began to collect her notes from the podium, when one last student hailed her.

"Ms. Box," a plump boy with blonde hair and freckles called out. He turned and glanced at the ridge. "Is it true that the next door neighbor to this ranch is…crazy?"

"You mean Lander Iron Feather?" Nicky replied without missing a beat. A disgruntled frown tugged at her lips. "Absolutely! I just met that guy in person, and my best advice is to stay far away. If you ever see him on our grounds, notify me immediately and I'll have him arrested. Got that?"

The boy's eyes grew wide. Surprised by Nicky's venom, he whispered to the girl next to him.

Nicky paused, realizing her response had been rather over the top. "Just remember that he went to this school once, too," she backpedaled a little, "and it probably left scars on his soul. People like Lander Iron Feather are the reason I'm determined to change things around here. Believe me, Bandits Hollow doesn't need any more sociopaths like him."

∽

From inside the Owl's Nest at the Iron Feather Brothers Ranch, Lander leveled a dark look at a speaker that had been broadcasting Nicky's every word. He'd planted the tiny receiver, the size of a thumbtack, under the collar of her khaki shirt that morning while she was in his net.

While she was caught in his kiss…

"Sociopath, eh?" Lander muttered, echoing Nicky's sentiments. "Well my dear," he tossed a glance at a box of small espionage devices that he often tucked into his pockets, "all's fair in love and war. And *business*."

Given that Nicky had admitted she was Thorne Wilson's granddaughter, Lander considered bugging her a worthwhile risk to uncover her true intentions—which he suspected might not be entirely altruistic. After all, Thorne Wilson was a very wealthy man. How convenient that she'd showed up the minute he was deemed no longer in his right mind or able to protect his will.

Picking up his spyglass and setting it against the Owl's Nest window, Lander focused on Nicky's beautiful face in the outdoor amphitheater on the neighboring property. The lens made her features so clear it was as if she were in same room.

"Yes, Nicky Box," Lander affirmed in an acid tone, "things are changing around here all right. And I can't wait to see what plans you *really* have for Thorne Wilson's assets. See you tomorrow when you head to that ridge."

Out of habit, Lander slipped his fingers into his front jeans pocket to feel for the familiar wolf bones he'd inherited from his ancestor, which always assured him of his plans. Digging deeper, he failed to detect their smooth shapes. Puzzled, he yanked out the pocket lining. When he glanced down at the empty fabric, it hit him—

They were gone.

7

"Damn her all to hell!" Lander swore under his breath as he headed back to the ridge the following afternoon. "Talk about sociopaths—she'd better return those bones, or I swear to God I'll shoot her."

It turned out Nicky Box was indeed a pickpocket. Only this time she'd snagged a priceless heirloom, one Lander felt had helped to create his empire. This was far worse than trapping her in a big-game net, in his opinion, and he fully intended to press that point with a Smith & Wesson.

Pulling up his stallion Danáskés in a thick grove of trees, Lander once again observed Nicky from high on the hidden knoll. Sure enough, she'd returned to the ridge like she'd promised her students, with an old Jeep and a school van parked nearby. A dozen teens were standing around with clipboards, cataloging trees that had been cultivated by the Utes, along with another staff member for support. Nicky stood in front of the group, pointing out various features on a pine that proved it had been bent into various shapes long ago.

"Bet she's aiming to trespass again," Lander grumbled to himself. "When I confront her, she'll probably try to blackmail me with the bones to get her way."

Lander nudged his stallion to move through the shadows along the ridge until he was within earshot of Nicky.

"Okay," she addressed the students, proud that she'd memorized each one by name before embarking on the outing, "please write down the GPS coordinates I gave you for this tree so we can record it for the forest service. As we discussed earlier, certain features indicate it's a direction tree with angled branches that communicated something important to the Utes. Can anyone tell me what you think the message might have been?"

"Well," a dark-haired girl with glasses named Jill ventured to guess, "two of the branches are raised to the right, and have marks showing they were bent in that direction. Maybe there were a couple of trails or creeks over there?"

"Excellent, Jill!" Nicky replied, beaming. "Later this semester, we'll consult with a Ute elder and a forest ranger to see if they can confirm our findings. Now what about the funky, zigzag branches that are higher up on the same tree, which also have ligature marks?"

"A storyteller tree, maybe?" mentioned Chris, a tall, slim boy with dirty blonde hair. He scanned the handout Nicky had given them of common tree formations and glanced up hesitantly. "I mean, if sacred trees can have more than one function?"

"They can! Good work, Chris," Nicky said with a pat on

his back, delighted by the students' keen observations. "Since it requires generations to alter a single tree, sometimes a tree will be designed to communicate a direction, and later will be used to convey a story that was also important."

"What's the story?" asked Susan, a short girl with curly hair.

Nicky sighed. "The Ute elder we talk to next month might be able to tell us, based on tales that were passed down. Or the story may have been lost in time. But if we catalog our own story tree with the sapling we planted this afternoon, hopefully our records will preserve the new start of the Sun Mountain School for posterity. Most importantly," Nicky pointed to the sapling now set firmly into the soil on the ridge, "this young tree will now provide a safe home for all our prayers and dreams."

Nicky was particularly pleased that she'd gotten the students' input on creatively bending the sapling's branches. And she encouraged them to whisper their dearest hopes to the tree while they angled the branches upward to show a joyful rebirth for the school. Then she had them tie the yucca ropes they'd woven to the slim trunk to keep the branches in place.

"Any other types of trees on this ridge?" Nicky asked the group. "Remember, this was a common route for the Utes, so there should be several examples. If you don't see bent branches, a sacred tree can also be one with bark that was peeled for medicine or food—"

"Ms. Box!" gasped a boy named Dan in a strained voice like he'd seen a ghost. "There's the crazy neighbor!" Dan darted behind Nicky and pointed between the trees. "I think he's got a rifle. I heard he shoots poachers and anybody else he doesn't like. None of us even heard him coming—"

"Of course we didn't." Nicky set her fists on her hips, squinting to detect Lander in the shadows. "That's because he comes from a bunch of outlaws who know how to sneak up on people. Well hello, Lander Iron Feather!" Nicky waved to him in mock friendliness. "Fancy meeting you here! Any reason you're *stalking* us today? Please don't play the trespassing card again—we're obviously on the Wilson side of the fence."

Lander urged his stallion into the bright sunlight and dismounted, then sauntered over to the barbed wire. He gazed up and pointed at the zigzag branches on the storyteller tree they'd mentioned earlier.

"Let's see, today's story is…you're a *thief*, Tavinika Box," he accused loudly so all the students would hear. "Is that what you want your sapling to commemorate? Good thing you warned your students yesterday that you're a criminal. That way they'll know the *real you*."

Nicky sucked air—

How on earth had Lander eavesdropped on my speech? she wondered. She watched Lander fold his arms in smug satisfaction, enjoying the sight of the teens gaping at her, waiting for an answer.

"Where are my wolf bones?" Lander demanded. He brazenly leaned over the fence, not caring if his shirt was punctured by the barbed wire, and stared at her nose to nose. "Wonder how the school board will react when they find out you've broken the law—*again*."

"Wait a minute!" Nicky set her chin in defiance. "How is that any different from illegally spying on me? Or trapping me in your crazy net?" She pointed at the prophecy tree where they'd met the day before, which looked surprisingly unthreatening now after the net had been reburied in the ground. "If you don't want me to rat on you to authorities," she warned, "you'd better allow us to catalog the sacred trees on your side of the fence, too."

"I knew it!" Lander huffed. "You're attempting to blackmail me with my ancestor's wolf bones. I guarantee if anyone contacts authorities, it will be me. When I call my brother in the police force again to tell him—"

Lander cut short his own diatribe, his attention diverted over Nicky's shoulder. "Wait a minute," he said, squinting hard, "who's that over by the fence?"

Nicky swiveled and spotted one of her students. He was a Native-American boy with long black hair named Riley, who'd wandered off about a hundred yards to look at more trees. Lander had noticed him just as he'd accidentally gotten his leg caught in a tangle of stray barbed wire. Before Nicky could even call out his name, Riley had tumbled to the ground and begun writhing in pain as he tried to wriggle free from the barbed wire.

With lightning speed, Lander vaulted over the fence to the Wilson Ranch side and dashed over to Riley. When he reached down to carefully unravel the barbed wire, Riley cried out.

But it wasn't from pain—

It was fear.

Lander recognized the stark look in Riley's eyes.

The teenager recoiled at the sight of him, as though certain that Lander was going to…

Hit him.

Lander pulled back his hand.

Deep in his soul, he remembered what it was like to be on the wrong side of that barbed wire fence as a teen at the Wilson Ranch. You could get dragged out of bed and beaten at any moment for the smallest infraction. God forbid you ever showed pain, anger, or other emotions, and you certainly never dared to defend yourself—unless you enjoyed spending time in solitary confinement. Any reaction only encouraged more abuse.

Especially at the hands of someone who looked...

White.

Lander glanced down at the strands of blonde hair that tumbled past his shoulders, wincing when he realized that the boy couldn't possibly know that his father was part Ute and his mother was full Apache. Cautiously, he looked Riley in the eye.

What he saw stabbed him in the heart—

It was like peering into a soul mirror.

Riley's eyes were filled with the familiar terror of one who'd been beaten many times, never knowing when or where the strikes would come next. Clenching his teeth, Riley squeezed his eyes shut and waited for the inevitable blows with all the stoicism he could muster.

A knot formed in Lander's throat.

"I-I won't touch you," Lander promised. He held up his hand for Nicky and the others to stay back for a second. "Unless you want me to. Here," he yanked a piece of baling twine from his back pocket and gazed at the nasty gash that had torn through the boy's jeans and wounded his shin, "tie this below your knee to slow down the bleeding, okay?"

Riley edged open his eyes. He studied Lander's face to

detect whether this stranger could be the slightest bit trustworthy. The sincerity in Lander's gaze made him relax a little. He accepted the baling twine and followed Lander's instruction to secure it around his leg.

Lander dug into his pocket and held up his cell phone. "I'm texting my ranch doctor to come here right away," he said, punching his finger at his phone and pressing send. "I'm pretty sure you're going to need stitches with that deep cut on your leg."

"Will it hurt?" Riley asked, trembling.

Lander leaned down to scrutinize the wound. The barbed wire had sliced the boy's leg to the bone.

"No. The doctor will use a strong anesthetic," Lander replied kindly. "You'll be as good as new in no time. But you're going to have to take it easy while you recuperate."

At that moment, Nicky broke past the small crowd, defying Lander's warning to keep her distance. She rushed to the boy's side, her face horrified at the sight of his gash.

"Oh my God, Riley!" Immediately, she ripped apart the bottom of her black t-shirt a few inches above the hem until she had a long enough stretch of fabric to tie it beneath Riley's knee and make a better tourniquet than Lander's thin baling twine. Riley allowed her to carefully adjust her makeshift cotton bandage to slow down the blood flow just enough without being too tight. In a swift gesture of maternal instinct, Nicky clutched Riley's hand and tenderly placed her palm against his cheek, staring into his brown eyes.

"Riley, I know you're in pain right now. Be strong for me, sweetie," she encouraged, squeezing his hand. "We're going to get you to a doctor right away." Nicky shot a glance at the staff member who'd accompanied them on the trip. "Joe, bring me the Jeep. I have to transport Riley to an emergency room —*now!*"

"He'll lose too much blood," Lander asserted in a forceful tone, loud enough for Joe to hear. "Even if we take my helicopter."

Lander pointed to a Hummer that was already racing up the ridge and only two hundred yards away, stirring up dust as it nearly reached the top. When it arrived at the barbed-wire fence, it came to a halt. "There's my ranch doctor. He'll take expert care of Riley."

"Riley doesn't need a veterinarian. He needs an emergency physician!" Nicky protested.

"Doctor Connor is *not* a veterinarian," Lander assured her as two men stepped out of the camo-colored Hummer with a red cross on the side and went to the back to grab a stretcher. "He's a full-time MD at the Iron Feather Brothers Ranch, where wranglers work every day with unpredictable cattle and horses. We have a state-of-the art emergency room for dislocations, broken bones, stitches—everything."

The men hastened with the stretcher to the fence line and swiftly cut open the barbed wire with clippers so they could easily step through. When they spotted Lander, they rushed to his side in seconds. One of the cowboys, an African-American man with gray sideburns, kneeled down beside Riley.

"How's our patient doing, boss?" the man said, surveying the boy's wound with a keen eye. He slipped a sterile bandage over it to contain the bleeding.

"He's a tough one," Lander replied. He smiled and set a comforting hand on Riley's shoulder. "Riley, meet Doctor

Conner, a highly-decorated wartime physician who received a purple heart for his valor in Afghanistan. He'll get you fixed up in no time."

Riley nodded, and the two cowboys quickly cut him free from the barbed wire around his leg and tied a medical-grade tourniquet above his wound. Then they shifted him onto the stretcher and proceeded to carry him to the Hummer.

"Wait!" Nicky cried, boldly charging after them. "I can't allow Riley go to a doctor without my supervision!"

"Just remember," Lander's lips crinkled at the corners as he caught up to her, "you asked for this."

With that, he grabbed Nicky around the waist and hoisted her into his arms, holding her close against his broad chest.

"Joe, take the kids back to the school in the van," Lander commanded Nicky's staff, whether Nicky liked it or not. "We'll call you when Riley's out of surgery."

Lander marched with deliberate strides through the hole in the fence to his horse, despite Nicky's kicks and punches, and he carefully set her on the back of his stallion. Before Nicky could get a word in, he'd already pinched the barbed wire together and stretched the fence closed around a post, then hoisted himself into the saddle in front of her. After he gave Danáskés a hard kick, the horse bolted forward like a rocket. Lander turned to Nicky with a wicked smile.

"Hold onto me tight, honey!" he cried as his horse barreled down the ridge with mind-boggling speed. "This is gonna be one hell of a ride."

8

"You owe me," Nicky stated with her arms crossed, in spite of the fact that she'd just witnessed a successful surgery on her student Riley. The boy was sitting up in bed, recuperating in a room adjacent to the Iron Feather brothers' emergency center, drinking a rich, chocolate milkshake especially prepared for him by Lander's French chef.

"Excuse me?" Lander replied. "Didn't I just provide medical assistance to your student—along with ambulance service—free of charge?"

"Those loose strands of barbed wire Riley got tangled in were *brand new*," Nicky sniffed. "They didn't even have rust on them. Obviously, they were left on the Wilson Ranch property when *you* put up the fence on the ridge. Which means we have some talking to do, Lander Iron Feather, or I'll sue."

"Sue!" Lander spit out. "First you steal the wolf bones

from my pocket, and now you want to *sue me* for taking care of your student? I should have security throw you out—"

"They can do so, but I'll see you in court. Riley would never have gotten that nasty gash on his leg if you hadn't been negligent about leaving wire around when you built your fence."

Lander's mouth slung open. For the first time in as long as he could remember, he couldn't think of a single thing to say.

Damn, this woman's a piece of work, he thought.

A master of deviousness.

"Listen," Lander finally said, after drawing a breath to collect his thoughts, "if you just pony up the wolf bones, we'll call it a draw. All right?"

"What wolf bones?" Nicky taunted in an innocent tone. The sly sparkle in her eyes betrayed that she knew she had Lander over a barrel.

Lander clenched his teeth as well as his fists, resisting the urge to lose control and explode right in front of her.

"Where…are…my…wolf…bones," he enunciated slowly, his eyes burning. He heaved out a breath and closed his eyes for a moment as if repeating a mantra in his head for anger management.

"Well, well! Looks like I've found your Achilles heel, haven't I?" Nicky teased, enjoying the situation far too much for Lander's comfort. "Let's see, *you're* responsible for my student getting hurt, and now you want some mysterious wolf bones as well? What else do you think you're entitled to—the moon?"

"*You're* the one threatening to sue after my doctor fixed up your student. Fine thanks I get for helping out—"

"Helping out—what a lovely term," Nicky retorted. "In fact, that's exactly what you can do if you want to avoid a lawsuit."

"What the hell are you talking about?" Lander pressed.

"You know," Nicky mused, tapping her lip, "you have such a lovely ranch here. I've seen pictures of it in *Vanity Fair* magazine. The editors drooled over the exquisite decorations throughout the main mansion, which apparently has a ballroom that rivals Versailles. All gold and glittery. And you have a French chef to cater to your every whim!" Nicky twirled a finger through her long hair, acting sweet and guileless. "What a perfect location to hold the school prom in two weeks. That is, if you want to avoid the lawsuit I mentioned. Of course," she ran her finger tantalizingly over Lander's collar, lingering on his hard chest, "you'll foot the entire bill as well."

"P-Prom?" Lander gasped, stunned.

To his bewilderment, Nicky had just turned the tables on him to swing a deal as artful and as cunning as any he'd ever cooked up.

"Let me get this straight. You want me to hold a *prom* on my property for the school's students and pay all expenses so you won't sue me?" He arched a brow. "I want to see that in writing—"

"Oh, I have a better idea," Nicky answered with another twinkle in her eye. "You'll get confirmation exactly the same way you sealed the deal with me. This time, you're in *my* net, Lander Iron Feather."

At that moment, Nicky seized Lander's face and planted a kiss on his lips, her hands grasping his jaw with an impact that left him reeling. Though she was simply making her point in the same cocky way he'd treated her, she couldn't deny that the delicious taste of him was tempting enough to remain lip-locked for quite a while. Nevertheless, as Nicky swiftly broke away, she laughed like a gambler who'd won a bet.

"Sealed with a kiss! Who's the winner now, Lander?" she teased. "It's such a shame, isn't it—I've heard when it comes to deals, you *hate* to lose."

"Woman, I'd throw a thousand proms to get another kiss like that," Lander replied in a devilish tone, making sparks wriggle up her spine. It took all of Nicky's might to resist his wicked charm and refrain from letting him get under her skin again. But then Lander dipped his head and threw her the coldest stare she'd ever seen. "Now where are my bones."

"If you're so good at the hand game, shouldn't you already know where they are?" Nicky challenged. "I've heard the best hand game players border on being…well…psychic."

"So you *admit* you have them," Lander growled.

"Maybe." Nicky threw her chin up in defiance. "What else do you think you can do for my school?"

She sure is stubborn, Lander thought. *And* greedy…

Yet secretly, he couldn't help admiring the fire in Nicky's eyes—and her willingness to do whatever it took to get the very best for her students. Lander's face may have remained gruff and thoroughly unreadable in that moment, but there was a soft spot deep inside him that melted at the big heart Nicky obviously had for the kids.

After all, she'd been one of them once. Just like him. And she knew intimately what their struggles felt like, along with their hopes and dreams. A prom…a place to dress up and pretend to be an adult for a night, full of first dances and hopefully first kisses. It was everything they should have had as teens, but never did—

How could he say no?

As though psychic herself, Nicky spied the brief lapse in Lander's granite front, and she gave him a wink. "They get to you, don't they?" she whispered with a self-satisfied smirk. "Those kids have a way of sneaking into your heart."

"You missed your calling, Nicky. You should have been a lawyer," Lander observed, shaking his head. "Because you're one tough-dealing cookie."

"I considered it for half a second," Nicky replied. "But I think I can do more good here, with the school."

Lander couldn't argue with that, especially when he spotted the compassionate look in Nicky's eyes when she glanced over at Riley to check up on him. The boy had happily finished his milkshake and was devouring a plate of roast beef and potatoes au gratin, adhering to the old adage to eat dessert first.

"He's only fourteen," Nicky whispered with a lump rising in her throat. "He's really good at math, and he wants to build suspension bridges someday." She paused, noticing the way Riley heaped his potatoes to form an arch over his meat, using several roasted carrots for support. "I heard that before I came here, a staff member beat him within an inch of his life. I fired that son of a bitch, of course. Riley deserves to create the future of his dreams…"

Nicky's words trailed off, but Lander spotted the soft gleam that formed at the edges of her eyes.

She gives everything she has to provide for these kids, he thought.

"You know, a prom would be a nice thing to do for the students," he remarked thoughtfully. "We never had one back when we were at the school. We never had any form of...celebration."

"So instead of meeting you in court," Nicky insisted, keeping their conversation on track, "the school prom will start at six o'clock in the evening on the second Saturday of this month. Don't worry, I'll have my staff arrange the music and transportation details ahead of time. See you then!"

Nicky wiggled her fingers in Lander's face before turning to head toward Riley's bed. As she picked up a pair of crutches to help him leave the surgery center, she glanced up and caught Lander's intense stare.

"That's all well and good, Ms. Box," Lander informed her, switching his emotions lightning fast to a tone of ice. "But you'd better bring those wolf bones to the prom. Or your ass is the one that will be summoned in court."

9

Nearly two weeks later, Nicky stood beside an antique dresser in her school director's cabin, putting clean clothes she'd folded into a drawer. When she reached into the laundry basket for her favorite khaki shirt, she chuckled over how she'd washed it a while back, only to discover Lander's small spy device rattling around afterwards in the dryer. No wonder he knew exactly what I'd said, she sighed, when I made my first address to the students! Setting the shirt down, she picked up the tiny spy device she'd placed on the dresser for safekeeping and held it up to the window in the afternoon light.

The bug was black and smaller than a dime, and Nicky had found two small holes in the khaki fabric where he'd secured the tiny prongs to her collar. Surely this thing no longer works, she thought, after drowning inside a washing machine for an hour?

The possibility made her nervous, but as Nicky examined

the bug between her fingers, a mischievous idea crossed her mind. She brought the spy device to her lips.

"Can you hear me, Lander Iron Feather?" she challenged in a cocky tone. "Because if you can, you're the scum of the earth! Oh sure, nicknames like that probably make you proud. But why on earth did you *spy* on me—so you could hear what I really say to students? By the way, they think you're crazy, too."

Nicky shook her head, feeling a bit silly and seriously doubting that Lander could decipher her ramblings from a laundered electronic device. "It's too bad you're nuts," she muttered, "given that you're so goddamned handsome, enough to make most women's underwear melt." Nicky threw up her hands. "Why do the crazy ones always have to be drop-dead gorgeous? And too arrogant for anybody's good?"

Nicky slipped the bug into her pocket to take with her to the prom that evening, just to relish the look on Lander's face when she pulled it out and taunted him. She still could hardly believe he'd agreed to host the event, even though she did have his back against a wall. Twisting open the latch on her jewelry box on the dresser, she peeked at the spot where she'd hidden Lander's beloved wolf bones. A slight tremor slipped down her back.

Nicky knew about the hand game—she'd watched her grandmother play it with friends during pow wows on the Ute reservation. Every summer, they'd line up two separate teams on parallel benches and participate in the age-old guessing game of who had the colored or the white bones. One team did the guessing while the opposite team hid the bones in their hands or behind their backs, singing songs in Ute and drumming to distract the other side. It became a test of almost...supernatural...skill, where the best players always seemed to intuit where the right bones were. Nicky turned over the wolf bones in her hand, wondering if the fact that she was holding them enabled Lander to somehow *see* her along with the bones in her cabin. After all, folks who were good at the hand game were known to consult ancestors and receive sacred songs from spirit guides to help them win. Did this otherworldly assistance include...visions...too?

Another shiver snaked its way down Nicky's spine.

"That man's not only crazy, he's pure trouble," she whispered in defiance to any spirit that might be lingering near the bones. "So what if he's spooky talented at business deals and killer good looking? Near as I can tell, he's just another gun-toting, alpha-wolf type with an attitude—hardly the boyfriend material my grandmother had in mind."

Nicky tucked the wolf bones inside her jeans pocket alongside the spy device, half-hoping they might help her navigate a bright future for the school, the way they were rumored to aid Lander in business. Then she ran her hand through her long black hair, checking the window to see how much light there was left to head into Bandits Hollow. She needed to pick up the corsages and boutonnieres she'd ordered for the students for the prom before five PM. It was the only extravagance she could afford after emptying the school endowment for recent improvements. Just as Nicky leaned over to pick up her purse, a fleet of black stretch limousines began to roll up the dirt road, kicking up clouds of dust until they parked beside her cabin. She knew before he developed dementia that Thorne Wilson used to entertain wealthy luminaries from the ranching world at his home in order to broker deals. But she'd never seen such guests bother to stop by the school before.

"They must be lost," Nicky muttered. She grabbed a map of the Wilson Ranch featured on an old brochure and stepped out her cabin door. Walking up to the first limousine, she waved her hand.

"Hello?" Nicky addressed the driver, who was in a classic chauffeur uniform with a black cap. When he rolled down his window, she handed him the map and pointed to the imposing, white mansion on a hill a quarter of a mile away. "Thorne Wilson's home is over there. You'll find plenty of room for parking beyond the carriage porch in front of his house."

The man merely smiled and stepped out of the vehicle. "You must be Tavinika Box," he said, giving her back the map. "I was warned you might try to steer us away. I assure you," he motioned with a white-gloved hand at the six other stretch limousines behind him, "we're here for *you*."

"W-What?" Nicky sputtered. She swiftly totaled the cost of such an over-the-top luxury in horror. "This must be a prank. Did some teenager call you to come over here?"

"No," the driver replied calmly, "Lander Iron Feather." He pulled out an official-looking order form from his coat pocket and unfolded it, holding it up to Nicky. "It says right here that we're to load up all the students from the Sun Mountain School at three in the afternoon to attend an event at the Iron Feather Brothers Ranch. Along with their chaperones, of course."

"But the school prom doesn't start until six o'clock. And I still have to pick up the flowers. I don't understand—"

"Mr. Iron Feather said you wouldn't," the driver informed her in a matter-of-fact tone. "It's supposed to be a surprise. And the flowers are already taken care of. Now, if you'll kindly step inside the vehicle Ms. Box, we can fulfill our orders and pick up the rest of the students for transport."

Flustered, Nicky pulled out her cell phone from her purse and dialed the Iron Feather Brothers Ranch, but no one answered. Then she yanked the spy device from her pocket and held it to her mouth. "Lander Iron Feather," she insisted, "I swear to God, if you can hear this, you'd better tell me what the hell you're doing!"

A low chuckle issued from the tiny device.

"Then it wouldn't be a surprise," Lander's familiar voice replied. "Better pack up the kids before those limos take off—they've got orders to bring you back to the ranch within thirty minutes. By the way, when you pay top dollar for spy devices, they still work even if you throw them to the bottom of a lake. See you soon, Nicky."

∼

O*h my God, he must have heard me in the cabin!* Nicky cringed to herself as the limos departed down the long, dirt driveway of the school to head to the Iron Feather Brothers Ranch. *That means he heard me say he's gorgeous, too,* she thought, wringing her hands until they hurt. *Good thing I mentioned he's a heap of trouble, so he knows I couldn't possibly be attracted to him. Because I'm* not.

I'm *really* not...

Everyone with half a brain knows Lander Iron Feather is unstable *and* impossible, Nicky convinced herself. The fact that he's handsome only amplifies that effect.

As the stretch limousines maneuvered up the twisty mountain road to reach their destination, Nicky did her best to perfect her resting bitch face. Luckily, she'd had plenty of practice at biting the insides of her cheeks and presenting herself as an ice queen from her years in modeling. Nevertheless, a blush suffused her face when the limousines finally crossed under the timber-framed entrance to the Iron Feather Brothers Ranch and came to a halt in front of the main mansion. Drawing a deep breath, Nicky set her lips into a hard, flat line and jutted her chin, prepared to give off the air of a woman who's never been intimidated by a soul in her life.

Even if it was a lie...

When the chauffeur opened her door, Nicky stepped out on the driveway and crossed her arms, glaring at Lander who was standing a few yards away on a lawn near a gazebo.

"Lander Iron Feather," she called out in a preemptive strike, "I hope you've got a good explanation for sending limousines to pick up my students three hours early, when we have perfectly good buses at the school—"

"Look around, Nicky," Lander cut short her scolding. He swiveled and waved his hand at the dozen mysterious racks of clothes positioned behind him. Then he met her gaze with a twinkle in his eye. "The dressing rooms are right over there—boys on the left, girls on the right." He slanted his head at two cabins across the lawn that matched the timber and stone architecture of the main mansion. "What's a prom without formal wear?"

Nicky blinked several times, her jaw sliding open. It was then she realized that the racks contained reams of fancy dresses and tuxedos.

They were for the kids...

Without warning, the students jumped out of the limos and dashed toward the racks, whooping like they'd won the lottery.

The unbridled joy on their young faces brought tears to Nicky's eyes.

Lander...bought...formal clothing, just for them? she thought. To make their prom extra special? Stunned, she glanced around the ranch, noticing there were several salon chairs accompanied by hairdressers and barbers positioned near the clothing racks, plus tables that contained rows of flowers—the corsages and boutonnieres she'd ordered in Bandits Hollow.

"Just so you know," the chauffeur from her limousine mentioned as he rolled down his window, "Mr. Iron Feather footed the bill for all of this. You might consider thanking him." As soon as the last students stepped out of his vehicle, he drove forward, leading the way for the other limos to park past the main mansion near a barn.

Nicky slowly unfolded her arms, amazed at the girls who were holding up dresses from the racks and giggling over whether they complimented their hair and eye colors, while the boys draped tuxedos at their shoulders to see if the sleeves and trouser legs were long enough. As soon as they made their choices, Lander's ranch staff pointed them toward the salon chairs to have their hair done by professional beauticians. Nicky had to giggle at a few of the boys who stubbornly shook their heads and refused to get haircuts.

"I don't get it," Nicky admitted as Lander walked over to her, beaming with pride. "From the first moment I met you, all you seemed to want to do is kick me off your land, along with any kids who dared to get near your fence. The only reason you agreed to hold this prom is so I wouldn't sue. Why the change of heart all of a sudden, when you clearly don't have one?"

Lander had been studying the ground while she spoke, and as soon as Nicky finished, she noticed the muscles in his jaw flexed, as though he were wrestling with a dark memory. For a moment, he shifted his boot over the gravel driveway, turning over a couple of jagged rocks to hide their sharp edges before he glanced back up at the kids.

"Every teenager deserves a prom," he finally said. "A special night while they're still young and full of dreams."

The fractured edge in his voice made it sound like he'd never had the chance to be that kid, as if hope had been irrevocably stolen from him a long time ago. Nicky wasn't sure, but she thought she saw Lander wince.

He nodded at the teens, who continued to ransack the clothing with big grins on their faces, chattering a mile a minute. "A prom is something you and I never had," Lander said, his voice low and serious. "Something no teen from that school ever got." He turned and gazed at Nicky with a bitter determination that couldn't quite overtake the haunting touch of loss in his eyes. "Guess you could say I wanted to do things right."

"Why, Lander Iron Feather," Nicky gasped in amazement, "is it possible you've developed some semblance of goodwill lately? I never thought I'd see the day."

"Neither did I!" boomed a voice from behind them. Nicky and Lander whipped around to see a gray-haired woman wearing a bright lavender rodeo shirt with yellow, appliqued roses and matching purple cowboy boots. "And if you ask me, this event of yours is headed straight to hell!"

Lander held back a smirk at the woman's brashness. "Nicky Box, meet Nell Granger," he said, wrapping an arm around the woman's shoulder and giving her a surprisingly warm squeeze, "owner of the Golden Wagon Hotel and Restaurant in Bandits Hollow. She also happens to be the closest thing to a second mother for me and my brothers. So watch out—she's been known to box ears if you get on her bad side. What troubles you this afternoon, Nell?"

"I'll tell you the very definition of trouble, young man," she stated, wagging a finger at him. "You asked me to help your fancy-schmancy chef serve up good ol' country eats, and he hasn't listened to a damn thing I've said." Nell planted her fists on her hips. "Whoever heard of making scalloped potatoes with beurre blanc sauce and Gruyere cheese? And he had the nerve to butcher my pecan pie recipe by adding cognac, of all things."

"Don't worry," Lander assured Nell, just as she was building up steam. "I'll have a talk with Francois right now. Come with me, Nicky," he urged.

To Nicky's surprise, Lander hooked his arm in hers and began to march toward a large chuckwagon spewing smoke from a dark flue, which looked to Nicky like a giant food truck built out of an oversized prairie schooner.

"Wait a minute," Nicky protested, halting in her tracks. "I thought we agreed to use your elegant ballroom for this prom. So far, everything's outdoors."

Lander gave her the side eye, as though it should be obvious. "Think about it, Nicky," he replied with a trace of impatience in his voice, "when you were sixteen, did you want to be inside a stuffy ballroom, dancing underneath dusty chandeliers while some orchestra plays classical music?"

He pointed at a nearby barn that was as tall as the Iron Feather brothers' mansion. Its giant wood doors were slid open wide, giving Nicky a glimpse inside the rustic century-old structure. The pine floor had been polished to warm, amber sheen. When Nicky glanced up, she spied pastel chiffon sashes with dangling silver stars that draped from the rafters, which were lit by strands of delicate champagne lights. The sight was so lovely it made her breath hitch.

"Or would you rather dance to country music inside a heritage barn decked out as the most beautiful western dance hall on earth?"

Nicky felt herself tremble a little, but she steeled her back and relied once more on her resting bitch face. Yet she was pretty sure Lander must have felt her subtle reaction, detecting her vulnerable tremor through his arm linked in hers. Despite her desire to appear cool, a lump slowly inched up her throat. This sweetly decorated barn was everything she could have dreamed of as a teenager. Speechless, she gazed at the long rustic tables inside the barn, covered by crisp linen runners and elk antler candelabras, each one featuring golden candle spires with flickering flames.

Lander allowed their silence to hang between them, making no attempt to fill the gap with words.

He simply let Nicky breathe in the romantic sight, and she had to wonder if there might be a tender spot inside him taking it all in as well. Could Lander possibly go back in time and let himself be that teen who longed for a prom, allowing the excitement to trickle into his soul?

Could *she?*

After a long pause that felt like minutes, Lander turned toward the chuckwagon.

"Francois," he stated firmly to the dark-haired chef who looked distinctly uncomfortable dressed in a red-checkered apron and a cowboy hat. "You listen to everything Nell Granger tells you, all right? We're serving teenagers tonight, not heads of international conglomerates. They want their favorite foods without any foreign embellishments. Okay?"

Francois sighed and slanted a gaze at Lander like he was out of his mind.

"See?" Lander mentioned to Nicky with a slight upward turn of his lip. "What's a man to do—even the help think I'm crazy."

"No," Nicky whispered. She slowly spun on her heels to do a 360 and take everything in. "This isn't crazy. It's not crazy at all."

Nicky swallowed hard, choking back how touched she really was, but her voice cracked against her will anyway.

"It's downright…beautiful…Lander."

"Just like you, after you get a move on!" Nell startled Nicky with her sharp tone as she marched toward her again, only this time holding the handle of a large basket lined with red bandanas and filled to the brim with cornbread. Nicky followed her nose to face her, struck by the yummy, heavenly scent.

"You don't want to be the only one around here in jeans, do you?" Nell insisted. "Time to come with me and put on your dress! And Lander," she said in a maternal tone, arching a brow, "get your butt over to the boys' dressing room cabin this minute and peel yourself out of those dirty ranch clothes for a tux. You're as dusty as a horse!"

Before either one of them could respond, Nell headed to Nicky and grabbed her by the arm, whisking her away to the girls' dressing room cabin for an impromptu fitting.

And for the life of him, as Lander watched Nicky stride across the lawn, her lithe hips swaying to the rhythm of her steps, her long black hair draping to her slim waist and glistening in the afternoon sunlight, he suddenly felt her absence yank on a corner of his heart. A place he hardly knew existed.

The twinge was unfamiliar and unsettling, hidden in a deep nook within his chest that he thought had been cauterized years ago—and so calloused now he could no longer trust it.

Yet try as he might, Lander couldn't will the odd sensation to stop. The lyrical timbre of Nicky's voice, her fiery attitude and fierce dedication to her students, clung to the edges of his thoughts like a lingering fragrance. Of all people, Lander knew his frenetic business schedule and womanizing reputation hardly made for a long-term liaison with a lovely stranger who somehow kept getting under his skin.

But damned if it wasn't hard to stop staring at her perfectly round ass and legs so long they made him ache to run his fingers along every willowy inch—and maybe his tongue as well. As Nicky opened the door to the dressing room cabin, Lander couldn't help wondering if Nicky's complex allure might turn out to be an uninvited poison. Or a balm for his soul…

But one thing Lander knew for certain: He wasn't about to put on an entire musty tuxedo for a country barn dance as suggested by Nell, no matter how big of a fit she threw. One of the black coats over his torn jeans would do just fine.

And as he watched the two women disappear into the cabin, he folded his thick arms across his broad chest with a smile toying at his lips. Then he resolved to be the very first one to dance that evening in the old barn under the twinkling lights—

With Nicky.

10

"The theme for tonight's prom is Rope the Stars," Lander informed the students with a glint in his eyes. "The future is yours for the taking. May this evening always remind you to dream big."

Lander stood in front of the long tables inside the barn where his staff had served dinner, and he pointed to a wall featuring glittery lights in the shape of a lariat. The bright constellation was surrounded by a giant gilded frame, large enough to surround several students for a picture. Beside the frame were tiaras, hats, feather boas, and even a couple of ropes on a bench for the students to use as props, along with a vintage Polaroid camera.

"First, we'll finish our meal." Lander winked at Nell and gazed greedily at the plates of ribeyes, scalloped potatoes and green beans on the tables with baskets of cornbread on the side. "Then everyone can take turns at the selfie station while the band plays music for the dance. After the dance is finished, we'll proceed to the carnival area."

The students glanced at each other, confused.

Lander gave the go ahead to his staff, who wheeled open the large doors at the back of the barn to reveal an acre of antique carnival rides that had been set up behind the old building. All at once, the lights of the tilt-a-whirl, carousel, and shooting galleries were turned on with blinding brightness, in contrast to the soft twilight hues that had begun to descend on the ranch.

The students gasped.

"Don't be wolfing down your dinners just to get to the carnival," Lander warned. "Our culinary expert tonight, Nell Granger, went to a lot of trouble to make sure your meals are perfect. No carnival rides till after your plates are clean and you've chosen partners for at least one dance."

At that moment, Lander spied Nicky stepping out of the girls' dressing room cabin.

The students weren't the only ones to gasp that night—

As she walked across the lawn to the barn with her hair swept up in a sleek chignon, Nicky looked every inch the supermodel in a strapless gold gown with a fitted brocade bodice that perfectly highlighted her caramel skin and statuesque physique. A couple of whistles erupted from the tables, but Lander stared the boys down, his penetrating brown eyes turning as cold as stones in seconds flat.

"Let's give a round of applause for the new school director," he announced in a firm tone, demanding respect, "who spearheaded this prom tonight."

Nicky heard clapping as she stepped over the threshold

into the barn, and she swiftly glanced behind her, wondering if some guest of honor had arrived.

Lander held up a glass of sparkling cider, nodding at the students to do the same. "To Ms. Box," he called out for a toast, clinking his glass against the ones held by nearby students. "The woman responsible for dreaming up tonight's event."

With that, Lander motioned for the band to strike up their instruments, and they began to play a dreamy country tune full of hope and longing. Before all the students, Lander stepped up to Nicky in his black tuxedo coat over threadbare jeans and held out his calloused, weather-beaten hand.

"Ma'am," he said, tipping his cowboy hat while his eyes brazenly roamed over her curves as if she were a goddess who'd just alighted on earth. "You look...*spectacular*."

Lander paused, allowing time for the students' giggles to die down. "May I have the first dance?"

Nicky dropped her gaze for a second, feeling self-conscious—especially since Lander looked indecently handsome with his long blonde hair draped over his wide shoulders in a black tuxedo coat, a five o'clock shadow giving his granite-cut face just enough rough-hewn allure to make any woman's breath catch. Naturally, he wore the coat over ripped jeans that were stained and dusty, probably from ranch work he'd been doing since the crack of dawn. Hesitant, Nicky risked checking Lander's eyes for sincerity, feeling like she'd suddenly regressed to a sixteen-year-old school girl with a swirl of adolescent expectations rising in her heart. Like usual, Lander's expression was as quicksilver as it had been on the ridge when he'd dared to kiss her—full of charm and an easy, rugged grace that she knew could switch on a dime. Yet in that moment, Nicky realized what Lander was really up to—he was showing the students, who'd had little social coaching in life, how to brave up and pick dance partners.

"Why, of course, Mr. Iron Feather," she accepted loudly with a curtsy, hoping to bolster the students' confidence. "I'm delighted to go to the dance floor with you—as long as you serve me one of those big steaks afterwards."

The students responded with more giggles, and Nicky flashed a bright smile, the one she always kept in her arsenal for modeling—more of a clever mask than a genuine register of emotion. As the band launched into a sweet rendition of Lady A's *If I Knew Then*, she followed Lander to an open area in front of the musicians and lightly set her hand on his shoulder, allowing her feet to follow his in a casual country waltz.

The last thing she expected from Lander was for him to be as fluid as water...

Nicky had hit dance floors before, of course, but the bad-boy billionaire types who constantly pursued her had proven many times that money hardly equalled grace. In fact, she'd lost track of how often her toes had been stepped on by overly eager men pumped up on alcohol and Viagra who struggled to remember her name.

But dancing with Lander was easy.

Too easy...

The way he set his palm firmly on the small of her back, like it belonged there—like they belonged together, entwined as the music played—only fed the adolescent sparks that crept up her spine. Lander boldly pulled her close so her breasts skimmed his chest like an invitation—maybe even an *invocation*—that there was a whole lot more where that came from. Yet in his strong arms, Nicky didn't feel like they were dancing in a barn at all, more like they were gliding on clouds. Who would ever guess that a ranch-hardened cowboy with a juvenile rap sheet as long as his own arm could suddenly turn an old barn into a…

Dream.

Nicky closed her eyes for a moment, trying to maintain her composure in spite of all those reckless sparks that kept sweeping through her, which by now had shuttled down to her toes.

Damn his sexual chemistry…

Charm is Lander Iron Feather's crack, Nicky reminded herself adamantly, knowing from supermarket tabloids that he regularly left scores of broken hearts in his wake. It's the drug he pushes on unsuspecting women, she thought, only to cast them aside like yesterday's news.

"Come on now!" Nell called out to the students, disturbing Nicky's cautionary line of thought. "Finish up those dinners quick-like and show us what you can do. I guarantee nobody's getting a slice of my pecan pie till I've seen each one of you dance a few rounds!"

Nicky smirked at Nell's overbearing warmth, thrilled to see a few of the students nervously rise to their feet and fumble to choose partners while the others finished their meals. Nicky deliberately made her waltz steps a bit more exaggerated, hoping they might copy her moves, when she felt Lander tug her even closer.

Really close—

Until she was absorbed into his hard, muscular chest. The warmth of his breath tickled against her neck, oddly tinged with the tell-tale scent of aged whiskey.

That wasn't only sparkling cider he'd put in his glass, Nicky realized. Despite her better judgement, a part of her secretly loved him for that. Yes, Lander Iron Feather was every bit the rule-breaking renegade, which was precisely why he'd amassed such a large fortune at his young age. But why, oh why, did he have to be heart-poundingly good looking to boot?

"Happy?" he whispered low into her ear, without the slightest break in his smooth steps.

Nicky's heart skipped a beat.

What did he mean? The prom, or being so tight in his arms that the music of the country waltz felt like it had fused them into one person?

Nicky nodded out of cursory politeness. "Who wouldn't be? This prom is…*perfect*," she spilled a bit too fast, feeling vulnerable as those words escaped her lips. Holding her breath, she leaned back and was surprised to catch a glimmer of genuine rawness in Lander's eyes.

A rawness she knew too well—

He's getting the prom dance he never had, she thought. The one she never had. The one by its very absence since they were teens had left a giant hole in their hearts.

Maybe it wasn't too late after all…

Nicky stole a glance at the vibrant selfie station and charming decorations Lander had arranged throughout the barn—not to mention the blinking, vintage carnival rides that she'd noticed had been set up outside. Could it be that the famously calculating Lander Iron Feather really *does* have a heart?

Be careful, Nicky thought, doing her best to stay grounded. This isn't a make-believe photo shoot, like your modeling days—this is real life. And the crazy-as-a-fox ranch neighbor is actually dancing with you, probably just to check off some box he'd been deprived of in adolescence. It doesn't necessarily mean you or the kids matter to him—

"You matter," Lander whispered, interrupting her train of thought. He studied her eyes with a gravity that left her startled.

The hair stood on the back of Nicky's neck, her heart quickening. Had he somehow read her mind? He couldn't possibly have a spy device rigged to her brain.

"W-What?" she stammered.

"Everything about tonight *matters*, Nicky," he insisted. "You, the kids—all of it. And no, I didn't read your mind. I simply took a wild guess, based on what your body and eyes have been telling me all day." A ghost of a smile etched Lander's lips, and he leaned seductively for a moment beside her ear. "Don't forget, I heard you mention that you think I'm handsome." His eyes danced mischievously. "*Goddamned handsome* is the way I believe you put it."

Heat flooded Nicky's cheeks, and she wished she could crawl into a hole beneath the old, rustic barn and die. Does he really have to rub it in, she cringed, after eavesdropping on me in my cabin? Don't let him fluster you, Nicky scolded herself, her back stiffening. That's Lander's superpower—he probably tries to rattle every woman he comes across. Struggling to keep her wits separate from the embarrassment spiking her cheeks, she stubbornly returned his gaze.

"Fess up, Lander," Nicky snapped, scrutinizing his face. "How many women have you brought to this ranch? I've seen the tabloids that parade all the beauties you've blown through. The outlaw billionaire who does everything his own way, leaving broken hearts on the roadside. It's no secret you're one of the world's most eligible bachelors. So why do you stalk women like a voyeur and listen from a distance to their conversations? Don't tell me, let me guess: Are you afraid of intimacy?"

"Are you?"

The way Lander took in her eyes, with a hint of whiskey— and male desire—lingering on his skin, practically screamed for Nicky to let go and lay her head on his toned chest, wondering if his heartbeat could possibly match hers. A tangle of nerve endings snapped through her system, making this simple barn dance a whole lot headier than she'd bargained for.

"Nicky," Lander said, "I also heard you admit to a student you're a model. One look at Google confirmed you're no stranger to the world's richest men who've tried to claim you. Before you came back to Bandits Hollow, you were one of the highest-paid women in fashion."

"You *researched* me online, based on your sneaky intel?"

With a huff, Nicky yanked her hand from Lander's shoulder and reached into a hidden hip pocket in her gold gown. She pulled out Lander's spy device and dropped it to the barn floor, crushing it with her foot. Then she lifted her gaze to him with a taunting twinkle in her eye.

"I...probably...deserved that." A crooked curl of lip threatened Lander's cheek as he glanced down at what was left of the device, now scattered in pieces. The way he restrained his amusement hinted that he secretly admired Nicky's moxie.

"Why were you spying on me?" she demanded. "Does it all come down to that total lech thing?"

Lander's mouth tightened to keep from creasing upward, betraying that he'd enjoyed that comment, too. "I only turn on the device from nine to five, if that's what you're thinking. Not that I have scruples. But even I have to take a break once in a while."

"You're not answering my question," Nicky pressed, re-crushing the remnants of the spy device every chance she got while they circled in their dance.

Lander cocked his chin for a moment, the muscles in his jaw working as if he were reluctant to acknowledge her accusation of espionage. As the band launched into Brett Young's *In Case You Didn't Know* to keep up the lazy tempo, he cleared his throat and looked her in the eye.

"The timing of your arrival was rather...sketchy...Nicky."

"Sketchy? You're calling *me* sketchy—the same guy who spied on me?" She searched Lander's eyes, her expression becoming indignant. "It-it's the money, isn't it? Thorne Wilson's money. Let me make one thing clear—it's no picnic to discover his poisonous blood runs in your veins. I would *never* accept a dime from that asshole except to keep running the school. For all I care, he can burn his fortune. I'm here for the—"

"Kids," Lander finished her sentence.

He turned his head, gazing out over the awkward

teenagers in formal wear who stumbled to navigate their waltz moves without stepping on too many toes. When his eyes returned to Nicky, that piercing rawness came back again.

"It's pretty obvious the kids are your first priority," he said. "And from what I've seen about your modeling career, you're not exactly hurting for cash." Lander tipped his forehead toward hers, a rare vulnerability surfacing in his eyes. "I…I was wrong about you, Nicky."

His hand gripped hers so tightly that a sharp breath escaped her lips.

"Oh," Lander loosened his grip without apology. "But I do have to point out that you never answered *my* question, either."

Nicky's gaze darted back and forth for a moment. "What question?"

Lander licked his lips, relishing the innocent look on her face like a wolf who'd cornered his prey.

"Are *you* afraid of intimacy?"

11

Nicky's breath hitched—

All at once, she felt like a wild animal trapped in a cage. A tremor tumbled through her, which she assumed Lander must have felt from his firm grip on her hand.

Was she afraid of intimacy? How can you be afraid of something you've never had?

It was common knowledge that Nicky had dated a roulette of high-rolling men, the kind who'd make most ordinary women seethe with jealousy. But deep inside, she knew she'd never really let any of them near her heart, much less into her soul. They were simply a glamorous way to pass the time, to artfully distract her from looking at her life—or lack thereof. Nicky's lips twitched for a moment, but she wasn't able to form words in her defense.

Because Lander was right.

And the glint in his eyes confirmed he'd nailed her—

She was just as relationship-phobic as he was.

Nevertheless, Nicky glanced around the room at the teenagers, trying out their first attempts to be genuine ladies and gentlemen, even if they were dancing clumsily inside a dusty, hundred-year-old barn. It was true, maybe she *had* resisted real relationships in her adult life. But these kids were young, and despite all the tragedies that had brought them to the school, the sweet, vulnerable looks on their faces indicated that they still dared to nurture…

Dreams.

Nicky smiled at the sight of her students, who were priceless to her beyond measure. Her heart felt full in that moment—as full as when her grandmother used to tell her she was strong and could do anything—and it made her feel emboldened.

"Tell me the truth, Lander. Do you *still* want to destroy Thorne Wilson and all of his assets?" Nicky asked, narrowing her gaze. "Word gets around about your real motivation to be the top rancher in the state, you know. If you destroy him, you destroy the school."

She paused, her heart climbing into her throat.

All at once, Lander's eyes became cool and unreadable, the way Nicky imagined they did whenever he was in the midst of a high-stakes business deal. Then he stared straight at Nicky with a raised brow.

"You run the school now," he said, his tone laced with skepticism, "and Thorne Wilson has *nothing* to do with it?"

"That's right," Nicky confirmed. "I have his endowment for operational money, plus whatever I can fundraise through grants and donations, pitching in as much of my own finances as I can. But now that he has dementia, I have total free rein to steer the school in a positive direction. Everything's changed since we were there. Come look at it, Lander."

"Why, because you need me as a donor?"

"No," Nicky said, swallowing hard. "Because I need a… friend. Someone who's been there and can give me ideas for ways the school can grow. There are other programs I want to start, independent of Wilson's money. Between the two of us, we could heal the school and its legacy."

"Oh," he replied sarcastically, cocking his head. "So you want me as a *strategic* type of friend, one with very deep pockets. Everyone's favorite kind."

Nicky rolled her eyes. "I'm serious, Lander. Where would the kids go if you succeeded in bankrupting Thorne Wilson and forced the school to close? Foster homes? I'm not a big fan of the guy either, but you and I both know the school is the only real chance these kids have. Try stepping out of that fancy mansion of yours for half an hour and meet me there some time. Let me show you the improvements I've made. The students are more excited than they've been in ages, and so am I. Will you consider it?"

A smile crinkled the edges of Lander's mouth, and he tilted next to her ear. "Only if you give me back my bones, like you *promised*," he whispered. Then he fell quiet for a moment, causing Nicky to dread what his next demand might be. "*And if you accompany me to the pool hall this Saturday, my lovely mercenary friend.*"

For all of his charm, Lander's suggestion felt more like a thinly-veiled threat than a request. The heat of his breath against her neck made her tremble.

"Do I have choice?" Nicky whispered back, dropping her

palm to keep it over the pocket of her gown. Right now, those wolf bones were the only leverage she had.

"You decide," Lander said, his gaze suddenly made of ice. "Burying Thorne Wilson in business deals has been my single greatest pleasure in life over the last five years. It would take a hell of a lot to steer me otherwise, Nicky."

"Well, if I *happened* to return your precious wolf bones," she countered, bartering for all she was worth, "and um, you make a *generous*, tax-deductible contribution for student programs, what pool hall would we go to?"

"The Outlaw's Hideout Bar and Grill in Bandits Hollow," he replied. "They've got a large billiards room in the back that usually draws quite a crowd."

"Wait a second." Nicky halted from following Lander's waltz steps, suddenly recalling the stories she'd heard about that place when she was a kid. It was where cowboys typically went after payday to compete at darts, pool, poker—and to show off their latest female conquests in order to make each other jealous. Their efforts usually ended up in drunken brawls over who got to take the prettiest woman home. "Let me get this straight," Nicky backpedaled as she began to grasp Lander's intentions. "You want me to be your *arm candy* for that night, don't you? To distract other cowboys during pool and make them envious, like some fabled Lady Luck."

Lander's eyes glinted, totally unfazed at being caught. "You said you wanted a contribution for the school, right?" he replied, enjoying Nicky's unease. "Given your former career, this wouldn't be the first time you've looked glamorous for cash."

"Lander Iron Feather!" Nicky burst, giving him a sharp shove. "I *refuse* to be anyone's paid escort!"

"Of course not—you'd be my date."

"I'll have you know I used to make ten grand a day per booking," Nicky hissed, poking her finger into his chest. "And I only worked with the world's top photographers. These weren't exactly smoky, back-room bar regulars—"

"Ten grand, huh?" Lander folded his muscled arms and tapped his chin. He narrowed his gaze and leaned into Nicky's face, meeting her nose to nose. "Then I'll double that in my donation to the school."

Nicky's cheeks swelled crimson and she balled her fists, but she couldn't help doing the math in her head. Twenty grand would be enough to finance state-of-the-art equipment for the new chemistry, biology, and physics labs she wanted to incorporate into the school's STEM programs.

Gritting her teeth, Nicky's knuckles creased white, and with all of her being she resisted the overwhelming urge to smack him. She heaved a slow breath and counted back from ten so she wouldn't have to face assault charges in front of the students. Then she gave Lander a wicked glare. "I will only go to the bar for *one hour*—got that, cowboy?" she spit out. "And I expect your contribution before midnight that Saturday. In cash."

"Sounds like a plan," Lander said, his eyes glinting as though he'd won a bet.

"No parading me around like I'm your girlfriend, either. *Comprende?*" she hissed, her eyes turning to dark beads. "And I wear whatever the hell I want, not some slinky outfit to impress cowboys."

Lander mulled over her last request and shook his head.

"Nope," he replied. "You'll be dressed to the nines like it's a Broadway opening. All glittery and," he dropped his husky voice a few notches as he brazenly scanned her curves, "utterly gorgeous."

Furious, but far too tempted by a quick twenty grand for her school, Nicky plunged her hands into her gown pockets, where she couldn't stop fiddling with Lander's wolf bones. Surprisingly, they began to turn warm against her fingers, and she half-wondered if it was because she wished she could set this manipulative man on fire.

"God damn you, Lander Iron Feather," she whispered under her breath, only to see him grin broadly with the same arrogant smile that had made him a fixture in the tabloids. Nicky lifted her chin in defiance, tempted to throw Lander's wolf bones at his face just to see how fast she could wipe off that smile. Despite her frustration, however, that twenty grand was just too good to pass up. "So," Nicky reiterated, deliberately pushing the envelope of their deal, "after we go to the pool hall and I get my…donation…you'll come out to the school next week and look it over. Then seriously think about becoming, shall we say, an ongoing financial *friend* to the school?"

"Is that your code word for *benefactor?*" Lander squinted, not fooled for a second. Yet he appeared to relish Nicky's feverish tap dance on behalf of the kids. "Let's see, first you hit me up for the prom, and now you want me to bankroll your school? Plus you haven't even given my bones back." He shook his head in amusement. "And people call me the wheeler dealer."

Despite the levity behind his comment, Lander's eyes creased to a venomous glare. "Beyond the donation Saturday night, Nicky, I'm not promising you a goddamned thing—"

"But you're open to suggestions, right?" she bounced back persistently. "And don't forget those great tax write-offs. Ooh!" she pointed at the selfie station, eager to switch the subject before Lander changed his mind. "Isn't it time to get our pictures taken? That lariat lit up inside the gold frame is amazing." To Lander's surprise, Nicky boldly grabbed him by the hand and began to drag him across the barn.

"Damn, you're determined." Lander shook his head. "Do you always get your way, Nicky?"

"With a tiara on top!" she winked. Nicky picked out a rhinestone crown from among the props on the bench and set it on her head. Then she grabbed a more masculine-looking plastic crown with fake gemstones and whipped off Lander's cowboy hat, positioning it on top of his blonde hair. "Here, you can be prom king for the night," she smiled whimsically. "As long as you remember who's queen around here."

"Somehow…that suits you," Lander noted. He turned and grasped the Polaroid camera. "Try putting on a few other props, and I'll snap your picture."

Just when Nicky discovered a leather belt with a holster and a pistol among the props and slipped it around her waist, several students walked up to the selfie station.

"Wait," one of the boys said, tugging at her arm. "Can we be in the photo, too?"

"Oh, of course," Nicky replied, startled and a little bit flattered. She smiled warmly at him. "Grab some props and join me inside the frame."

Before she could say another word, a passel of kids came over and rifled through the cowboy hats, feather boas, and tiaras. Then they squeezed into the frame, all smiles and giggles. Before long, more students joined, and it became like a dare to see how many kids they could fit into a Volkswagen Beetle. Over a dozen kids crammed up so tightly against Nicky—standing on their tip toes, kneeling, or lying down—that she couldn't help busting out laughing.

"This is gonna be great!" one of the girls smiled, staring up at Nicky from the floor. She swung her feather boa so it that caught Nicky around the neck and gave her an affectionate tug. "You're like a mom to all of us."

Mom...

Goosebumps threaded over Nicky's skin, and her breathing came to a halt.

The girl had actually called her...*mom*.

Choking up a little, Nicky relished the feeling of being squished between the students as if it were a big, crazy family reunion. She hadn't experienced this feeling of belonging in years, and to her, it was like a warm salve soothed over a fractured part of her soul that she'd never quite known how to fix. Wrapping her arms around as many kids as she could reach, she beamed with everything she had in her, her grin rivaling the brightness of the lariat twinkling over their heads.

Only this time, Nicky's smile was for *real*.

At that moment, Lander deftly swirled a rope over his head with an easy cowboy familiarity, like he'd done it a thousand times, and lassoed the group as though they were a captured outlaw gang. When he yanked the rope tight, it made the kids laugh.

"I told you it's possible to rope the stars," Lander reminded them. "You're all stars tonight."

With that, he dropped the rope and grabbed the Polaroid to snap their picture, which sent the students into fits of belly laughs until they collapsed onto the barn floor in a clumsy heap.

A big, messy, wonderful heap. All arms, legs and jiggling bellies that brought tears to Nicky's eyes. She couldn't help herself—she laid beside the students on the old barn floor and kept laughing until her stomach hurt.

"Ma'am," said Lander, walking up to her and holding out his hand to give her a lift. "Would you like some help up?" He glanced back at the dining tables. "There's a ribeye on a plate over there with your name on it."

Nicky shook her head. "No way. I'm staying right here till the last kid gets up," she whispered, attempting in vain to restrain her giggles. "I've done nothing but have picture after picture taken of me for the last five years, playing everyone but myself. And for once, Lander, I'm inside a silly gold frame being exactly who I want to be."

12

Nicky creaked open the door of the Outlaw's Hideout Bar and Grill in the early evening on Saturday, allowing her eyes to adjust to the dim light of the vintage, stained-glass lamps that hung from the ceiling. True to form, she wore a mini dress in metallic peacock colors with a halter neck and a cutout décolletage that set off her tan cleavage. The sultry outfit was already a showstopper, and Nicky had no intention of pimping her self-esteem any further for Lander's whims *or* his money. So she'd stubbornly put on a pair of black leggings underneath the mini dress to complete her look, making it less likely to show too much thigh. The only other concession she made to glamour was a pair of fire-engine red Louboutin heels with pretty sashes that tied around her graceful ankles.

As far as Nicky was concerned, Lander either approved of her get-up for his deal or he didn't. And if he dared to haggle about his donation, Nicky was going to tell him to shove it up his ass, along with the wolf bones she fully intended to return. After all, he *had* already paid for the prom—God bless him—and anything else he decided to pony up was gravy. She didn't need to lower herself if he was going to renege on his promise.

The second the door fell shut behind her, a row of cowboys who were bellied up to the bar turned their heads so fast they nearly got whiplash. Their mouths dropped in awe.

Nicky sighed…

It was her superpower.

Moments like this capitalized on her God-given assets, which was only pleasurable if she liked the attention of a bunch of half-drunk, dusty cowboys. Nicky could have set her watch for when their whistles filled the air, and like usual, it made her eyes roll. Unfortunately, she never did get the hang of enjoying such regard from strangers, and she hoped she'd find Lander soon so she wouldn't have to endure watching the men's drool actually pool onto the bar top.

The tall bartender, a grizzled man well into his sixties, glanced up when he saw Nicky. He squinted at her face with a flare of recognition in his eyes. The intensity of his focus made her feel awkward, especially since she'd never been inside this place.

"Good evening, ma'am," he said, still studying her features. "By God, you have got to be related to…"

Nicky cringed while he mopped up a glass of whiskey that a patron had just spilled, fearing he might mention Thorne Wilson. It was true—she knew she'd inherited his height and long limbs from the occasions she'd seen him back in school, but she prayed none of his dark soul had filtered down to hers.

"Tavachi Cloud," the bartender finally finished his

sentence, tossing his wet dishtowel into a nearby sink. "You're the spitting image of her." He motioned to a framed photo of Nicky's grandmother on the wall, which was hung beside other photos of cowgirls through the years. She was wearing a cowboy hat with a tiara positioned on the hatband, smiling like she owned the world. The sash that cut diagonally across her chest said *Miss Outlaw Days 1970*.

Nicky had forgotten that her grandmother used to compete in barrel racing and pole bending in local rodeos, since she was never one to brag. But her sensitive connection to horses was something Nicky had always aspired to emulate.

"Her beauty was renowned in three counties," the bartender continued with a gleam in his eye, as if the memory were still fresh. He gave Nicky a warm smile. "Sure looks like it runs in the family. You her granddaughter or something?"

Heat rifled Nicky's cheeks. As a girl, she'd never thought of her grandmother as attractive to men, though it was no secret that her long, straight hair and cheekbones to die for perfectly set off her stunning brown eyes and full lips. To Nicky, Tavachi was the epitome of inner warmth and strength, her beauty coming from her soul and the boundless well of love that she freely gave to others.

"Y-you're right," Nicky stammered, unable to deny from the photo that she *did* resemble her grandmother in her younger days. "Tavachi Cloud was my *kagu-chi*."

The bartender nodded at the Ute word for maternal grandmother, and he topped off a drink for one of the cowboys. "Her beauty wasn't the only thing that made her remarkable around here," he added. "She's the only one I've ever heard of who had the guts to stand up to Thorne Wilson, even though she was a young slip of a gal. She took her baby and disappeared far from his grip, when she could have sued him for millions in support. There's plenty of folks who admire her to this day."

"So *that's* where you get your mettle," a familiar voice commented from a darkened corner of the bar. As Lander stepped into the light of the stained-glass lamps, Nicky noticed he had bemused expression on his face. "Your grandmother was a fire cracker, just like you."

The glint in his eyes showed he approved of Nicky's outfit, despite the fact that she'd thrown on a pair of leggings under a designer dress. The way the fabric of the dress clung to the curves of her waist and breasts made it obvious why she'd become a top model.

"I'll take that as a compliment," Nicky replied, folding her arms. "Apparently, the women in my family have a noble history of *defying* men." She narrowed her gaze at Lander. "And turning down their money if they get too out of line." Nicky sank her hands into her dress pocket, where Lander's wolf bones were buried. For a few moments, she felt them jiggle beneath her fingers like Mexican jumping beans.

"Ready to head to the pool tables?" Lander asked. He leaned close to her ear and whispered, "The bones always like it when gambling is about to take place."

Goosebumps trickled down Nicky's neck. How had he known the bones shimmied beneath her fingers?

With a shrug, she dismissed the coincidence and followed Lander to a room at the back of the bar with three pool tables, where two men were already playing against opponents.

Two *extremely handsome* men—

Who were every bit as tall and rugged-looking as Lander.

Nicky held back a gasp. One of them resembled him, with the same stone-cut jaw, sharp cheekbones, and imposing stature. But his long hair was dark, not blonde, and his wide shoulders appeared even impossibly broader.

Dillon Iron Feather? Nicky thought, her mind reaching into the cobwebs of memory. Lander's oldest brother?

She'd caught rare glimpses of the Iron Feather brothers back when she was a teen at the Wilson Ranch, where boys and girls were kept separate at all times. The rumor mill had said they were part Apache, part Ute, and part white, "mixed breeds" who for some reason earned an exceptional degree of abuse from Thorne Wilson. As defiant as they were handsome, everyone said they were unbreakable—and the biggest criminal badasses in the county—which was why they'd been sent to the school.

At the next pool table stood the middle brother Barrett, Nicky surmised, as intimidating and good-looking as his other two brothers, but with short dark hair and a particularly arresting stare.

"This is Dillon and Barrett, my brothers," Lander confirmed, introducing Nicky to them. "It's sort of a tradition for us to play pool here once a month, whenever we can."

The two men nodded at her, and Nicky couldn't help noticing there was a keen sense of appraisal in their eyes, as if she were hardly the first woman Lander had brought here. Nicky returned their stares unflinchingly, hoping to give them the hint that they needn't worry about her being girlfriend material. And secretly, she hoped the unflappable mask she'd perfected in her modeling days might also let them know she wasn't the least bit intimidated.

Because she was...

Everyone knew the Iron Feather brothers had hardly gotten a good shake in life. Yet they'd made something of themselves with their extraordinary, multi-million dollar ranch and commercial enterprises.

But Nicky's childhood hadn't been a picnic, either. She might not have their massive assets, but like them, she hadn't let Thorne Wilson's school destroy her. Still, to have all three of the Iron Feather brothers in one room was a jolt to anyone's system. Not only because they were astonishingly handsome and quite possibly lethal, but because even Nicky could feel the anger that always seemed to simmer beneath their skins. The three of them didn't say much—they didn't have to. They were big, determined men with a strangely threatening way of swallowing the entire space around them. Within seconds of stepping near the brothers, Nicky could already tell she'd better hold onto herself in order not to be derailed by their intense presence.

At that moment, she spied several other people who'd begun to filter into the billiards room. They either leaned against the wood-paneled walls or aimed for the rows of folding chairs that lined the edges of the room to sit down.

Audience—

They're audience, Nicky realized. Onlookers who'd come specifically to watch the Iron Feather brothers play pool.

Before long, a crowd of about thirty people stood around the perimeter of the billiards room. Nicky felt fortunate to have grabbed one of the chairs, many of which had "reserved" signs taped to the seats, and she wondered how she could possibly sneak out in an hour. What was she supposed to do during the pool tournament, anyway? Be Lander's cheerleader?

No way.

That hadn't been expressly part of their deal, as far as Nicky could recall. And she'd had enough of plastering on fake smiles during her career to keep up such a superficial game anymore. Sticking with her decision, she stood to her feet and headed over to Lander at the pool table, pulling his wolf bones from her pocket. While he angled his cue for a practice shot, without a word, Nicky brushed beside him and expertly deposited the wolf bones into his jeans.

"Wow, that's quite a shot," she remarked, confident her ghost-like fingers were so smooth from years of practice that Lander probably hadn't detected the slip into his pocket. "Good luck tonight," she offered, giving him a pat on the shoulder.

Now she was free to go any time.

Nicky returned to her seat and checked her watch. She would spend exactly one hour here, as they'd discussed, and then she'd see if Lander was going to make good on his promise to give her twenty grand in cash.

And if he didn't?

Well, that'll be the last time he'll see me, Nicky resolved. If he didn't intend to become an ongoing benefactor for the kids' sake, her dealings with Lander Iron Feather would come to a close.

"So, who are you rooting for?" a pretty woman with knockout curves and long blonde hair said as she plopped onto a chair beside Nicky. She glanced her up and down. "You don't seem like the usual hoedown honey who's here to ogle the Iron Feather brothers. For starters, you're not wearing cut-offs that are so short they reveal the edges of your lingerie." The woman sighed. "Every time one of the Iron Feather brothers leans over to make a shot, I guarantee you're going to hear the room groan. With pleasure, that is."

Nicky scanned the room, a bit startled by the crowd—the woman was right. Most of the audience was made up of rhinestone cowgirl wannabes whose shirts and shorts were so tight she wondered how they could breathe. Like clockwork, when Lander leaned over to make another practice shot, light moans threaded through the audience.

Nicky bit her lip—Lander really did have an amazing ass.

"See?" The woman beside Nicky chuckled, giving her the elbow. "I'm Dillon Iron Feather's wife, Tessa. Believe me, I've seen it all. Luckily, the brothers are so competitive they rarely take notice of the hopefuls."

"The hopefuls?"

"The women who try to snag the attention of the richest and best-looking ranchers in Colorado. But that doesn't mean they won't snap pictures on their cell phones of the men's… um…assets. A girl can dream, right?"

"Well, I'm *not* here to dream," Nicky stated flatly. "I'm Nicky Box, by the way. The new director of the—"

"Sun Mountain School at the Wilson Ranch," Tessa completed her words, grabbing Nicky's hand to shake it. "I know. Rumors travel fast in this small town. Everyone says you've completely transformed the place, for the better." Tessa sought Nicky's eyes with a tender gaze. "That's why I wanted to introduce myself—to thank you." She glanced at the Iron Feather brothers around the pool tables. "What you're doing is incredible for the kids, and the fact that it's happening is helping all of them heal. I've seen it myself in Dillon—the relief that comes from knowing what he experienced won't ever happen to another kid again. And that the school is in good hands."

Nicky's eyes became slightly watery at the edges as her throat cinched. She hadn't thought about the legacy for the school's former alumni as well as her current students—that she might be playing a role in healing for everyone involved.

"Keep up the good work," encouraged Tessa, giving Nicky's knee a pat. "And let me know if there's anything I can do to help. Oh, look—here comes Lainey, Barrett's wife."

A slim woman with an athletic figure and honey-brown hair smiled from across the room and walked toward them, sitting down in another chair next to Tessa. She gave her a quick squeeze around the shoulders.

"Lainey," Tessa said, "this is Nicky, the new director of the Sun Mountain School."

"Oh my gosh!" Lainey replied, clutching her chest for a moment before giving Nicky an enthusiastic wave. "Nice to meet you! Barrett's already told me what an impact you've had on the kids. We're really glad you've come to Bandits Hollow."

Nicky returned her compliment with a smile, swallowing self-consciously. She had no idea other people in the community would be so…grateful.

"All right, everyone," Barrett called out, snapping Nicky from her thoughts. He stood in the middle of the billiards room and addressed the audience. "My brother, Lander Iron

Feather, is going to shoot the first round of Eight-Ball tonight with our fellow rancher from Bandits Hollow, Hank Goodacre. Out of courtesy, we need everyone to keep their voices low during the match, and please," he urged, "*no* flash photography." He glared at the scantily-clad women who stood along the walls with such an icy stare that they tucked their cell phones into their cut-offs. "The betting tonight starts at ten grand."

All at once, Nicky spotted a group of well-dressed men in Stetson hats and Lucchese boots who were filing into the billiards room. They sat down on a row of reserved seats at the opposite side of the room with solemn stares.

"High rollers," Tessa whispered to Nicky. "A dozen or so top ranchers fly in from places like Tulsa and Houston each time the Iron Feather brothers play. It's a rich man's amusement, I guess you could say. But the stakes are real."

Nicky eyes grew wide when she saw Lainey nod in agreement. This wasn't a typical Saturday-night pool game after all—

It was the secret Vegas of the Rockies for those who could roll big.

Really big.

The eager women along the walls smiled and winked, hoping to score the affections of the out-of-town ranchers as well. Their flirtations were cut short, however, when Barrett held up a coin to bring the room to silence. He ordered Lander and Hank to make their calls as he flipped the coin in air and set it on his arm.

"Heads!" Barret stated. "Looks like Hank Goodacre will

do the first break." He racked the balls into a triangle and gave the two men an official nod. "Game on, boys."

Barrett crossed the room along with his brother Dillon, and the two sat down on reserved chairs on the other side of Nicky. With a loud crack, Hank's cue broke through the balls. Although he did a fairly decent job, the way the balls rolled across the green felt into mediocre positions made him cringe.

Surprisingly, Dillon paid little attention to his pool skills.

"So, I hear you run the Sun Mountain School at the Wilson Ranch these days," Dillon whispered from beside Nicky with a cocked brow. "Quite the job."

Nicky was surprised to hear him talk at all, like a stone-cut figure from Mount Rushmore wired for sound. He didn't bother to introduce himself either, like his wife. Apparently, in typical arrogant Iron Feather brother fashion, he assumed Nicky knew who he was.

And he was right.

"Lander told me he held the prom for the kids at our ranch the other night." Dillon looked Nicky over, making her jittery under his hard gaze. Then his eyes softened a little. "That must have meant a lot to them."

"It did," Nicky replied. "It-It was a dream come true for the kids, to be honest. Thank you," she said in all sincerity, "for letting us use your facilities."

Dillon nodded slowly, and Nicky got the peculiar impression he was *feeling* her presence more than listening to anything she said, as though he could somehow measure her soul. The thought made her fidget.

Dillon cleared his throat. "Lander also told me you'd do

anything for those teenagers," he mentioned without looking at her. "I believe he...admires...you."

A rush of tingles arced up Nicky's back. Seriously? Practically all Lander's done since I returned to Bandits Hollow is torment me, she thought. And then there's his crazy obsession for competing with Thorne Wilson. "Well, near as I can tell," she sighed, "he's hell bent on destroying the school's owner. Which certainly will impact the school's future."

"We all have our addictions," Dillon replied. "Winning is Lander's. Except when it gets in the way of his heart."

"His heart?"

Dillon stole a glance at Nicky. He inclined his face to the pool table again. "Just watch."

Nicky fixed her gaze on the game of Eight-Ball, watching Lander bumble one shot after another—to the point of ripping the green felt near the edge of the pool table. His opponent Hank appeared to be beating him blind. Nicky folded her arms, intrigued to see something Lander wasn't good at for once. The crowd gasped when Hank's turn came up and he banked a lucky shot that made Lander's face burn with indignation. As the game progressed, Nicky became riveted when Lander failed to sink another one of his balls into a pocket. Furious, Lander clenched his cue with a white-knuckled grip and boldly snapped it over his knee in half.

The murmurs of the crowd swelled into a seismic rumble.

"That asshole's cheating!" Lander cried out, his fists balled in rage. "He's gaming the goddamned system somehow. Who the hell makes shots like that?"

Barrett leaped from his chair and grabbed Lander by the arm, yanking him into a corner of the billiards room before he could take a swing. Hank merely smirked like he was a sore loser.

Although one of the bar employees handed Lander another cue as if his legendary temper were merely routine, it was clear Lander's game was headed downhill.

Dillon released a long breath at his over-the-top display. "My brother's known for being crazy as well as one of the world's best negotiators," he whispered, his lip curling into a hint of a smile. "Which means he's a damned artful liar."

"Liar?" Nicky replied. "How could he possibly be lying right now—"

"Keep an eye on his next shot."

Nicky studied Lander while he poised his cue. Just before he made the shot, he loosened his forefinger ever so slightly, barely detectable unless someone was really looking for it. As he struck the ball, the cue imperceptibly slipped.

Nicky's breath hitched.

"Hank's ranch is heading into foreclosure," Dillon mentioned in a low tone. "Lander's been challenging him month after month, if you get my drift."

Nicky's mouth dropped.

Lander was doing all of this for…charity?

"Why?" she whispered back. "He could just give the guy the money."

"Because cowboys don't take hand outs," Dillon replied. "He's preserving the man's dignity. And contrary to popular belief, he doesn't sleep with every woman he flirts with, either. He just puts on the crazy Casanova image to keep businessmen—and pretty little sharks—at bay."

Sharks…

Nicky studied the room. Sure enough, the women along the walls were practically drooling while standing with their backs arched and their breasts shoved forward as though offering Lander an all-you-can-eat sexual buffet. Their sprayed-on tans and shrink-wrapped clothes were enough to make Nicky wince.

Another failed shot had Lander cursing in a rage like the Tasmanian Devil. Dillon shook his head, then squinted at Nicky. His penetrating stare made her shift in her seat.

"Who gave you those earrings?" he said.

She lightly brushed one of the dangling turquoise earrings with her fingers. "M-My grandmother. They're old—"

"They're more than old," Dillon pointed out. "They're Lander Blue."

Nicky's stomach knotted, unsure of what he was after. They matched her pendant that had been lost to the Mediterranean Sea.

"My mother named my brother after that stone," Dillon asserted. "The most valuable turquoise in the world, because our ancestor had a piece of it in his medicine pouch that we inherited. He'd traded a horse for it long before white people discovered Lander Blue in the 1970s. Back in the day, my mother could hear it sing. She said it was Lander's song."

Nicky felt unnerved by his words—she'd heard that certain people could hear tones coming from the turquoise, but she didn't know if it was true. "I-I used to have a matching pendant, but I lost it off the coast of France, in a bad accident."

Dillon eyes rested on hers. "Be careful, Nicky."

"What do you mean? Why are you telling me all of this?" she asked, feeling distinctly uncomfortable.

"Because I saw the way he looks at you," Dillon said flatly. "And I can tell the war has already started."

"The war?"

"Between his head and his heart. My mother said the Lander Blue stone has the brightest color with the darkest matrix—just like Lander's soul."

In that instant, Lander snapped another cue in half by bashing it on the floor and stomping it with his boot. When he turned to glance at Dillon, his lip rose into the fleeting ghost of a smile. Then his gaze lingered on Nicky.

"See?" Dillon said. "If you look close, the wolf bones jump in his pocket every time he sees you. And that means only one thing."

Stunned, Nicky's throat suddenly felt dry and tight— Dillon had *seen her* return the bones to Lander's pocket, when Lander himself hadn't even detected them. She sucked in a breath, waiting.

"They want him to take a gamble on you."

Nicky's heart began to race, when she happened to spy a tall old man who'd stumbled into the billiards room. Frail and wiry, he leaned heavily on a cane, and he was dressed in a dark coat over pajamas and slippers. All at once, he lifted his cane in the air and waved it dramatically until the chatter in the room fell silent.

Nicky's heart nearly stopped—

It was Thorne Wilson.

His eyes narrowed to bullets when he spotted her across the room, and he began to hobble toward Nicky, wheezing.

Then he pointed his crooked cane at her with the all dark energy of the devil.

"You! Thief!" he called out in a hoarse voice laced with poison. "Daughter of that bastard bitch! Thought you could take the school from me, eh? Well, it's on *my* ranch, and I'm not handing it over to anybody! I'm *not* senile, and I'll fight you in the highest courts."

Eyes blazing, Thorne pounded the floor with his cane, making the wood thunder. "Mark my word," he growled vehemently, "the charter says I only have to give thirty days' notice to shut the school down." He glared into Nicky's eyes, jabbing a gnarled finger in her face. "And as far as I'm concerned, you just got it."

13

Lander greeted dawn the following morning at the Iron Feather Brothers Ranch like he always did, watching the sun's rays settle on the barns and slowly warm the backs of his horses and cattle that angled their bodies toward the horizon like sundials. It was his quiet morning ritual, a private time to collect his thoughts without the constant demands of business, where he could consider his next moves for the brothers' ranching empire. But on this particular morning, as soon as he distributed alfalfa to the livestock and checked the water tanks, he aimed his truck straight for the dirt road that led to the Wilson Ranch.

With twenty grand in cash tucked into his pocket.

Along with the wolf bones…

Lander was surprised Nicky had secretly returned the bones to his jeans last night without first snatching the money he'd pledged. For a seasoned pickpocket, he thought it was odd that she'd left the bar with less than she came in with, especially since he hadn't noticed her clever sleight of hand. As much he admired her finesse, a clench in his gut hinted at her reasons. He figured Nicky was far too independent and stubborn to allow herself to be beholden to him for very long. Nor did she give a rip about his fleeting attention or favors like the other desperate cowgirls in the bar. And after her grandfather's humiliating tirade, Nicky was probably in no mood to stick around for any kind of payout.

Word had spread that Thorne Wilson had snuck out of his mansion that night during a shift change with his staff. Pajamas and all, he'd managed to escape from the house and into his old truck, then found his way to Bandits Hollow, probably after checking the director's cabin to find Nicky and realizing it was empty. Most people in Bandits Hollow liked to frequent the Outlaw's Hideout Bar and Grill on Saturday nights, and he must have guessed Nicky would be inside.

It had only taken a few minutes for Lander's law-enforcement brother Barrett to call Thorne's staff to alert them that Thorne had gone AWOL. By the time his handlers arrived to pick him up, the old man had become disoriented again and forgotten where he was. Despite Thorne's occasional episodes of clarity, dementia had already taken a toll, and no one could predict from moment to moment how lucid he might be. During all of the commotion, Nicky had silently slipped out of the bar.

Lander could hardly blame her.

Who wants to be hailed in public as the "daughter of that bastard bitch" or be accused of seizing the school in some bizarre act of greed? As he steered his truck up the gravel road toward the director's cabin, Lander shook his head, wondering if any of Thorne's threats could possibly be true. Surely with his dementia diagnosis, he wouldn't be able to change the charter to close the school, as he'd claimed. But one thing Lander could bet on: Nicky hadn't gotten a wink of sleep last night. She cared far too much about the kids to take Thorne's proclamations lightly, and her mind was probably still racing over his cruel taunts. As soon as Lander drove around the last bend, he spied the director's cabin and noticed Nicky's lights were on, though it was only six o'clock on Sunday morning.

The wolf bones in his pocket began to dance.

Lander pulled up within a hundred yards of Nicky's cabin and cut the engine. He drew in a sharp breath.

Never in a million years did he think he would come back here.

He slowly surveyed the grounds of his nightmarish adolescence, so different now from when he'd attended the school five years ago. The razor wire separating the school property from Thorne's homestead was gone, though there was still a chain-link fence along one edge of the campus that Thorne had installed to keep students away from his mansion. Despite this harsh boundary, Nicky had painstakingly revamped the rest of the campus, painting the dorms and school buildings in warm, inviting colors and planting cheerful landscaping with shrubs and flowers. Lander's gaze continued to roam over the property, when he spotted a weather-beaten structure next to an old barn, about the size of a garden shed.

His entire being went stiff, every muscle in his large frame snapping to attention.

Lander's fingers gripped the steering wheel until his

knuckles flashed white. It took all the willpower he had not to break the damn thing in half.

Before him was the notorious solitary confinement shack—

The wolf bones in his pocket stilled and turned to ice.

They had a different name for the shack back then, of course. It was called the "attitude adjustment room", conveniently outfitted with a large padlock on the front of the door so students couldn't escape. Along with thick blankets padding the ramshackle walls.

So no one could hear them scream.

Lander sealed his eyes shut for a moment, trying to repel the dark memories.

It didn't work—

His breathing became ragged while images flooded his mind of kickings and severe beatings. Bullwhips and belt lashings. Even a two-by-four that had once been aimed at his head.

Nicky must not have known the purpose of the shack, Lander thought, since it was only the most "insubordinate" boys who were sent there. Or she would have demolished it weeks ago…

As Lander stared at the old structure, everything within him had to fight the urge to grab his rifle that very second and pump so much ammunition into the shack that it collapsed into a million pieces. His fists exploded on the dash, pounding with all his might until it cracked. Despite his violent outburst, Lander couldn't erase the image of Thorne's beady eyes all those years ago, the way he gloated while a staff member held him down so Thorne could choose his favorite weapon for "obedience reminders." Thorne always laughed after he finished his beatings, claiming Lander would thank him later for "mainstreaming" him into civil society. At age fourteen, long before the growth spurt that broadened his chest and made him tower over most men, Lander had been too small and wiry to succeed in fighting back.

He'd just had to take it.

Creaking open the truck door in the soft morning light, Lander stepped into the cool air, his eyes fixed on the primitive shed that had never ceased to torment the edges of his mind. How many times had he howled after receiving blows, crying into the early morning hours until exhaustion finally reduced him to sleep?

Lander had lost count.

For him, the abuse eventually transformed into his defiant badge of honor, which Lander suffered in gritty silence, just so Thorne could no longer have the pleasure of hearing him scream. By his sophomore year, no matter how many times Lander was sent to the shack, he always met Thorne's blows with his wide, cocky grin. Then he'd brazenly taunt Thorne to lock him up until the day he died, so he'd have the eternal pleasure of haunting his ass until he went mad.

What sweet justice that Thorne is finally losing his mind, Lander thought.

Yet it was in that same, godforsaken shack in front of Lander that he learned to rely on the wolf bones.

At night, Lander used to swipe the bones from his ancestor's medicine pouch that Dillon secretly kept beneath his mattress, slipping them into his jeans pocket during the daytime in case he was sent to the shack.

Whenever Lander was confined to the shack for the

smallest transgressions—unfinished homework, failing to answer a question in class, glancing the wrong way at staff—he occupied himself by singing the hand game songs his Ute father had once taught him. Then he would flip the wolf bones in air, hour after hour, like dice. Over time, Lander began to realize that the bones appeared to respond to his thoughts. If the dark ones happened to land with their tips up and an icy feeling spread over his wrist, it meant a certain boy he'd trusted in the past was going to turn on him and become a snitch or a bully. But if the light bones landed on their tips while a warm tingle moved up his arm, it meant a new kid at school would become a loyal ally, even during a fight. Soon, Lander began to trust the bones for guidance about everything. Depending on the way they fell, he could even tell how many days in advance an event might occur. They became his survival mechanism—

Because the bones always had his back.

So why had they begun to vibrate every time he got close to Nicky?

Lander inhaled a deep breath. She was certainly stunning—any fool could see that for a mile. He folded his large arms, turning to study the sacred tree on the ridge that he used to go to for solace after spending grueling hours in the shack. The bones shivered whenever he got near the old pine as well, and he examined the way the morning sun glimmered off the pine's branches that wrapped around its trunk like an embrace. There was always something special about the prophecy tree, something that inexplicably whispered to his soul and put him in contact with a surprisingly tender part of himself that he thought had been consumed in angry flames. A lot like…

Nicky.

Lander swiftly bit back that thought.

How could anyone *not* be taken in by her fierce determination and beauty? It wasn't his fault she was drop-dead gorgeous—and equal parts demanding, irascible, and sometimes downright sneaky.

But damned if she didn't get to him…

The only reason I'm here right now, Lander reminded himself, is to give her the money. Because I keep my word—

A great horned owl hooted on the ridge, interrupting Lander's thoughts. Its call echoed off the nearby barn and school buildings. He spied the bird on top of the sacred tree as it lifted its wings and slowly soared from the ridge, dipping low over his head.

All at once, the owl alighted on the ground beside a boulder next to Nicky's cabin. Its dark silhouette fell against the rock in the morning sun like a projection onto a screen.

Lander did a double take—

He'd seen that kind of image before.

An owl's likeness on a rock, one that Dillon had shown him on a Ute pictograph from over a century ago, etched into stone with minerals like hematite and ochre, as well as the artist's own blood.

The sight made the nerves skip down Lander's spine.

That rock Dillon had shown him belonged to their ancestor Iron Feather—

It was a special communication between him and the Ute

tribe, representing an oath they'd once made with each other that lasted to the present day.

Deep inside, the owl's abrupt presence troubled Lander, and his thoughts wove through the implications when the bones in his pocket began to stir. The owl gave another hoot and took flight, just as Nicky's silhouette moved in front of her window.

Lander headed toward the cabin without making a sound.

He didn't want Nicky to detect he was there quite yet. So he maneuvered downwind with silent phantom strides, his path tracing from shadow to shadow, like his parents had taught him whenever they went hunting. Closing in on Nicky's door, he lingered in the dark recesses of a nearby pine. Then he sank his hand into his pocket one more time for the wolf bones.

This was the one secret his relatives never talked about—

The way you could still your heart and sense a person's… soul…through the bones. Especially if he or she was nearby.

To Lander's surprise, the bones shuddered against his fingers. Then they began to feel heavy under his grip, pulsing with a steady rhythm.

Like the beat of a human heart.

Nicky's big heart…

Warm tingles danced up his arm again.

At that moment, Nicky swung open her cabin door. From his place in the shadows, Lander noticed her eyes were red and swollen, moist at the edges, yet her face remained stoic. She held a cell phone to her ear, her mind caught up in conversation. Then she quickly scanned the area beyond her door as though she'd heard the owl's call, too.

Nicky winced.

"Look, Bradley," she said, "I know I've cashed a ton of stock lately to finance improvements to the school and hire the best teachers. The endowment wasn't nearly enough to cover everything. What if we try an aggressive approach for the rest of my portfolio? Maybe I could pull out more funds and rebuild the school elsewhere? Oh, right…it's a breach of contract if I withdraw before two years."

Nicky bit her lip, deeply regretting that she'd put the rest of her earnings into *Bar Profitieren Gruppe*, a Swiss investment membership that would sue her if she didn't maintain her twenty-four month commitment. Frowning, her forehead creased into lines. "How about a loan?" she sought desperately. "Gotcha…not enough upfront collateral. Well, thanks for trying. Let me know if you think of anything, okay? Talk to you later."

Nicky clicked off her phone and quietly slipped it into her jeans pocket. Then she buried her head in her hands and began to sob, her shoulders racked with grief. When the owl called once more and she saw it swoop to a nearby tree, she drew a few halting breaths and shook her finger at it.

"Is this your way of telling me to go back to modeling?" she cried, her fragile voice cracking. Tears streamed down her cheeks, and she threw up her hands. "Well, in case you didn't get the memo, there's not much demand for supermodel has-beens," she said bitterly. "It-girl one minute, forgotten the next! And now I'm portfolio rich and cash poor, dammit—with no more investments I can liquidate."

"You could try investing this," Lander stated as he

emerged from his place in the shadows. He held up his thick wad of cash, fastened together by a rubber band.

Startled, Nicky swiveled in his direction and nearly jumped out of her skin.

"What the hell are you doing here?" she snapped, her voice choked with a combination of fear and fatigue. She gulped a few breaths to calm down, then narrowed her eyes to slits.

"Don't you *dare* say you feel sorry for me," Nicky threatened. "This is probably a celebration day for you, right? The school you hated so much will finally be closed. Say bye-bye to all those awful memories! Everything will be gone, including the kids—"

Nicky's body began to heave with sobs. She buried her face in her elbow, attempting to hide her tears so Lander wouldn't see.

Lander moved toward her, but she peered over her arm and glared at him.

"Stay back!" Nicky spit out. "And keep your goddamned money! What good does it do my kids now?"

My kids—

Lander felt a snag in his throat.

Nicky had said *my kids*—

Rather than spew one of his usual cocky comebacks fueled by a sly grin, Lander gradually approached her until his presence loomed over hers. He stared into her eyes.

"I make good on my promises," he stated with deep resolve. "You came last night, after I told you I'd give you the money. For *your* kids."

Nicky glared at him suspiciously. "I thought you lost

everything to Hank Goodacre," she corrected. "If you can call it that. Your brother Dillon filled me in on your way of, you know, handling charity. Besides, there's no need for a donation to the school now. Thorne's determined to shut it down."

"You believed that old coot?" Lander sighed and crossed his arms. "He's a catankerous damn fool who's just jawing—"

Before Lander could finish, Nicky had turned on her heels and marched into the cabin to her dresser. She snatched two pieces of paper and returned to the porch. She shoved them into Lander's face.

"Jawing, huh?" she countered. "Try these on for size."

Lander grasped the documents and briefly scanned their contents. One was an official statement signed by a psychiatrist claiming that after thorough psychological testing and analysis, Thorne Wilson is in perfectly good health with excellent cognitive faculties.

"Well, I'll be damned," Lander said. "Guess with enough cash, you can pay off anybody to certify you're sane."

"Oh, it gets worse." Nicky closed her eyes for a moment, restraining her emotions. "He's not only going to shut down the school in thirty days. He's determined to bulldoze the property so it looks like it never existed—buildings, amphitheater, chain-link fence—everything. And evict the kids, of course, sending them to God knows where. Then he's going to log the whole ten acres—including the sacred trees on the ridge."

Lander gazed at the second document in amazement. "No way—"

"Yes way," Nicky insisted. "I found the eviction notice from the lumber company nailed to my door when I came home last night, along with a copy of the psychiatric evaluation. The eviction notice states that everyone has to be off the premises in a month. Oh, and Thorne Wilson has gathered a team of lawyers to sue me and the school board for claiming he has dementia and taking control of the school."

Nicky glanced down at the wad of cash in Lander's hand. Despite her will to appear composed and brave, her lower lip began to tremble. "L-Let's just say," she stammered, "there's not much point in taking your twenty grand for the school anymore."

Without another word, Lander enfolded her in his arms. Nicky hated herself for it, but his chest felt so warm and strong and inviting that she couldn't help crumbling against his hard muscles. Secretly, she relished his secure grip, while the scent of him enveloped her like a warm blanket, filled with the aromas of barnwood in the sunshine along with traces of alfalfa and fresh mountain air. Before she knew it, she'd completely buried her face in his faded Carhartt jacket. In that moment, Nicky felt strangely protected, even though her world was falling apart. Despite her desire to pull away, the strong maleness of him drew her like a magnet. She wanted to allow herself sink into the safe fold of his arms for hours, but she forced herself to snap to attention.

"W-Why did he bother to leave the school to me, anyway?" she stuttered, her body trembling against her will. "I mean, if he never wanted me to run it! And now he plans to destroy everything and log the ridge?"

Lander gave her a gentle squeeze, one that made Nicky pause. It was comforting, of course, but also the kind you offered to someone in grief because things really were that bad. He brushed back her hair with his palms and grasped her temples.

"He's pure evil, Nicky," Lander said solemnly, studying her tear-stained face as though some part of him wished he could shield her soul. "Thorne Wilson knows *exactly* what will break your spirit—and hurt your grandmother's memory the most. He couldn't keep Tavachi Cloud, and he couldn't buy her off, either. Everybody for a hundred miles knows that. So he wants to destroy everything that was hers. Especially *you*."

Lander searched her eyes. Then he turned her shoulders to face the solitary confinement shack.

"See that?" He pointed at the building. "Girls didn't end up in there like the boys. We nicknamed it the suicide shack, because of the vile things Thorne did inside. It wasn't enough to banish kids to solitary confinement—he had to beat them within an inch of their lives, leaving permanent scars of his cruelty." Lander rolled up his jacket and shirt sleeve, showing the lash marks on his skin to Nicky in the early morning light. "I remember one kid couldn't take it anymore, so he ended his life by and hanging himself from his own belt tied to the rafters."

Shock riddled through Nicky's body from this revelation. Lander leveled a hard gaze at her, his jaw set like stone.

"That's why I've spent my whole career derailing him," he said, his voice bordering on a hiss. "The other kids didn't have two older brothers at the school or the hand game bones for support. Because of me," Lander's eyes burned like they had the power to banish Thorne to hell, "Thorne Wilson lost over five-million dollars in business deals last year. It's the only reason I haven't shot him and his goddamn shack to pieces yet. Because killing Thorne Wilson would be *far too easy*."

Lander's entire being tightened into a vessel of hate. His dark eyes became so deadly it made Nicky's breath catch, and she took a step back.

"I want Thorne's empire to slowly disintegrate before his very eyes," Lander vowed. "While he watches every single thing he ever loved or owned slip from his fingers and be destroyed. Believe me, Nicky," he growled from deep in his throat, "I'm just getting started."

The rage and determination in Lander's expression left Nicky rattled to the bone. Yet she still couldn't see any way to alter her fate or secure the students' future. "Listen Lander," she said urgently, "I realize you have every right to be hell bent on revenge. But it's taken you five whole years to make a dent in Thorne's plans. I've only got thirty days—"

"Watch me," Lander challenged, his eyes regarding her with a dark, sinister focus. The bones grew hot in his jeans pocket, and the tingling had changed, igniting into a savage fire that leaped up his arm.

Let it burn, Lander thought, reveling in the sensation spiked with pain.

Let it burn…

14

"I don't get it," Nicky said. "How can you possibly destroy Thorne's plan to bulldoze the school and the ridge? If a doctor deemed he's of sound mind, he can do whatever the hell he wants—"

"Except for one thing," Lander replied, lifting his chin defiantly. "Thorne's side of the ridge might not be his."

Nicky's eyes flared. "What do you mean, *might not be his?*"

"You've seen the sacred trees on the ridge." Lander's stern lips shifted into a faint smile. "I distinctly recall you were listening to one right before you got hung up in my net." His eyes glinted for a moment, then narrowed. "What did the tree say to you, Nicky?"

Nicky bit her lip, appearing jittery. "I-I have no idea what you mean—"

"Don't lie to me," Lander warned in a gruff tone. His harsh, penetrating gaze gave her a glimpse of his ferocity in business deals.

"What…did the tree…say?" Lander pressed.

Nicky's heart hammered against her chest. *How did he know I was listening to the prophecy tree that day?* she wondered. *Were those wolf bones really some kind of conduit to people's souls? Or had Lander heard the tree as a teenager, too?* Nicky chewed the insides of her cheeks, trying not to appear flustered.

Because the truth was, a few weeks ago the tree *had* spoken to her—

About *him*.

At first, Nicky had thought it was simply the soft tones on the breeze that rifled through her hair as it whisked past the tree's branches. But then she heard words, just like when she was a teen at the school.

Welcome home, the gentle voice had said, somewhere between a whisper and a hum. Its encouraging cadence reminded Nicky of her grandmother.

The wolf will help you, pia-muguan, the voice continued.

If you let him…

In that moment, Nicky dared to peer into Lander's eyes, which suddenly appeared as intense and wolfish to her as any she'd ever seen, making her shudder. For the first time since her accident in France, her heart caught sight of what Iron Feather's riddles might mean.

Is Lander really…the wolf? As preposterous as that seems, she thought, *he certainly is dedicated to derailing Thorne Wilson. But will he consider helping to create a* real *future for my kids?*

Nicky twisted her fingers, avoiding his stare that brought beads of perspiration to her brows.

"This isn't just about a school building, is it?" Lander said, studying Nicky's face as if he'd stripped back layers of her soul. "Think about it—I can buy any goddamned school I want a hundred times over. Hell, I could hand one over to you today, if you asked for it."

Lander glanced at the spot where the owl's shadow had cast against the rock, then up at the trees on the ridge. The sun's rays beamed through the prophecy tree, highlighting the upper limbs that reached for the sky in a peculiar wishbone shape, making the top branches glow with light. The sight looked strangely like a doorway to Nicky, giving her goosebumps.

"This is about the *trees*," Lander said with an arched brow.

He pointed at the ridge.

"That sacred tree told you you'd make it, didn't it? Back when you were a teenager, just like me. It's more than centuries old—it's the keeper of your heart, your home. The center of everything you do here for the kids. Because it helped you survive."

Lander's eyes locked on Nicky's.

"You *are* that tree for them now, Nicky," he said. "It's the whole reason you're here."

Lander scanned the path the owl had taken earlier from the ridge to Nicky's cabin as though everything suddenly made sense to him. He tilted his head and regarded Nicky with a sharp look. "That tree gave you the courage to come back here, didn't it? It called to you—through Iron Feather."

Nicky felt lightning rip through her, exposing her vulnerabilities to Lander in a nano-second. "W-Wait, you never explained why this property might not belong to Thorne

Wilson," she countered too quickly, cringing that her defensiveness betrayed that he was on to something. "I only have thirty days left here, you know," she said, eager to change the subject.

Without a word, Lander unzipped his Carhartt jacket and unbuttoned his flannel shirt at the neck, his fingers working steadily down to his tanned, muscled chest. When he opened the shirt wide, Nicky gasped—

There, over his heart, was a tattoo of an owl.

It was drawn in an ancient, stylized fashion, the way one might see etched onto a rock as a petroglyph. Or a pictograph…

Lander nodded at the ridge.

"There's a reason the owl guards that ridge, Nicky—local legend claims that location's watched over by my ancestor Iron Feather. Some say the owl *is* Iron Feather."

He tapped the tattoo on his chest.

"Rumor has it that the Utes once let my ancestor live on a pocket of their land in return for bringing home their children," he explained. "This tribal symbol on a rock meant he had their permission, since the tribe trusts stone more than paper. When Dillon found a rock with this image where the Bandits Hollow Gang used to have their hideout, the BLM honored it rather than face lengthy legal action from the tribe. Nicky," Lander closed his shirt and jacket, "I have reason to believe the Utes encouraged Iron Feather to use the ridge, too."

"Why?" Nicky shook her head. "I mean, if they'd already let him use another parcel for the Bandits Hollow Gang?"

Lander gazed at the sacred tree on the ridge, at the way

the sun shined through the odd wishbone formation of branches at the very top like a gateway. He grew solemn for a moment, as though weighing his thoughts.

As though weighing Nicky…

"Because Iron Feather was the most elusive outlaw in the West," he stated as if testing her mettle. "Some people claim he could…cross dimensions…to avoid capture. And he used the sacred trees to do it. Those trees are considered to be…portals."

"Portals?"

"Doorways—to other dimensions," Lander replied. "The Utes didn't want him to be caught so he could continue his work for the children. No one can ever prove if the legend is true, but this morning it finally hit me—there might be a pictograph somewhere indicating that Thorne's side of the ridge doesn't really belong to him. If we can locate that rock and prove this ten-acre parcel, including the school, was designated to Iron Feather a century ago, we might be able to have the property legally stripped from Thorne Wilson."

Tears collected in Nicky's eyes—from hope this time. Cautiously, she allowed herself to release a thin breath of relief. Lander was nothing if not cunning, and his steel determination bolstered her spirits a little. Yet there was still something that left her mind puzzled.

"Wouldn't you have found the pictograph when you bought half the ridge and put up your barbed-wire fence?"

"I would if it had still been there," Lander replied matter-of-factly. "Someone as crafty as Thorne isn't going to leave it around on the property once he'd taken ownership—particularly after hearing that Dillon had reclaimed the

Bandits Hollow Gang's hideout." Lander glanced up at Thorne's large white mansion sitting high on a hill nearby. "My bet is that the pictograph is somewhere in his house."

Lander pulled his cell phone from his pocket to check the time. Then he leveled his gaze at Nicky, full of challenge.

"The Rocky Mountain Cattlemen's Symposium is tomorrow night. Every year they hold it at a different ranch, and this year it's at Thorne's place. Come with me to talk to my brothers this afternoon," he offered. "We're branding at the ranch today, and both of them will be there. If you approach them and tell them about the school's crisis, they might agree to help us search for the pictograph during the symposium. After you assist with branding, of course."

Nicky examined his face. "I'm confused—you mean, your brothers might help me locate the pictograph in Thorne's *house?* Wouldn't that be against the law without a warrant?"

"Not if it's in plain view. And my police officer brother just *happens* to see it during the symposium," Lander pointed out. "Thorne doesn't get to choose who comes to the event—the invitations are sent by the Rocky Mountain Cattlemen's Association. And Thorne's so arrogant, he probably displays the pictograph on a shelf under a spotlight so he can laugh at it every time he passes by."

Nicky cocked her head. "Then why don't *you* ask your brothers for help?" she protested. "I hardly know them—"

"Because they aren't exactly going to be pushovers for saving a damn thing on Thorne Wilson's land," he argued. "When they hate him as much as you do. Especially considering that we could buy another school any day of the week—but that won't spare the sacred trees. We need Barrett to keep things legal." Lander folded his arms and appraised Nicky with a wicked gleam in his eye. "Besides, you are *far* underestimating the power of a beautiful woman—especially on the Iron Feather brothers."

"My, my," Nicky replied, enjoying his flirtation more than she cared to admit, "do you realize that's the first inappropriate thing you've said to me all morning? Watch out, you're in danger of losing your rep as an opportunistic asshole and a lech—"

To her astonishment, Lander seized her for a kiss.

His mouth worked over hers in a hard, claiming kiss, boldly drinking from her lips like he'd been dying of thirst since dawn. In that moment, Nicky's whole body was thrust into a whirlwind, caught up in a swirl of sensations—the warmth of his rock hard-biceps and brick-like chest as he wrapped his arms around her—blurring any recall she had of where she was that morning. He was all Lander—all male heat and muscle and desire—closing his body in on her in a way that left her breathless. Nicky couldn't help running her hands up his back like they belonged there, fused to the taut muscles beneath his jacket. Something about Lander's ferocity, that same reckless aggression that made the whole business world shudder, intoxicated Nicky and only made her want more. She could have sworn she spied steam rising in the crisp air to envelope them, and her heart pounded so hard she thought it might burst through to meet Lander's chest.

Because unlike the kisses he'd swiped before, there was a subtle shift inside him that trickled down to Nicky's very core…

This man *knew* her.

He knew all about her relationship to the tree. How it gave her crucial strength and support during the most vulnerable years of her life.

And he'd already sensed the tremors of her hopes and fears as sure as a seismograph, due to their similar history, as well as her desperate longing not to let down the kids.

Lander could peer into the most hidden parts of Nicky's heart that few people in the world would ever understand. And the way he held her so tightly told Nicky he wasn't merely claiming another kiss. He was trying to find a lost piece of…

Home.

Perhaps it was simply the dream—

The barest possibility of a place to belong.

The very thing they'd both been deprived of in adolescence.

Lander's kiss dared to whisper to Nicky that such a place might exist, right here, right now, even for broken people like them.

If you were bold enough to take it—

To hell with the consequences.

Despite all sensible logic, Nicky felt her body dissolve into his raw embrace as though they'd become one being.

Just like the arms that curled around the prophecy tree.

Sparks rippled through Nicky's spine, flowing into her breasts and thighs. She couldn't stop imagining herself crushed against Lander's skin, naked and entwined, with only the heat remaining between them. Sliding her hands up to his broad shoulders, her fingers suddenly developed their own will and began to tear at the fabric of his clothing.

God almighty, she thought, stunned by her own craving, if

I weren't the school director and standing in front of the dorms right now, I might have already lost control and stripped this man bare.

"Nicky," Lander broke away and warned in a low seductive tone, one that went straight to the currents snapping through her skin, "don't ever believe I'm *not* an opportunistic asshole or a lech."

He tweaked her chin with his usual brash smile. But then a soft glint surfaced in his eyes, as though a secret part of him hoped he'd swiped a bit of her soul this time as well as that kiss.

"Especially when it comes to *you*."

15

All at once, Nicky heard an odd, scuffling sound—and it wasn't from the butterflies colliding in her stomach. She turned her head, her attention drawn by a disturbance among several teenage boys in the distance.

"Fight!" she declared, promptly stepping away from Lander.

Though Nicky began to sprint as fast as she could toward the boys she'd spied grappling on the ground near a dorm, she was no match for Lander. Within seconds, he'd dashed past her to reach a circle of teens who stood around the two fighters, gaping at the vicious swings they hurled at each other and calling out bets. The moment Lander broke through their wall, with stunning strength, he lifted both warring boys by their collars to separate them.

The two boys were wiry and only a fraction of Lander's size. One boy reacted by throwing a savage punch to his face, drawing a burst of blood. Lander simply hauled in a deep breath and gave both boys a hard shake, dropping them to the ground like rag dolls. With street-fighter swiftness, he reached into his jacket pocket and pulled out a coil of wire, the flexible type used to repair fencing. Instantly, he looped the wire around their hands and feet and gave it a tight twist, cutting off the ends with a pair of wire clippers. The other boys' faces fell in astonishment, and they bolted for the dorm entrance before Lander could wrap them in his wire as well.

"How do you like rassling now?" Lander remarked to the two boys who remained wriggling on the ground. He stood over them with a nonchalant look on his face, like a rancher contemplating whether to haul a couple of calves to market.

"You're hurt!" Nicky exclaimed when she made it to Lander's side, spying the blood that trickled from a gash on his forehead. Her mouth dropped at the lightning-fast way he'd tied up her students to prevent more violence—and at how they looked surprisingly unharmed, despite the fact that they were spitting mad.

Lander held up his hand to keep Nicky from speaking for a moment, knowing she'd demand that he set the boys free immediately.

"Lemme go!" insisted one of the boys, kicking and screaming until the wire pressed against his flesh. "Don't you get it?" he cried, his cheeks beet-red in frustration. "We're losing our home! Who cares how much we fight now? We're just gonna end up in juvenile hall or some crappy foster home anyway."

Lander sighed—clearly, the teenagers had already heard the rumors about the school closing, due to how fast gossip traveled in town. He sat next to the boys on the ground.

"Because you're fighting the wrong enemy," he said, gazing in the direction of Thorne's mansion.

"What would *you* know about our enemy?" the other boy sputtered bitterly. "Aren't you the crazy neighbor living it up in some bazillion-dollar ranch?"

"Plenty," Lander replied, "since I went to this school myself. How many times has your fighting made a bit of difference to Thorne Wilson?"

The boys glanced at each other sheepishly. When their muscles finally relaxed a little, they gave him a shrug.

"Thought so," Lander said, exhaling a long breath as though this were the oldest story on earth. Once satisfied that the boys had calmed down, he snipped their wires and helped them to get untangled.

"You know, my dad used to warn me about people like Thorne Wilson," Lander said, tossing them a hard glare to make sure they stayed put and listened. "He told me a story once about how Coyote, *Yogho-vu-chi̱*, was always baiting Wolf, *Sinae-vi̱*, for a fight. When they ventured north for an epic battle, many people went to see it for entertainment, kind of like the circle of kids that were watching you fight just now. But ice started to form ahead of them, and it began to surround everyone and reach for the sky. The people were trapped and couldn't cross it. Coyote got scared and said, 'All these people will never make it across this big sheet of ice. Quick, let's run ahead of them and go somewhere else to battle, or we'll die, too.' But Wolf didn't say a word. He simply howled to the sky, and his friend Owl, *Múu-pu-chi̱*, came and cracked the ice apart so the people could cross safely. Coyote hung his head and was the last one over."

Lander folded his arms, staring down the two boys sitting beside him as though testing them. "So tell me, who's the biggest enemy in that story?"

The boys rubbed their hands and feet where the wire had been, mulling it over.

"Coyote?" mentioned one boy with an uncertain look.

Lander shook his head.

"How about the ice?" replied the other boy. "It's the biggest enemy, since it could have frozen them to death."

"Almost," Lander replied. "It was the battle itself." His fingers slid thoughtfully to his chin. "It took a very long time for me to understand my dad's story. The idea of the fight distracted Coyote and Wolf from noticing that the ice was growing and they were in danger. They needed to face the *real* enemy—their desire to battle each other—and work together with Owl to help everyone survive. Only then could they beat the threat of the ice and live."

"If you understand the story so well, does that mean you're the wolf?" one of the boys asked with desperation in his tone. "And you'll help us? Help save our home?"

"Tell you what," Lander said, shooting a reassuring glance at Nicky. "I'm shorthanded for branding at my ranch this afternoon. If you two promise to help me with the cattle, I'll pay you a day's ranch wages and won't charge you with assault for this cut on my head." He wiped his brow and stared at the crimson dripping from his fingertips with the anticipation of needing stitches. "Then I'll see what I can do about that enemy of yours."

"So you'll save our school?" the other boy pushed with heartbreak in his voice.

Lander bristled for a moment, his jaw clenching. He spotted the scars on the boy's arm, indicating he'd been whipped badly by Thorne in the past, too. All at once, Lander's fists closed so tightly, his entire being exuding rage, that the two boys became alarmed and inched away from him.

"Mark my word," Lander vowed while pressing his fists into the grass, barely able to restrain his anger. "I will *never* lift a finger to save a goddamn thing of Thorne Wilson's," he said in a lethal tone. Glancing at the trees on the ridge, his gaze grew startlingly cold. "But I'm more than happy to work with my brothers to take whatever that monster holds dear. Just so we can sit back and watch his pride go up in flames."

16

Clouds of dust roiled in the distance as Nicky drove the school Jeep beneath the timber-framed entrance to the Iron Feather Brothers Ranch. Squinting at the windshield, she aimed for the billows of smoke and dirt that climbed to the sky. It was no secret where branding was taking place that afternoon. The cacophony of lowing cattle and ranch hands barking orders created a chaos that made Nicky anxious, wondering how her students might fit in to this rugged scenario. If they'd never helped with branding before, how were they going to navigate such a bedlam of noise, animals, and dust? She scanned the vast ranching spread, hoping Lander would give them quality direction as she drove beyond the main mansion and the barns to several back corrals that were filled with calves. When she brought the Jeep to a halt, she spied Lander emerging from the haze.

He sauntered up to her side of the vehicle with an easygoing stride. His thumbs were looped into his front pockets, and he smiled broadly, every inch the good-looking cowboy even though he was smeared from head to toe in dirt.

Damm, Nicky thought. *Dirt only makes him look handsomer.*

"Welcome to branding day," Lander said, glancing at the two boys and a girl sitting in the Jeep. "Best event all year—this is where the magic happens."

"Magic?" Nicky stepped out of the Jeep, her voice doubtful. She motioned for her students to hop out as well.

"Sure," replied Lander, turning for a moment to check the progress in the corrals. "This is the day all our calves become official Iron Feather brothers stock, belonging to one of the top USDA prime beef herds in the world. Branding may subject their hides to intense heat for three whole seconds, but after that, they're the most pampered cows on earth."

"Oh," said Nicky, self-conscious that she couldn't tell one Angus calf from another if her life depended on it. They all looked rather uniformly stout and black, which she assumed was the point. "So Lander," she said, getting down to business, "this afternoon I've brought my students from the school, like we discussed. You remember Jonathan and Mark from the, um, *incident* earlier this morning?"

"You mean the fight?" Lander smirked, enjoying the hint of red that climbed up the rebellious boys' cheeks. "You bet. See these stitches?" He pointed to the fresh scar held together by surgical laces over his brow. "You're gonna work this off today, boys. But don't worry, I'll make sure you get paid like men."

Lander grinned with his usual killer charm at the three

students, making even Nicky's breath catch. "Who's the lovely young lady?" he asked pointedly.

The girl with wavy red hair and freckles bit her lip, returning a shy smile.

"This is Amanda," Nicky replied with pride. "When she heard at lunch time that I was bringing a couple of boys over here to learn ranching skills, she begged me to come. She aspires to running her own ranch someday, and she's hoping you'll show her the ropes. Right, Amanda?"

The girl nodded. Despite her reticent nature, the determination in her pale blue eyes was palpable.

"My kinda girl," Lander approved with a glint in his gaze. "You're in the perfect place to learn ranching first-hand. Not only are we branding and vaccinating hundreds of calves, but Maribelle Ryman is due to arrive later today to discuss buying a top Angus bull. She happens to have the largest cattle ranch in Texas owned by a woman, and she's very supportive of other women in business. But I warn you," Lander checked the sun's position in the sky to gauge the time, "watch out for her Chihuahua named Galveston. She spoils him like a baby, and he's got a hefty Napoleon complex."

Lander shifted to examine the dusty action going on in the corrals. "As you can see," he addressed the students, pointing to a corral loaded with calves and a few people on horseback, "right now we're separating the calves one at a time from the herd so my brothers Dillon and Barrett can rope their heads and heels to keep them still. Once a calf is caught, the branding and vaccinations begin, which will protect the calf's life from respiratory and bacterial diseases. C'mon, I'll take you to the coal pit and show you how everything works."

Lander led the way to an empty corral and climbed over the wood fence to step inside, waiting for Nicky and her students to do the same. As soon as they joined him, he advanced to a wood-fire coal pit in the ground and picked up a branding iron that had been sitting on top.

"The stainless-steel feather at the end of this rod marks the Iron Feather brothers' brand," he continued, carefully holding up the red-hot iron with his gloved hand. He gave one of the ranch hands a signal, and the man opened a small gate separating the empty corral from one that was packed with calves. Nicky spotted Lander's brothers, Dillon and Barrett, on horseback near the gateway, ready to rope. Behind them, she also recognized their wives, curvy and ivory-blonde Tessa and athletic and honey-brown haired Lainey, on horses as well, helping to herd the cattle inside the large back corral. When Tessa and Lainey saw Nicky, they gave her friendly smiles and waves. Then the two women returned to their assignment by gently cutting off one of the calves from the large herd and ushering it toward their husbands at the gateway, where the calf bolted through the opening to the center of the next pen. In a shot, Dillon and Barrett tore after it while swinging their ropes. Nicky was astonished at how fast they headed and heeled the calf, leaving it mewling in the center of the corral with their ropes around its head and back ankles, forced to a shaky standstill.

"Let's go!" commanded Lander as he trotted over to the calf and gestured for the students to follow. They watched as he set one gloved hand on the calf's head and a knee onto its belly to press the calf to the ground. Then he placed the hot branding iron onto the calf's hindquarters and rocked it slightly for a couple of seconds while the smell of burnt fur filled the air and the wide-eyed calf let out a squeal. Quickly, he lifted a syringe from his jacket pocket and pierced the calf's neck, administering a vaccine within seconds. Afterwards, he peeled Dillon's and Barrett's ropes from the animal and set it free, giving a nod to a man at the other end of the corral. The man opened a gate and let the calf loose to join the rest of the herd that was free-range grazing outside.

Nicky blinked several times, reeling at how quickly the process had been completed.

"Our goal is to be as fast as we can so we stress the calf as little as possible," Lander told the onlooking students. "In spite of how harsh branding might seem, it's necessary to prevent our cattle from being stolen. Rustling didn't just happen in the old days—it's picked up in recent years as a fast way for meth addicts to get cash. Each cow they steal fetches up to three-thousand dollars, and I've already lost ten head this year. That's thirty grand if you do the math, so it makes sense to go to this much trouble to establish ownership."

"Can't you just use the tags on the cows' ears to identify them?" Amanda asked in a timid tone, her brows creased as she watched the next calf being funneled toward the branding corral.

"Good question," Lander replied, impressed. He gestured for one of his ranch hands to approach who'd been sitting on a fence with an electronic tablet. Lander returned his iron to the coal pit for the moment and took the tablet from his staff. To Amanda's surprise, he handed it to her.

"As a matter of fact, we *do* use tags to register what's been completed for each calf," Lander explained. "See tag number forty-three on the spreadsheet—the calf I just branded?"

Amanda scanned the document and located it with her finger.

"Check the boxes beside it to indicate forty-three has been branded and vaccinated, then type in today's date. Tags help us keep track of our herd's progress, but the problem is that they're easily cut off by rustlers. Tattoos in the cows' ears aren't much better, since most quick-sale barns don't bother to put cattle in chutes to check their markings. Old-fashioned brands are still the best way to deter theft."

Lander crossed his arms and narrowed his eyes at the boys. "Now, what I need from you two is to join Buster at the cooler beside the fence, where you'll put on sterile gloves and help him mix the vaccines and fill syringes so we're ready for each calf. While you're at it, Amanda will record all the tags and what each animal received. Ready?" Lander motioned for the boys to catch up to Buster. "Time to get to work!"

As the boys headed over to the experienced ranch hand to receive instructions, Nicky fastened her gaze on Lander. "So what do I do?" she smiled, proud to see her students taking on responsibility.

"Besides stand there and look beautiful?" Lander remarked with an upward curl of his lip, enjoying the eye roll Nicky sent his way. "Tell you what—you can shadow me while I brand, and call out the tag numbers for Amanda, in case it's hard for her to see them."

"Roger," Nicky nodded as she glanced over the corrals, doing a swift head count of the staff. "But there's something you should know," she said in a clipped, accusatory tone. "I'm onto you, Lander Iron Feather."

"Oh?" He arched a brow.

"I couldn't help noticing that you actually have *plenty* of ranch hands around here. You don't need a lick of help to finish branding this week, do you? It doesn't take a couple of wolf bones to see through you." Nicky eyed Jonathan and Mark for a moment, who were learning to mix vaccines by the cooler. "You can't fool me, Lander. You used to *be* one of those boys who got into too many fights at school, huh?" She regarded his face with a decidedly knowing gaze. "That's the *real* reason you gave my students a break to work here, isn't it?"

Lander dipped the rim of his cowboy hat. "Guilty as charged," he admitted. "And if they do a good job with the syringes, next time I'll let 'em help wrestle the calves down for branding instead of wrestling each other. You'd be amazed at how proud those kids are going to be after finishing tough ranch work."

"So…are you committing to hiring them for the whole week—with *pay?*"

Amusement flickered across Lander's face. "Always maneuvering benefits for the kids, aren't you?"

Nicky lifted her chin. "Guilty as charged," she chided, setting her hands on her hips. "I refuse to apologize for wheeling and dealing on behalf of my students."

"Nor should you." Lander tilted his head toward the corrals. "Looks like my brothers are fixing to rope another calf. You ready?"

Nicky swallowed a halting breath, prepping herself mentally to engage in this wild, time-honored ranching tradition. But then she surprised Lander by grasping his arm and giving him a tender squeeze.

"Thank you," she whispered with all the sincerity she could muster, leaning into his ear. "I mean that. You're giving my kids a chance to get work experience in the real world. That's something few employers are willing to do because of their histories, and I'm really grateful."

Lander studied his dusty boots for a moment, as though allowing her words to trickle inside. He checked his brothers across the corral on horseback, who were smiling and chatting leisurely with their wives astride their horses near the herd. When his gaze drifted back to Nicky, for the first time she thought she spied a look that resembled…longing…or perhaps even envy…settling deep into his mahogany eyes. Then Lander slowly regarded her face, his focus following the curve of her forehead and cheeks before resting on her eyes with an intensity that startled her, as if he were once again searching for that lost piece of home.

"Don't mention it," Lander said softly.

He glanced back at his brothers and their wives once more, then cleared his throat.

"It's the least I can do," he added. "Any kid of yours, Nicky, deserves a break."

17

By the time dinner rolled around, so many cattle had been branded that Nicky was ready to collapse. After the first few calves, Lander showed her how to administer vaccines while calling out tags, leaving her exhausted once they'd handled over a hundred head. Nicky's nose and mouth felt gritty from inhaling dust, yet out of stubborn pride, she forced a cheerful smile when the dinner bell finally rang at six o'clock. Lander's chef Francois served fried chicken with velouté sauce and corn pudding topped by pralines at outdoor picnic tables, inviting everyone who'd worked that afternoon to come eat. Recalling Nell's disdain for his prom recipes, Nicky carefully inspected his French interpretation of the southern-style fare, but the smell was so divine she couldn't resist diving right in. When she glanced over at Jonathan, Mark and Amanda wolfing down their meals at another table, she noticed they were glowing with pride from the hard day's work—just like Lander predicted.

"Holy moly, girlfriend!" Dillon's wife Tessa gushed as she sat down across from Nicky and motioned for her husband to do the same. "You sure worked your butt off today! If I didn't know better, I would have pegged you as a seasoned ranch hand."

"My muscles are screaming otherwise," Nicky cringed with a half-smile, rubbing her shoulder. Secretly, she was thrilled she'd earned Tessa's respect. "How about you?" she asked. "Did cutting cattle take its toll?"

Tessa hitched up her messy blonde ponytail and smirked, pulling a small vial from her denim jacket pocket. "I have one word for you," she said adamantly. "Motrin. Believe me, we'll all be sleeping soundly tonight."

Dillon sat at the picnic table beside Tessa, and soon Barrett and his wife Lainey joined them. Their plates were piled high with comfort food, and just like Nicky, they devoured several bites before coming up for air.

Lainey brushed back the wisps of honey-brown hair from her forehead and gave Nicky a wink. "Bet you've never been this hungry in your life," she smiled, scanning the others at the table who were gulping down food. "Tessa and I gave up Pilates and spin class long ago for ranch work cardio. We've never been fitter."

"I'm really impressed both of you helped herd cattle," Nicky mentioned to the women after another spoonful of corn pudding. "Did you know how to ride before you married ranchers?"

Lainey and Tessa shook their heads, but the expressions on their faces told Nicky they were just as proud as her students for participating in the grueling ranch labor.

"Lander likes branding to be a big family event," Tessa explained, watching him talk to Francois by the chuck wagon. "He's downright obsessed with making every brand perfect." She lowered her voice. "I think he believes we give cows good vibes if the Iron Feather family works together and personally bonds with the herd." Tessa kept her eye on Lander as he headed toward their table with a plate of fried chicken. "The fact that he invited you and your students to participate today says a *lot*," she confided in a hushed tone. "He's never done that with any other woman before."

"It's called chemistry," Lainey ribbed Nicky with a sly grin. "I've seen the way he looks at you. Sure, Lander may pretend he's a hound dog to the press. But he's pure Iron Feather brother, through and through. Which is code word for loyal —*if* the right woman comes along. Something tells me, after vaccinating calves for six solid hours, you've become a front runner."

Nicky's cheeks engulfed in heat, and she dearly hoped her students at a table a few yards away hadn't heard those words and spied her blush. Lifting her gaze, she dared to sneak a peek at the imposing presence of Dillon and Barrett across from her, both of them even taller than Lander and just as heavily muscled. Though the brothers remained stone-faced while eating their meals, Dillon startled her when his dark eyes arrested hers.

"You brought your students with you," he observed. He narrowed his focus, his granite gaze appearing to look right through her. "You must be very proud of them."

"I am," Nicky replied sincerely. "They mean the world to me."

Dillon studied Nicky's features like he had a hidden radar tucked inside his brain that could detect the nuances of her character. "You took them out of their regular environment and showed them a different world," he noted. "Rolled up your sleeves and worked with them side by side."

While his face appeared emotionless, Dillon's sheer intensity made Nicky fidget at the picnic table.

"That speaks well of you. And your…school," Dillon mentioned in a stilted tone, as though reluctant to compliment some former enemy. "No one ever bothered to do that back in my day."

"Thank you," Nicky replied as Lander sat down at the table. "I consider it a privilege to work with my kids. But the truth is," she paused, her heart tumbling as she summoned the courage to tell Dillon the news, "the school won't be around much longer."

Barrett stopped chewing and tilted his head. "What do you mean, won't be *around?*"

Nicky realized then that the brothers hadn't heard the news as fast as her students. She darted a glance at Lander, desperately hoping for his assistance. This was it—the critical moment to explain the fate of her beloved school and see if Dillon and Barrett could find it in their hearts to care. After all the horror they'd been through at the Wilson Ranch, Nicky couldn't blame them if they didn't. For all she knew, they might be the first to cheer while the school was being torn down. Nevertheless, she pressed her palms together under the picnic table and uttered a silent prayer—

To their ancestor Iron Feather.

"What she *means* is," Lander cut in with a grave tone,

setting down his fork, "Thorne Wilson intends to bulldoze the school—*and* the trees on his side of the ridge—within thirty days."

"The trees?" Barrett's brows furrowed. His gaze shifted from Lander to Nicky and back again. "Thorne never gave a damn about that school—I get it. But why the trees?"

Lander's eyes locked on his brothers with a searing gaze.

"Payback," he insisted. "Nicky dared to transform the school, the ultimate heresy to Thorne. He's always wanted to keep it a place of hate and destroy anything good that could possibly grow there."

"Including…the trees," muttered Barrett, mulling it over in his mind like the trained detective he was. "Cultivated by Tavachi Cloud's people." He shoved the pralines on top of his corn pudding around with his fork, slowly piecing things together. Then he threw a look at Lander. "The only woman Thorne ever tried…and failed…to love."

Lander didn't reply.

He simply folded his arms and stared at his brothers, allowing the facts he'd reported to sink in. Then he carefully unbuttoned his flannel shirt from the collar down to his chest to reveal the owl tattoo, an old symbol his brothers knew so well they could trace it in their sleep.

Dillon's jaw worked back and forth at the sight, as if wrestling with Lander's information against the legacy of their ancestor. He checked Barrett's eyes, which were creased with questions.

"You took over the Bandits Hollow Gang's parcel," Lander said pointedly to Dillon, tapping his tattoo, "when you found the Ute's owl pictograph on the land."

He glanced up at the fence line on the ridge that separated his property from Thorne's.

"You know about the old legend of the portal as well as I do," Lander asserted. "How folks claim our ancestor relied on the power of the trees to escape. What are the odds that the Ute stashed another owl pictograph on the ridge, giving Iron Feather claim to use it?"

"You would've found it a long time ago," Dillon replied, his voice testy.

Lander shook his head. "Not if Thorne pocketed it after hearing you settled on the outlaws' former land. He may be evil, but he's not stupid."

Lander clenched his hands together in a big fist on the table and cleared his throat. "If Thorne *does* have the pictograph, proving the ridge and nearby school parcel don't really belong to him, we might find it in his house. Rumor has it he doesn't trust bank vaults. And he loves to show off his collections in gilded cases, including frontier rifles, ancient baskets, and Ute war shirts and pictographs. They're like his sick trophies." Lander drew a deep breath, running his hand through his tangled, blonde hair. "The Rocky Mountain Cattlemen's Association is holding their annual symposium at his place tomorrow night. We *have* invitations, you know."

Barrett's gaze darted across the picnic table in disbelief. "What? Are you freaking kidding me?" he said. "You're actually suggesting we go to the symposium and snoop inside that bastard's *house?*"

"It's not snooping if it's in plain view," Lander persisted. "All we have to do is make sure *you* see it, bro. With your police camera, of course. Thorne would never in a million years expect us to attend, so he'll probably be sloppy and leave the pictograph displayed in one of his cases."

Nicky shrank back from the increasing tension between the brothers, her heart still hammering over the fate of her school. Yet when she slid a glance to Tessa and Lainey at the table, catching their warm, supportive expressions, she felt brave and sat up straighter.

"Those trees," she broke in, her voice quivering a little, "they're the spiritual heart of everything I do for the kids, the one thing that kept me going as a teen." Nicky swallowed hard to maintain her nerve, struggling with difficult memories. "My people have sculpted the trees according to sacred traditions for centuries. They're considered *living* beings—wise spirits who freely share love and healing, long before Thorne Wilson was even born. If the trees are cut down...it's...it's like destroying my ancestors. My home—"

To Nicky's surprise, Tessa squared her shoulders and leveled a stiff gaze at Dillon and Barrett.

"Would it really kill you to go to the symposium for half an hour?" Tessa glared at her husband. "You told me yourself you used to head to the trees on the ridge whenever your pain became too great at the Wilson Ranch." She shifted her eyes to Barrett. "I bet you did, too. All the Iron Feather brothers probably relied on those trees for...hope. Nicky's gone to enormous trouble to overhaul the school for the kids, to offer them a genuine future. Isn't saving the trees the least you can do?"

Lainey regarded Barrett with equal challenge in her eyes. "I assume the Rocky Mountain Cattlemen's Association issued the invites, so Thorne can't kick you out even if he wanted to."

She clutched Barrett's large, calloused hand and gave it a hard squeeze. "What have you got to lose?"

Barrett slowly shook his head, sealing his eyes for a second like he'd been forced to swallow bitter medicine.

"Pride," he said through gritted teeth. He shot a gaze at Thorne's mansion on the hill. "You really expect us to just stroll into his house of horrors tomorrow night? Where he brazenly displays sacred artifacts from our ancestors like gaudy trinkets he won on eBay? Everything that man has ever done was designed to make people like us feel small. Throwaways, half breeds—that's what he always called us. In between whippings, of course." Barrett issued a dark look at Lander. "I'd rather set his goddamned mansion on fire. Maybe then we'll get lucky and find the pictograph in the ash."

Nicky's heart plummeted to her heels. She knew she had no right to insist that the Iron Feather brothers relive the abuse they'd endured by helping her. She paused for a moment and dipped her head, fighting back tears, when she felt a warm hand gently caress her hair. As she glanced up, she was startled to see it came from Dillon.

"That pictograph," Dillon stated carefully, settling his gaze on Barrett and Lander, "has the potential to destroy Thorne—from the inside out. It's not just an old image on a rock. It's proof he could never own Tavachi. Thorne doesn't care about the trees. What he's been after all along is Tavachi's *magic*."

Tessa's and Lainey's breath hitched, appearing puzzled by his words. Nevertheless, Dillon's eyes bored into Barrett's.

"Iron Feather's not the only one who used the trees for escape," he said. "There's been talk that's how Tavachi got away from Thorne all those decades ago, with Nicky's mother in her arms. She knew the secret of the trees—how they can act as portals. As long as Thorne has that pictograph, I'm betting he believes he can still possess her somehow. I'm not saying it makes sense—obsessions never do. But I am saying that if the pictograph is in his house, the way to crush Thorne's spirit is by retrieving it." Dillon leaned forward and stared into Barrett's eyes. "Time to take a risk and claim that ridge back, bro. *Forever.*"

Barrett studied the red-and-white-checkered fabric on the tablecloth. His fists clenched tight and released, over and over again. Finally, he pitched a warning look at his brothers.

"Half an hour," Barrett relented. "We go to the symposium tomorrow night for exactly thirty minutes. And I swear to God, if that pictograph isn't in plain view, we're gone."

"Deal," replied Lander.

Dillon gave a nod to Barrett as well.

Nicky felt a wave of relief wash from her head to her toes. Nothing was guaranteed, of course, but at least now she had a slim ray of hope. She closed her eyes, allowing gratitude to course through her being. "Thank you," she whispered, lifting her gaze to the Iron Feather brothers. "Thank you so much—"

At that moment, Nicky's words were swallowed by the roar of an airplane over their heads. She gazed at the sky and spied an elegant, private jet with a lasso logo soaring above them. The plane carefully descended to land on a thin airstrip that extended beyond the barns and corrals. As soon as it came to a full stop, a side door opened and a set of passenger stairs was lowered to the ground.

"Well, ladies and gentlemen," Lander stood up and dusted

off his shirt, addressing the small crowd at the picnic tables, "it's showtime." A half-smile crinkled his cheek while he gazed at the stout woman in a leopard-print coat who started walking down the jet's stairs. "The Queen of Cattle has arrived. And believe me, Maribelle Ryman fully expects to be treated like royalty."

18

"Don't worry," Lander mentioned to Nicky and her students, who were eyeing the gray-haired woman with a dog in her arms as she stepped out of a black stretch limousine that had shuttled her to the corrals. The woman stood and tilted her chin in the air before she began to stride confidently toward them. "When it comes right down to it, Maribelle Ryman may act regal, but she's a total softie. Besides, she's not here for chit chat. She's here to meet Chester."

"Chester?" replied Amanda, appearing weary from recording cattle brands all day. She squinted at the Chihuahua in the woman's grip, who possessed a rather imperious gaze for such a small dog.

"Chester's one of my top Angus bulls." Lander inclined his head toward a corral circled by a tall, steel-rail fence that contained a massive black bull.

"Branding's only a fraction of the cattle business," Lander explained. "A big part of my job is breeding the best stock in the world. And selling them—for the right price. So listen carefully while I talk with Maribelle," he smiled in particular at Amanda, "because if you want to know how to run a ranch, auctioning livestock is a large portion of the business."

As Maribelle Ryman drew closer, the two boys began to chuckle at her over-the-top outfit, complete with a flashy, leopard-print coat draped over a teal rodeo shirt speckled with rhinestones and jeans that tucked into matching teal cowboy boots. Her silver hair was piled high into a bouffant, accented by a diamond-studded tiara featuring a lariat. Lander flicked a glance at the boys with an arched brow.

"Don't be fooled, young men," he warned, motioning for Nicky and her students to rise with him from their tables. "Before you write off Maribelle as some little old lady who can't stop reliving her 1968 rodeo queen glory, you should know that she won the women's reining world championship last year at the age of seventy-two. She may wear diamond rings the size of quarters, but she's a bonafide rancher who's earned every penny of her multimillion-dollar business. I encourage you to be on guard around her dog Galveston, though. I hear he bites."

"Lander Iron Feather!" Maribelle hollered when she got within earshot of him. "Come on over here give me a hug! How is it you get handsomer by the day?"

Lander gave Nicky and her students a wink. "Did I mention she's bossy?" He headed over to Maribelle and wrapped his large arms around her, engulfing her short frame, and gave her a big squeeze.

"I swear, it's simply a crime you're so good looking," Maribelle said, grabbing Lander's chin and moving it left and right to take in his deeply-tanned skin and stone-cut features, framed by wild blonde hair. "Fellas like you put a strain on all of womanhood," she chastised.

Then Maribelle's eyes narrowed as she scanned Nicky up and down with the same concentration ranchers use to study the conformation of prize cows. "Glory be!" she gasped. "Who's this fine young heifer?" Before Lander could answer, Maribelle boldly stepped up to Nicky and pinched both her cheeks as if to test her hardiness. "Why, she's a beauty! Tell me, darlin'—has Lander taught you how to herd cattle yet?" She peered into Nicky's eyes. "I swear you got cow in you," she asserted with conviction. "Yessiree. That's just something I can tell about folks right off the bat, whether they can cut it or not in ranching. And as for you, sweet thing," Maribelle turned and brazenly gazed into Amanda's pale, blue eyes. "You *definitely* got cow in you. What's yer name, honey?"

"A-Amanda," she stammered, taken aback by Maribelle's brash approach.

"Amanda wants to be a rancher someday, just like you," Nicky broke in, making Amanda blush. "It would be really wonderful if you could show her what you look for in a cow's conformation."

"Well, let's go then!" Maribelle prodded, pointing to the corral. "I love a girl who knows exactly what she wants. Lander," she insisted, "lead us to Chester."

"At your service," Lander replied, doing his best to hide his amusement at Maribelle's domineering tone. He began to walk toward the bull ahead of Maribelle, then settled his boot on the bottom steel rail of the corral to wait for the others to catch up.

"As you recall from my recent email, Maribelle," Lander said as soon as everyone gathered at the bull pen, "Chester is fourteen-months old and descended from Emulation, the greatest Angus breeding bull of the last twenty-five years. Though he's almost two-thousand pounds already, his offspring demonstrate particularly low birth weights, which contribute to easier calving. In addition, his calves routinely show high weanling and yearling weights."

"Which means they start off puny and grow like weeds, is that what you're saying?"

"Exactly." Lander's lip curled at Maribelle's straight-shooting response. "Chester's offspring grow like gangbusters, but their meat-to-bone ratios are higher than any other cattle in existence."

"Well, that's all fine and dandy, but you know I don't give two cents about birth weights and ratios," groused Maribelle, setting her hands on her hips. She examined the front of Chester's chest and the width of his barrel with a careful eye, her gaze roaming to his beefy hindquarters. "I have to *feel* whether a bull is right for my distinguished herd, straight inside my gut. A lot like falling in love. I like my bulls the same way I like my men—heavy in the chest, riddled with muscle, and chock full of testosterone. Here, honey—"

Amanda startled when Maribelle handed her the dog and proceeded to climb onto the steel fence. Once she reached the top, she slung her elbows over the last rail and slipped on a pair of leopard-print, horn-rimmed glasses to get a better look at the bull. Chester appeared piqued by Maribelle's attention, and he tossed his head and gave a loud snort, eyeing her in cocky defiance. Then he began to strut around the pen, clearly showing off for his audience.

"Hot damn! He's a feisty one, I'll give you that," Maribelle said, pleased. "And handsome as the devil—a lot like his owner." She turned to steal a glance at Lander. "Naturally polled, right? Born and raised on organic corn and alfalfa at the Iron Feather Brothers Ranch?"

"Yes ma'am," replied Lander, casually looping his thumbs into his jeans pockets. "And so far, all of his offspring have qualified for USDA prime beef, which only two percent of the country's cattle ever achieve."

"Well, hell's bells. That's quite impressive, Lander. You should be very proud." Maribelle slowly rubbed her chin, her brows knitting together as she scrutinized every inch of Chester's physique. Then she hopped down from the fence and swiveled on her boot heels to stare Lander in the eye. "How about seven-hundred?"

Nicky shot a glance at Amanda, whose eyes had flared wide. Seven-hundred dollars seemed a ridiculously low offer, considering Lander had told them earlier that even cattle rustlers get three-thousand per head. *Perhaps she thinks he'll give her a sympathy deal for old times' sake?* Nicky wondered, turning to her students to offer a puzzled shrug.

"Now Maribelle," Lander sighed in a patient tone, "you know as well as I do that Elation went for eight-hundred last year, and he and Chester have the exact same bloodlines."

"Are you really going to squeeze me for eight-hundred,

young man? A poor, old woman who's just trying to keep her herd afloat?"

"And who bought her second private jet last month to fly her top livestock home? It was in all the industry papers, Maribelle." Lander's mouth stretched into his famous pirate smile. "Don't forget, if you break Elation's record, it will put your ranching enterprise in all of the top financial rags. Heck, you'll probably be on the cover of *Forbes* holding up a pistol like Annie Oakley. We both know how much you *love* publicity, Maribelle. That is, unless you want to see Chester go to the Lonely Star Ranch in Dallas. Douglas put in a bid for nine-hundred this morning."

"Nine-hundred!" Maribelle shook her head with a huff. "Damn, you Iron Feather brothers drive a hard bargain." She gave Chester one last look, scanning his entire frame. Then she reached down to the ground to pick up a small, round stone. She rolled it between her fingers for a moment before she tossed it in the air and caught it a few times while appearing lost in thought.

"Here, sweetie," Maribelle finally said, handing Lander the stone. "I'll give you a rock for that fine Angus specimen. You know my word is golden, and I'll have the money wired to you right away. *If* you have your ranch hands load up Chester in my jet by the time I leave this evening. After a nice bubble bath, of course. I don't want him stinking up my brand new plane."

Lander reached out his hand to Maribelle's and gave it a firm shake.

"Agreed. We'll even make sure his bath has lavender

essence. But are you prepared for all the press attention you're gonna get?" Lander slung his arm around Maribelle. "Hope you have your body guards ready, because the minute you step off your plane, news crews are gonna come running. No man or woman in history has ever paid a million bucks for an Angus bull, and I expect to see your face plastered on *CNN*."

"That's fine by me—you know I live for applause," Maribelle said with a glint in her eye. "As well as to beat those big boys in Dallas. Don't blame me for making them crawl to breed their cows with Chester. I intend to charge a pretty penny to remind them who they're dealing with, and that handsome bull over there is about to become my cash cow."

"Can't imagine the Queen of Cattle operating any other way," Lander replied in a tone laced with admiration.

Despite the seeming casualness of their banter, Nicky and her students were sucking air.

Had they really just witnessed a million-dollar sale? Amanda, Jonathan and Mark checked each other's expressions. Then they looked at Nicky, who nodded slowly in stunned confirmation.

Chester began to paw the dirt like he'd heard them talking, and he arrogantly bobbed his head and trotted around the corral as if to indicate he was worth every cent. Galveston's attention was immediately drawn to the bull's proud gait, and he started to wriggle in Amanda's arms and issue a low growl. Before Amanda knew it, the Chihuahua wrenched from her grip and dove to the ground, yapping furiously. He ducked under the lowest fence railing and dashed into the corral to confront the large bull.

"No! Galveston—no!" Amanda cried, slipping through the fence and chasing after him without thinking. In seconds, she came face to face with a one-ton Angus bull snorting angrily at both her and a renegade Chihuahua.

"Get away from that bull!" ordered Nicky in her most ferocious school director's voice, squeezing between the railings and sprinting toward her. The instant she reached Amanda, she shoved her aside and scooped up Galveston in her arms. "Run for the fence!" Nicky commanded.

Amanda did as she was told and slid through the railings, then turned to peer back at Nicky in horror. Chester glared at Nicky with two-thousand pounds of attitude as he began to charge.

In the blink of an eye, Lander had already vaulted over the fence and ripped off his flannel shirt as he tore after Nicky. He tossed his shirt high in the air, which made Chester stop in his tracks to gawk at the moving object. Those few seconds were all Lander needed to envelope Nicky and the dog in his arms and dash toward the fence. When he reached the railings, he tossed her and Galveston over the fence to safety, sending them tumbling into the dirt before he joined them in a heap.

Nicky maintained an iron grip on the Chihuahua, though her eyes were closed and she was hacking hard, wheezing from the dust. When she dared to open her eyes, all she saw was Lander's big grin.

"You know," he observed, scanning her soiled cheeks, "that earth color looks good on you." He turned his head and spied Chester in the corral, stomping his flannel garment to pieces. "Damn, that was my favorite shirt, too."

At that moment, Galveston whimpered in Nicky's arms and perked up his nose to lick Lander's face.

"Wait a minute," Lander said with a cocked brow, "I thought you were supposed to be a biter. Truth is, you're a lover, not a fighter—"

"Takes one to know one?" Nicky teased. Nevertheless, her tender eyes told him she was deeply grateful for his quick-thinking courage.

"Only when it comes to *you*," Lander whispered with a sly smile. His lips hovered dangerously close to hers, and the moist heat of his breath sent goosebumps down her skin. In typical Lander fashion, he disregarded all propriety and sealed his lips to Nicky's—right there in public for a kiss—her students be damned.

A chorus of giggles erupted from Mark, Jonathan and Amanda. Soon, Galveston shoved his head between Nicky and Lander, letting out a growl like he'd gotten jealous. Then he gave Nicky a big, sloppy lick across her dusty cheek, making her laugh.

"Is that your way of thanking us for saving you?" Nicky sighed. She stroked Galveston's head and peered into his eyes. "Maybe you got the hint you're not quite as big as you think?"

"Boy, are you two in trouble!" Maribelle reprimanded, wagging a finger at Lander and Nicky as they struggled to disentangle their limbs. "You're a couple of damn fools to risk your lives for my senseless dog!" A smile crinkled her cheeks. "But I sure am glad you did!"

Maribelle reached out her hands to help Lander and Nicky stand to their feet. Nicky was still too rattled from the experience to release her white-knuckled grip on Galveston, and Maribelle was forced to pry the dog free from her fingers. As soon as she seized her Chihuahua, he let out a whine.

"No complaints from you, mister!" Maribelle scolded Galveston. "These folks did a great job of rescuing your butt." She pinned her gaze to Lander and Nicky. "And I insist you let me treat you both to dessert and drinks tonight at the Golden Wagon Restaurant. I always stop by to see my friend Nell when I'm in town. And in case you didn't know, it's best not to cross me, because I *never* take no for an answer."

"Far be it for us to disobey the queen," replied Lander, darting a glance at Nicky, who nodded in consent. He dusted himself off a little and patted Maribelle on the shoulder. "Isn't tonight's dessert special Nell's famous angel berry pie?"

"Did somebody say pie?" Nicky piped up, wiping the dirt from her brow. "Believe me, after six hours of cattle branding," she patted her stomach, only to make a cloud of dust rise up, "I intend to eat you all under the table."

"Is that a bet?" Lander challenged, lifting his chin. "Be prepared to put your money where your mouth is."

"Oh, I'll wager more than just money," Nicky taunted with a gleam in her eye. "If I win, you'll have to bring another group of my students here to gain ranch work experience."

"And if you lose?"

Nicky dropped her gaze to his weather-beaten boots and waved the foul air past her nose. "Then I'll personally shine those old boots of yours. *After* I wash them off with a hose to get rid of your, shall we say, cowboy cologne? Because in case you didn't notice, you stepped in a fresh cow patty in Chester's corral. But I warn you, Lander, I'm *not* going to lose. So you'd better make room in your schedule for more of my students."

Lander shook his head, thoroughly amused. "Always got an angle, don't you?" The wolf bones in his pocket began to jiggle as if to say yes.

"Of course!" Nicky replied with a sparkle in her eye. "Of all people, you should know by now not to expect anything less."

19

"On your mark, get set, go!" Nell Granger crowed, sitting beside Maribelle Ryman in a cowhide-covered booth at the Golden Wagon Restaurant.

Across from them, Lander and Nicky dove their forks into their servings of angel berry pie, a concoction of custard and meringue inside a flaky crust with huckleberries on top. They both wolfed down their desserts as fast as they could muster while everyone in the restaurant cheered them on with wild hoots.

Nicky devoured her piece with mercurial speed, holding her clean plate high for the other customers to see. "Ta-da!" She grinned in smug satisfaction.

"Atta girl!" encouraged Maribelle. She and Nell glanced at each other and clinked whiskey glasses before throwing back their shots. It was clear the dessert-eating contest had morphed into their excuse for a drinking game, and the other patrons in the restaurant cheerfully followed suit.

Dabbing her red-bandana napkin to her lips, Nicky was relieved to have won the first round, yet she was surprised after consuming a whole piece of pie that she didn't feel particularly full. When the waitress Kit came by in her yellow Victorian-era dress with the second round of desserts, Nicky narrowed her eyes and put on her best game face.

"Ready for rainbow cheesecake?" Lander grumbled, returning a dark look at Nicky. His disgruntled expression indicated just how much he *hated* to lose, which only emboldened her.

"Game on!" Nicky replied as Kit set down two slices of multi-colored cheesecake topped by red-icing stars at their table.

In anticipation of the next bout, Nell poured two more shots of whiskey for herself and Maribelle. With a swift glance, Nicky scanned the restaurant and noticed that the customers were tossing bills to the center of their tables, presumably for bets. Near as she could tell, this dessert-eating contest was quickly becoming the talk of Bandits Hollow.

"Focus, Nicky!" warned Maribelle, jolting her from her distraction. "Okay, you can start digging into your cake at the count of three." Maribelle held up three fingers high, ready to curl each one down. "One, two, three—go!"

This time, Nicky altered her strategy by foregoing the fork entirely. She picked up the cake with her fingers and proceeded to stuff the whole piece into her mouth until her cheeks were as swollen as a squirrel's. Squishing her palms against her face, she jammed the dessert as fast as possible into her throat. When she finally came up for air, she took a big gulp from her water glass to make the dessert slide down more easily.

"Done!" Nicky cried, grinning like a demon at Lander.

"Dammit!" He threw down his fork on his plate beside his half-eaten cake with a loud clatter, fit to be tied that he'd lost again. To Nell's astonishment, he grabbed her shot glass and threw back her whiskey without apology.

"Lander Iron Feather!" Nell reprimanded. "You don't have a lick of manners whatsoever! You know that?"

"Never claimed I did," he replied in an insolent tone. He brazenly swiped the whiskey bottle from the table and poured himself another glass. "What dessert's next?" he demanded. "I'm already down two, so I gotta beat Nicky at the next three to win. Luckily, I'm renowned in this town for my appetite. Remember the hot-dog eating contest for charity last year at the county fair? I brought in top dollar."

"I do indeed." Nell yanked the whiskey bottle away from him with a hard glare. "But Nicky's so tall she probably has a hollow leg, not to mention her competitive drive and heap of determination. Given her record so far, my money's on her." Nell tossed a twenty-dollar bill on the table and waved for her waitress to return. "Kit, bring on the chocolate mousse!"

Kit strolled over with two parfait glasses in her hands filled with a whipped, airy brown custard topped by curls of dark chocolate. She set them before Nicky and Lander and gave them two long spoons.

"You honestly think you've got room left for these?" Kit said. "They're pretty rich—"

"Try me," Lander challenged, his eyes drilling Nicky's.

"Alrighty, then!" Maribelle said, holding up her red-bandana napkin this time. "I'm going to drop this napkin, and as soon as it hits the table, time to chow down!"

Maribelle splayed her fingers open and let the napkin fall. The second it hit the tablecloth, Nicky and Lander began scooping madly from their parfait glasses. Once again, Nicky was scraping her last spoonfuls of dessert into her mouth in record time. She leaped up from the table with her spoon in the air and released a big whoop. The customers in the restaurant whistled and applauded, and she smiled, giving them a dramatic curtsy. Then she returned to her seat and met Lander's eyes with a self-satisfied smile.

"Well, Lander," Nell announced, "looks like Nicky just beat your ass." She perched her elbows on the table and leaned forward. "I do believe that's the first time in five solid years that anyone has ever beaten you at *anything*."

The muscles in Lander's jaw flexed tight. "How can you possibly fit all that food into your slim body?" he badgered Nicky. He quickly peeked under the table to see if she'd cheated by dumping part of her desserts on the floor. The rustic, wooden boards were clean.

"Nicky won fair and square," Maribelle gloated, pouring whiskey shots for herself and Nell. "Truth hurts, don't it?"

Lander regarded her with a lethal stare, but he didn't reply.

"So," Nicky's lips curled upward in triumph, "when are my students coming back to your ranch?"

"Name the date and we're good," Lander said flatly.

"Looks like you're getting soft on us," Maribelle chided. She lifted her chin to appraise Lander's features. "If you ask me, it only makes you better looking."

"What does?"

"Having a heart," Maribelle teased. "I watched the way you gallantly saved Nicky and my poor Galveston this afternoon." She leaned over the table and met him nose to nose. "So the bad-boy billionaire has a soft spot for ladies in distress and naughty dogs?" She slid her gaze to Nell. "When you gonna get this boy married off, anyway?"

"Now, you know it ain't up to me," sniffed Nell.

"Then who's it up to?"

Nell threw a look at an old, wanted poster on the wall of the Bandits Hollow Gang in the nineteenth century. On the right in the sepia-toned photo was a tall man in a dark coat and a flat-brimmed hat with long, black hair. Goosebumps scurried down Nicky's spine when she realized they were staring at Lander's outlaw ancestor, Iron Feather—the same man who'd appeared to her in the Mediterranean Sea.

"The stars, I reckon," Nell said with a knowing smile. She nodded at the poster. "And maybe an old owl or two. Did you know Lander's mother gave each of the Iron Feather brothers a piece of heirloom turquoise?" Her voice shifted, becoming soft and low. "She said it came from their ancestor's medicine pouch. Rumor has it that each stone foretells the women they'll have in their lives, almost like their mother knew all along she was going to be taken from them one day in that car crash. Dillon's stone is greenish-blue, like Tessa's eyes. Barrett's is skystone blue, matching Lainey's eyes. But Lander received the rarest stone of them all—a piece of Lander Blue."

"Damn," Maribelle said, squinting at Nicky, "her eyes are as brown as chestnuts. But if I had to wager, I'd say she's been winning more than a dessert-eating contest lately."

Nell shrugged. "The color of her eyes don't distract me a bit. If she's the right one, you never know how she might be connected to that Lander Blue turquoise."

Nicky bit the insides of her cheeks to hide her unease while her heart began to wobble. Sure, her eyes were just as brown as Lander's—but she was also the only at this table who knew that her grandmother had once given her a large turquoise pendant. Of Lander Blue, no less, along with matching earrings that she'd worn the other night at the bar. Through no fault of her own, that extraordinary pendant had been lost forever off the coast of France.

"What's the matter, honey?" Nell asked. "All of a sudden you look pale, like you've seen a ghost. Are those desserts turning in your tummy?"

"No, I'm, um—I'm fine," Nicky fibbed, disturbed by the peculiar change in conversation, along with the coincidence that both she and Lander had inherited similar stones.

"Maybe it's time for this young man to take her home," Maribelle observed. "The sugar rush alone is enough to make a person jittery, and I heard you've been branding all day to boot. I'm awfully proud of you, sweet thing," she told Nicky, "for showing those teenagers the true ranching life. You sure got a heart o' gold. And you know I'm always delighted when a woman can prove she can beat a man, even if it is at a dessert-eating contest."

Nicky smiled shyly, relieved the subject had changed. "Well, I think I might have to let out these pants a little," she replied, "but thank you, Maribelle. For being a great role model. It's been a real pleasure to meet you."

Lander stood to his feet and glanced at Nicky. "Shall we

get a move on?" he offered, sneaking a bill under his napkin for the waitress. "Probably best for you to turn in early and get some shut-eye if you intend to bring more kids to work at my ranch."

Nicky's eyes locked on the edge of the bill he'd tucked under the napkin for Kit—the number on the corner said *100*. When she stood up, she caught Lander's cool poker face.

"Sure," Nicky replied. She bit her lip for a second, mulling over his odd expression and generous tip. "Let's go."

20

As Lander navigated down the winding stretch of mountain road toward the Wilson Ranch, he noticed Nicky had fallen silent in the passenger's side of his truck, her brows furrowed in thought.

"Stomach okay?" he asked. "You've been quiet the whole ride home. Guess three desserts is enough to—"

"You know perfectly well I don't have a stomach ache." Nicky regarded him with a shrewd look. "Okay, I admit I was fooled at first, till I dug into that chocolate mousse at the end. It was hollow in the middle, Lander. Covered lightly with whipped cream." She raised a brow. "You slipped Kit a hundred-dollar bill so she'd make my desserts half portions, didn't you? No wonder I finished them so fast."

A devilish gleam arose in Lander's eyes, accentuated by the light of the quarter moon in the sky. Nicky could tell he was gritting his teeth to hide his smirk.

"You claimed Maribelle is the secret softy," she reminded him. "But I think you've got her topped by about a mile."

"You calling me soft?" Lander replied. "Them's fighting words in cowboy circles——"

"But you're a lover, not a fighter—remember? Just like Galveston."

"Lover, eh?" he replied in a low, husky voice, barely above a whisper. Lander paused, taking Nicky's joke more seriously than she'd intended, and he released a long breath as he scanned the darkness ahead of them. "Out of all the things I could spend my time doing in this big old world," he said with a sincerity that shook her, "I sure wouldn't mind proving that to *you*, Nicky."

Then he reached across his old Dodge pickup seat and gently grasped her by the hand. Ever so slightly, he gave her fingers a warm squeeze over the vintage, cracked leather. All at once, in the thin moonlight that streamed through the windshield and softly limned his rugged features, Nicky felt as if she were seeing a different Lander altogether. No longer the slick, rapacious businessman who emblazoned covers of financial magazines and tabloids alike. But simply a lonely backwoods cowboy, traveling in the dark on a dirt road in his blue pickup, hoping to win the attention of the woman who'd been lingering on his mind.

Nicky wondered if perhaps this was a hidden facet of Lander—of the young man he'd never been allowed to be. The Lander *before* he'd been sent to the Wilson Ranch. Someone tender, maybe even kind…

And as Lander's large, ranch-calloused hand gripped hers a bit tighter, Nicky felt her heart drum out of control. She hadn't realized until that very moment that she desperately needed Lander to be…

Shallow.

A two-dimensional lady killer whose familiar outlaw smile was spread all across the media. A man whose crazy reputation was so over the top it would be ridiculous to take him seriously. Because he wasn't *real*—

Just like Nicky, throughout her modeling career.

The famous Paper Indian who'd been masquerading as an international trend-setter for the last five years, and who'd marketed everyone else's clothing, products, style, and most importantly, *life*.

That way, Nicky never had to truly feel.

Because surely Lander Iron Feather, the notorious renegade billionaire, was far more artificial than she was. Which meant Nicky always had an excuse to never draw close.

Especially to *him*.

Nicky thought back to their barn dance at the prom, to the penetrating way Lander had accused her of being just as afraid of intimacy as she claimed he was. And dammit, with his warm, rough hand wrapped gently around hers, she swore she could feel Lander's pulse beating through his skin. No matter how artful she'd become at building up her emotional armor, she couldn't deny the fact that ever since she'd come back to Bandits Hollow, practically every time she'd turned around there was Lander and his big, beating…

Heart.

Doing everything in his power to make her life—and the kids' lives—better in any way he knew how.

Nicky didn't want to feel this. She didn't know *how* to feel this.

She could love the kids—

They were safe. They were *her* at that age: wounded, scared, and desperately searching for hope. For home.

But a flesh and blood man, who'd been through many of the same painful experiences at the Wilson Ranch? Who'd jet-setted around the world and played glossy roles for the sake of commerce? And who knew exactly how to cultivate the right image to keep people away—and to prevent anyone from exploring the tender, most damaged places inside?

That was *way* too close.

Lander briefly turned to take in the pearlescent hues on Nicky's face as they continued down the lost mountain road, with nothing between them but the longing she spied in his eyes and a host of moonlit possibilities. Nicky's breath hitched at the casual, country-style familiarity that had slowly begun to close in on her usual, safe distance. In an old truck that smelled like hay, axle grease, and day-old biscuits, somehow Lander's simple gesture of taking her hand had cleverly lifted the edges of her well-constructed masks. The school director facade, the modeling facade—hell, every disguise she'd thought about wearing—to expose the real and very vulnerable woman underneath.

Normally, Nicky would make light of such a moment with a snappy, sarcastic remark. But this time, any effort at words clogged in her throat. Up ahead, the porch light of her cabin shone through the darkness like a star, but in their thick silence Lander ignored it. Instead, he steered his old truck up a dirt side route that led toward the ridge and brought it to a halt. He killed the engine.

"What are we doing here?" Nicky asked, her fingers hovering on the door handle in case she wanted to bolt.

"Well," Lander's lips tugged into a hint of a smile, "I couldn't quite bring myself to call it a night when the stars are so bright. Did you know you can see the Owl Nebula this evening? Best time all year."

Nicky rolled her eyes. "Seriously? That's got to be the lamest cowboy excuse I've ever heard to park a truck in an isolated spot with a woman inside."

"Well, in cowboy terms," he cocked his head to one side, his focus lingering on her face, "if you're riding in a guy's truck after dark under the stars, doesn't that mean you're his *date?*" Despite the sharp angles of his roughcast features, Nicky caught a softness in his eyes that pierced her heart.

Lander swiped a glance through the windshield at the night speckled with stars. "Besides, you can't deny this glorious view. C'mon," he reached behind his seat to pick up a small, portable telescope with a tripod, "let's go take a look."

He stepped out of the truck and walked around to Nicky's door, opening it for her like a gentleman. Then he took her by the hand and headed up the ridge to show her the constellations. When they came in close proximity to the prophecy tree, Nicky halted in her tracks.

"Hold on, mister," she protested, staring at the old tree that was highlighted in the darkness with platinum hues. "This wouldn't be a ploy to get me strung up in your net again, would it?"

"Nicky," Lander said, cinching his arm around her waist,

"if I intended to ravish you right now, I certainly wouldn't need a net."

Nicky stilled, holding her breath and desperately hoping not to betray how infernally sexy he was. God as her witness, the very scent of him—a complex aroma of dried sweat tinged with dust and blended with the bite of sage and pine—had the power to unsteady her knees. Lander pressed his hard cheek against hers, his skin rough with stubble, yet his warmth deliriously inviting. Then he pointed to the wishbone configuration on the highest limbs of the prophecy tree.

"There," he said, aiming his finger at a hazy light cluster on the belly of Ursa Major. From where they stood, its position in the sky was right smack dab between the tree's upper limbs. "That's the Owl Nebula. It has two dark spots in the middle that make it look like the large eyes of an owl. My parents used to say it's my ancestor Iron Feather, watching over us."

Lander held up his small, battery-operated telescope. He punched in several digits on a side console to dial in the celestial coordinates and set it on the portable tripod.

"Here, take a look," he added, adjusting the scope.

Nicky grasped the cylinder to position it against her eye. "You never told me you're an amateur astronomer," she mentioned. "Though I *have* heard wicked rumors that you like to look through a telescope in the atrium on top of your mansion so you can spy on unsuspecting people." She smirked and opened her eye wider while she peered through the high-intensity lens. There was the bright Owl Nebula—a radiant disc of blue ringed in a striking circle of crimson, with two dark eyes in the center. The sight was so stunning it made Nicky pause.

"Wait a minute," she muttered, "what day is this?"

Nicky lifted her gaze and squinted at the top limbs of the prophecy tree that framed the twinkling constellation. Her eyes shifted to the position of the moon. "This is the first quarter moon in April, isn't it?"

She swiveled to face Lander. "When my grandmother passed away, long before I knew anything about our connection to Thorne Wilson, my mother took me on a night hike to this very tree. She said we had to be quiet, because we were on someone else's land, but there was something she wanted me to see. She showed me Ursa Major, in this same location, shining between the prophecy tree's limbs. Then she told me Tavachi was our true Mother Bear, our *pia-kwiya-chi*, always protecting us. At the time, I didn't understand what we were being protected from—but now I realize it was the influence of Thorne Wilson. Afterwards, my mother set down a bundle of sage and a ring of braided sweetgrass at the base of this tree. It was her offering to her mother, who she said inhabited the tree now, along with our ancestors."

Nicky gazed into Lander's eyes. "That's when I first heard the tree speak," she admitted. "Under the stars of the great Mother Bear. It said, *You are loved.*"

Nicky snuck a peek into the telescope again. The vivid blue of the Owl Nebula was the only thing she'd ever seen in her life that compared to the intensity of Lander Blue turquoise. The sight made goosebumps alight on her skin.

"Lander," she said softly, "when Nell was talking in the restaurant, and she joked that the owl would pair you off someday, she mentioned the turquoise in your ancestor's medicine pouch. You were named after that stone, weren't you? It was your mother's way of telling you that you're…"

"Rare?" Lander broke in. He ran his hand through his wayward hair and shook his head. "No," he corrected, gazing up at the constellation like the stars were speaking to him. "It was to imply that one day I'd meet…you."

Nicky tilted her head. "Why would meeting me make any difference?"

Lander looped his thumbs into his jeans pockets, releasing a bemused sigh. "Because unless that tumble we took after escaping Chester's corral knocked the sense out of you, you should've figured out by now that I'm falling for you, Nicky." He leaned in closer to her. "Why the hell would I eat three goddamned desserts and let you beat me?" He cocked a brow. "When you *know* how much I love to win?"

Winning…

Nicky shifted her feet and stared at the dark ground. How much of Lander's so-called attraction to her was genuine? Or based on stealing something out from under Thorne Wilson? She was his granddaughter, after all. And everything about Lander's association with her was designed, in one way or another, to help sabotage Thorne. Keeping the school, preserving the trees—they might seem like altruistic goals, but they also undermined Thorne's plans. What would happen to their "chemistry", Nicky wondered, once those goals were accomplished? Maybe the tabloids were right, and a woman like her would become just another footnote in yesterday's news—

"Let me in, Nicky," Lander urged, cutting off her trails of doubt. His dark eyes met hers in challenge.

Nervous, Nicky cast her gaze from the ridge to the distant glow of the porch light on her cabin. "Unfortunately, I'm already swamped with paperwork tonight. And since I have to leave in a month, my cabin's jammed with cardboard boxes—"

"I'm *not* talking about your goddamned cabin."

Lander's lips were so close that her heart raced, and she swiftly glanced aside. He lifted her chin to face him.

"All right, I get it—there's a lot of media gossip about me," he conceded. "Most of it's nasty, spreading stories about all the women I supposedly leave. But haven't you noticed yet that I'm not exactly leaving?"

"What if you're all about the chase?" Nicky burst a bit too quickly, causing heat to rush to her cheeks. "Have you forgotten I've burned through my own share of glamorous guys? It always ends the same, Lander—in flames. You've been my grandfather's nemesis for five whole years. Even if we manage to find the pictograph tomorrow night, and you succeed in ripping the school and ridge property away from Thorne, why would you need to stay connected with me? In a way, you'd have already won. Game over."

Without warning, Lander swept her up in his arms. He held her tight against his warm, hard chest.

"What the hell are you doing?" Nicky protested as he began to walk further into the forest.

"This isn't a game, Nicky," he said. "Can't you get a clue for once? I don't throw dessert competitions for nothing. Or hold expensive proms, or donate large amounts of cash, or spend an entire day teaching kids about ranching. I've been doing my damndest to chase your heart for some time now.

Because the moment I saw you, Nicky, I knew I was falling for you."

"Excuse me!" she shot back. "The first time we met I was captured inside your net. And as I recall, afterwards you pointed a rifle at me—"

"Like I said," a low chuckle rumbled deep in Lander's chest, "I live to win." But then his gaze turned tender, as though he wanted nothing more than to keep holding Nicky in his arms. "And to be perfectly honest, right now the word *winning* to me means a chance to finally get under your skin, like you get under mine. Not just for a night—but for as long as I can manage to stay there. Because one thing I know for certain is that you *are* that rare stone my mother warned me about."

"*Warned* you about?"

Lander's lip curled up a little.

"Because she knew you'd steal my heart."

"Then where on earth are you taking me?"

"To my home. I figured you're probably too stubborn to hike there willingly, so I'm giving you a lift. Be grateful—"

"What? You can't possibly walk with me in your arms all the way to your ranch! It's a quarter of a mile from here." Nicky wriggled fiercely, but it only made Lander's iron grip squeeze against her tighter.

"Can't I?" he taunted, heading deeper into the forest.

Despite the fact that his muscled arms and toned chest felt heavenly against her body, Nicky wrenched herself free from his hold and managed to plant her feet on the ground.

"Stop right there," she demanded, drawing back her arm

in case she wanted to take a swing. "You can't just haul me off to your fancy ranch house without my permission."

Lander gazed at her, puzzled. "I didn't say we were going to my house."

"Yes you did! You said we were—"

Lander gripped her by the shoulders and turned her to face a grove of pines on a nearby knoll. Then he pointed to an opening in the trees that was highlighted by rays of moonlight. Nicky spied the tops of long poles tied together and pale buffalo skin wrapped around a tipi.

"There," he insisted, "that's my real home. It belonged to my parents once, handed down from their ancestors."

Lander glanced at his boots for a moment, his features more raw than she'd expected to witness.

"I just really wanted you to see it."

Taken aback, Nicky's heart climbed to her throat. Perhaps Lander's method had been cowboy clumsy in its way, but now she could tell how much seeing the tipi really meant to him, and she felt touched. "That's," Nicky hesitated, getting a better look at the structure, "that's the place people say you go to before business deals. To cast the wolf bones and see your..."

"Future," Lander finished. "I've never brought anyone here before, Nicky. Not even my brothers, once our parents passed away and I set the tipi up here."

"I bet you tell all the girls that," she sighed.

Lander gave her a steel glare. "Nicky, what you're about to see is sacred to me. Don't come if it—if *I*—don't mean anything to you. Because I'm going to let you in on a little secret. I can build other schools. I can even call the elders of the Ute tribe to help me create more sacred trees. But the one thing I can't find is another *you*, no matter how much money I've got. Now I understand why Thorne was so obsessed with your grandmother."

Lander boldly stepped up to her and cupped her cheeks. He stared into her eyes. "You're beautiful and intelligent," he glanced up for a moment, "and you have a heart as big as that wide, starry sky." He scanned the shapes of the sacred trees in the moonlight on the ridge. "You *are* the strength and love these trees embodied for you when you were a teen. And in my mind, that makes you pretty rare."

Lander set his lips firm, his wolfish gaze drilling into her. "No matter what happens, I'm going to save your school and the ridge—not because I have to win against Thorne Wilson, but because it's the right thing to do. For you and the kids. So tell me, do you want to go inside my tipi tonight or not? Unless *you're* the one who's afraid of intimacy…"

Nicky desperately wished she still had her grandmother's pendant right now—some semblance of comfort and security that she could hold against her heart. She felt exposed next to Lander in the cool night air, as though he'd succeeded in tearing away all of her shields. But then she noticed the vein along his temple, throbbing hard in the moonlight, and she caught the searching look in his eyes. Lander was taking a gamble, she realized, risking the deepest part of himself by putting his heart on the line.

For *her*.

Right here, right now—

Nicky drew in a breath. She reached up to his collar and carefully unbuttoned his shirt down to his chest, exposing his owl tattoo. Then she placed her hand against his warm, hard skin, directly over his heart.

It was racing out of control.

"You know what your problem is?" Nicky asked.

Lander simply gazed at her with all the yearning in the world.

She shot a glance at his tipi and returned her eyes to his. "You talk too much."

With that, she sealed her lips to his for a kiss. Her fingers worked steadily to open the rest of the buttons until she could tear his shirt from his shoulders. She threw it aside in the air.

"Damn," Lander broke from their kiss, his lips rising in a crooked smile. "There goes another flannel shirt. Second one today—"

"Sh," Nicky scolded.

She took him by the hand, her grip firm and certain, and began to walk the few hundred yards toward his tipi on the knoll.

"Like I said," Nicky reiterated, "you talk *way* too much."

21

Lander carried Nicky inside his tipi and carefully placed her down on the floor in the center on a thick buffalo rug. From the top opening where the poles joined, rays of moonlight filtered down on Nicky's face, bathing her skin in a silvery essence that made her appear…

Magical.

Nicky caught a brief flinch in Lander's eyes, as if her beauty were so all-encompassing that it was nearly too much for him to take. For *any* man to take.

Bare chested, he lowered himself beside her and propped his head on one elbow, his gaze slowly tracing every inch of her body without saying a word.

Nicky couldn't help wondering why he wasn't hastening to remove her shirt, as she'd done with him outside. She opened her mouth to speak when he put his finger to her lips.

"Sh," he whispered, relishing the sweet bow of her pillowy mouth. His lip curled into a half-smile. "You talk too much."

Lander swept his palm over her cheek that appeared sculpted in the soft light. Then he paused to study her features as though memorizing her delicate curves and angles. Tenderly, he slid his finger down her chin and along her neck, leaving a trail of goosebumps skittering across her skin. Tracing a smooth line past her collar bone, he began to gently unbutton her shirt and unfurl it from her shoulders.

Lander took in the glow of the starlight on Nicky's bare shoulders as if she were a revelation. He settled his hand upon her heart, his palm simply resting there, as she had done with him earlier on his owl tattoo.

Only this time, it was Nicky's heart that was beating out of control.

Spilling his long, blonde hair onto Nicky's chest, he leaned over and reached behind her back to unclasp her bra, the warmth of his fingers sending her nerve endings on fire. Then he sat up and set her lingerie aside before gently working her jeans and underwear from her hips and legs. He hesitated for a moment to look at the wonder of her body while Nicky kicked free her boots. Silently, he ran his calloused hands over the swells of her tender breasts, moving down along the dip of her waist and curves of her hips. As much as Nicky wanted to swallow Lander whole in that moment, obeying without question the fiery craving that had begun to ache in her nipples and between her legs, she couldn't bring herself to interrupt his smooth, warm caresses. In Lander's total... reverence...Nicky had the impression he was taking his time to truly *feel* her as well as breathe her in—maybe even etch the throb of her heartbeat into his memory. His languid strokes enabled him to luxuriate in the planes and curves of her body, as though every inch of her skin was a rare flavor to be savored.

All of this was completely new to Nicky.

She was accustomed to demanding, high-powered types of men who couldn't wait to strip off her clothes, foaming at the mouth to see what a supermodel really looked like naked. More than once she'd heard a man mumble "bag of bones" when her back was turned, disappointed that she'd never gotten breast or butt enhancements—and forgetting that in the fashion industry "rail thin" was actually part of her job description. But here, lying on a downy-soft buffalo hide, Nicky's entire body snapped and sizzled with every nuanced stroke of Lander's fingers, and she couldn't help thinking that he was trying to feel her…

Spirit.

"Lander," Nicky whispered, hesitant to disrupt the heady, near-worshipful attention he paid to her physique, yet no longer able to restrain the reckless need of her taut nipples and burning core that demanded more, "I want to feel you. All of you—skin on skin."

Lander studied her exquisite nakedness in the silver light, his lips tugging into a smile. Reaching into his jeans pocket, he pulled out his wolf bones, one light and one dark, and set them next to the buffalo rug. Then he slipped off his jeans and cowboy boots.

Nicky's breath hitched in awe—

Lander's physique was lean and tanned and perfectly toned—and she realized in that moment that he was the single, most stunning creature she'd ever seen. With his wild, blonde hair that threaded past his shoulders, every muscle in his body was tight and bulging. Nicky's breath snagged in her throat as she found herself wanting to run her tongue over each hard, convex surface. Before she knew it, she sat up and was kissing his chest over his owl tattoo. Then she leaned him back against the buffalo rug to trace her tongue along his well-formed abs. She licked the bulges of his six-pack before her mouth sought his finely-muscled groin. Lander's penis was so hard and lance-like that she couldn't stop herself from taking his tip between her lush lips, relishing in his ragged moans of pleasure. Her pillowy mouth slid up and down the length of him until she felt his whole being shiver. Lander broke away from her hold and gently rolled on top of her, sinking his body down to Nicky's thighs. He traced his lips against her silky skin and then inched his shoulders farther down as his hand nudged her legs open. All at once his tongue penetrated her core.

Sparkling explosions rippled through Nicky. Lander's artful tongue circled her ridges and folds, undulating in a rhythmic, throbbing motion, until Nicky cried out and clutched his head, pulling him deeper into her as she grabbed fistfuls of his thick, blonde hair.

"Lander," she gasped, panting wildly as her legs writhed, "I don't want to come yet—not until you're inside me."

Lander continued to stroke her core gently with his tongue, stimulating her just enough to make her legs keep twisting in pleasure, but not quite enough to climax yet. Then he sat up and reached for a condom in his jeans pocket. As he rolled it onto himself, Nicky glanced at the smooth wolf bones by his side, glinting in the moonlight.

"What do the wolf bones tell you, Lander?" she whispered, sitting up and cupping his hard jaw in her hands. She searched his eyes. "I mean, when you're with *me*?"

The familiar outlaw smile stretched across Lander's lips. He stole a kiss as he reached to fondle Nicky's firm breasts in his palms. Then he pressed his mouth to her erect nipple and circled his tongue, sucking on one breast and then the other, all the while enjoying the way he could send her body into more shivers of pleasure. His mouth sought her full lips again, drinking from her until he had his fill.

"They say once I'm inside you," he broke away breathlessly, his gaze studying her eyes, "I won't ever let you part from me again."

"Is that a threat?" Nicky teased.

Lander shook his head, his eyes burning into hers.

"No, it's a *fact*, Nicky. That's the way the Iron Feather brothers are made. It's why we choose…very carefully."

He picked up the wolf bones from the rug and placed them into her palms. Nicky felt a rush of tingles sweep up her arm and spread across her chest, bringing a warmth that filtered into her heart. She glanced up at Lander, surprised, when he closed his palm over hers.

Lander kissed her delicately, his eyes meeting hers as if to ask if this is what she really wanted.

If *he* is what she really wanted—

Because in his dark, nearly predatory expression, something deep inside told Nicky that if she kept going, there was no turning back.

Lander would be hers for keeps.

And he wouldn't have it any other way…

Tightening her fingers over the wolf bones in her hand, Nicky glanced up at the top opening of the tipi, at the stars that twinkled above them. She felt the throb of Lander's heartbeat from his palm over hers.

"Don't forget," she whispered, returning his gaze as her lips rose into a smile, "I choose carefully, too."

Lander's jaw sliced back and forth, doing his best to restrain his overwhelming desire. Relishing the craving in his eyes, Nicky leaned forward to his ear.

"And right now, I choose you."

Lander clutched her face with far more force than he intended and enveloped her lips in another kiss. Then he leaned her back on the buffalo rug and swept his hand down to her thighs as he gently separated her legs. Suddenly, he plunged into her with all of his pent-up force in a way that left Nicky reeling. A rush of golden, sparkling light filled her vision and began to course in warm, liquid streams through her limbs, fanning out to her fingertips and toes. As Lander pumped harder within her, Nicky let go of the wolf bones and dug her fingers into his back. She grabbed his buttocks to anchor herself, pulling him in even deeper. She wanted to meld with Lander until they both became molten pools of light. Crests of hot pleasure overtook her entire body, building stronger and stronger until Nicky thought she might split into pieces. Crying out for more as currents of electricity spiraled from her core and shot to her limbs, Nicky's body became riddled in powerful waves of pleasure. The moment she climaxed, Lander collapsed against her, leaving them both fighting for breath. Their limbs remained tangled on the buffalo robe, and the two of them clung to each other like they'd just survived a storm—a delirious, wild, body-melting storm—while they shuddered and gasped sharply for breath.

Nicky trailed her hand gently down Lander's back, relishing the smooth heat of his skin as though they'd been fused together. Yet in the course of her caresses, she detected a peculiar, criss-cross pattern of ridges on his shoulders and lower back. For a moment, it made her breath hang still. A twist yanked on Nicky's stomach.

They were scars—

The marks from where Thorne Wilson had brutally whipped Lander as a teenager, all those years ago in the solitary confinement shack.

Nicky held her breath like she'd accidentally opened a door to a very dark room, and she sensed Lander stiffening at her touch. In that instant, Iron Feather's words came back to haunt her.

The wolf's heart is as dark as it is light.
But you are strong.
Strong enough for him.
Was she?

Was she really strong enough for this wild, unpredictable and renegade wolf? Who one moment could be as cold as a stone, only to melt her heart in the next?

But more importantly, Nicky wondered if the bruised and broken parts inside of her could have any hope of healing the dark and damaged places within him.

Lander's eyes bored into Nicky's as if he'd sensed her

thoughts. He slid the wolf bones from the buffalo rug into his hand and stared at their dark and light shapes.

"We can't change the past," he whispered with a heavy finality that rattled her. "All we can do is carve out a new future."

"And what do *you* want for that future?" she prodded.

Lander brushed the long strands of Nicky's black hair away from her forehead. He tenderly cupped her cheek.

"You."

His dark eyes implored hers, asking her the same question.

Nicky found herself trembling at the warmth of his touch, and she glanced at the wolf bones in his hand. Then her eyes swept across the tipi, the place where Lander often cast those bones to determine his future. He'd brought her here deliberately—he'd made space for her in the most sacred place he knew. And the one thing Nicky understood for certain was that being inside this tipi was like walking into Lander's soul. Forget his vast fortune, his arrogant masks, and his seemingly relentless drive to win at all costs. This was the place where Lander was vulnerable and real—both dark and light, and he refused to hide that fact from anyone. And now here he was, gazing into her eyes with all of the raw hope that had been brutally torn away from him at the Wilson Ranch. Only now, he dared to focus his longing upon *her*.

Nicky brushed a stray, blonde lock from Lander's face. She cupped his hard-edged, cheekbone and gave him a smile.

"Everything I want," she said, her grin stretching as wide as a thief, "is sitting right here."

When Lander glanced down, he realized his palm was

empty. In typical pickpocket fashion, Nicky had artfully slipped the bones away from his grasp without him even noticing.

"But from now on, Lander," Nicky warned, giving him a sly wink as she held up the bones, "if you want to peer at the future, you'd better damn well include me."

22

An owl's call pierced the air outside of the tipi at dawn, startling Nicky from sleep. She blinked hard, rubbing her eyes for a moment, and got up from the buffalo rug to open the tipi flap and peer outside. From their position on the knoll, she could see the grove of sacred trees on the ridge about a quarter of a mile below them, highlighted with glints of copper from the rising sun. The snow-capped mountains in the distance were painted in daybreak hues, and Nicky tilted her head, simply absorbing the rugged, wilderness beauty. Yet when the owl called again, its insistent tone reverberating through the pines, the sound set Nicky's teeth on edge.

All at once, her cell phone began to ring from her jeans pocket inside the tipi, which Nicky thought was odd for that time of day—only six o'clock in the morning. She headed back into the tipi to her pile of clothes beside the buffalo rug, giving Lander a drowsy smile after realizing he'd been roused by the sounds, too. Pulling her cell phone from her jeans pocket, she noticed the caller's number was from the school.

"Hello," she answered, "this is Nicky—"

"Amanda's gone!" the caller burst. Nicky recognized the woman's voice as her staff member Brenda, one of the dorm monitors at the school. "I just did a routine bed check, and I can't find her anywhere! Somehow she got past security, because they haven't seen her."

"Oh my God," Nicky gasped, "Amanda ran away? Did you question any of the other girls?"

"They said Amanda was really upset last night when she found out her dad didn't get paroled after his hearing. He's the only direct relative she has left. Apparently, he got busted for printing counterfeit bills, and it looks like he's committed for another twenty-four months."

"Poor thing, no wonder she's upset, if her dad's stuck in jail for two more years. I'll be right there," Nicky promised. "We'll start a search immediately. Tell the staff to get ready for an investigation as soon as I arrive. In the meantime, call the police—"

"No, *don't* call the police."

To Nicky's astonishment, Lander resolutely disagreed with her advice to Brenda.

"If the police come, they have to file an official report," he explained to Nicky, "which will go on Amanda's permanent record and mark her as more trouble to the court system. It may sound strange, but delinquent behavior is probably her way of identifying with her dad right now. I saw kids act like this all the time after receiving bad news when I was at the school. Amanda's a great kid who deserves a real shot in life.

Just give us two hours to find her. If we don't, then you can call the police."

"Wait Brenda, scratch that," Nicky told her staff member, realizing Lander had a valid argument. "I don't want Amanda's record to look worse than it already does from her stints at shoplifting. Give me till eight this morning to search for her, all right? In the meantime, you and the staff should check all of the usual places on campus. If she doesn't turn up, then we'll notify police."

"Okay," Brenda replied anxiously. "I'll ring you immediately if she turns up."

"Thank you—and good luck." Nicky clicked off her cell and turned to Lander, her brows knitted in worry. "Do you think Amanda might have tried to hitchhike to Canon City? Her dad is in the state penitentiary there."

"Amanda's a very smart girl," Lander replied, mulling it over. "Without any ID on her, she'd know they wouldn't let her in for visiting hours without being accompanied by an adult."

"Then where do you think she might have gone?" Nicky's voice rose in panic. "Could she have tried to hike to your ranch? For a sense of comfort, maybe? She seemed to really connect with being near the animals there."

"Good point," Lander muttered, gazing at the buffalo rug on the floor. He picked up the old wolf bones that he and Nicky had set beside the rug before falling asleep. Closing his eyes, he kneaded them between his fingers.

Goosebumps filtered down Nicky's spine. She wondered what Lander was feeling from the bones—if it was actually possible for them to connect him to one of her students. Deep inside, she prayed that the bones were becoming warm…

"C'mon," Lander urged. He slipped on his jeans and boots and headed toward the tipi entrance. "These bones have never failed me in business," his gaze lingered on the gentle curves of her figure before meeting her eyes, "or failed my heart."

Blushing at his compliment, Nicky swiftly put on her clothes and met Lander at the tipi door. He grasped her by the hand, his strong grip providing comfort as they both stepped outside into the cool morning air. Lander released her and picked up his shirt that they'd discarded the night before. He put it on, throwing on his jacket as well, and then he held out the bones to the early morning sun, its soft glow warming their light and dark hues. Slowly, he turned in the direction of his ranch buildings and corrals, which Nicky could barely see in the distance beneath a layer of fog. Lander opened his eyes and shook his head. He held out his palm to Nicky.

"Touch them," he insisted, nodding at the bones.

Nervous, Nicky did as he asked. They felt chilled against her fingertips, making her stomach sink.

"Amanda's not at my ranch," Lander concluded. He swiveled and walked a few yards in the opposite direction. Then he glanced back at Nicky.

"They're getting warmer the more I veer away from the ranch," he confirmed. He inclined his head to the sacred grove of trees down the hill from the knoll.

"Tell me something—was Amanda with you that day when you went to the ridge to catalog the trees?"

"Yes," Nicky replied, curious what he was after.

Lander's eyes narrowed, keen on the barbed wire fence that separated his property from Thorne's. "Did she like that activity?"

"I-I think so," Nicky answered. "She couldn't stop talking about it at dinner that night. She seemed to feel a kind of... kinship...with the trees. The same way I did at her age." Nicky paused to correct herself. "I mean, the same way I still do."

Lander held out the wolf bones for Nicky to touch again. Holding her breath, she rested her fingertips on their smooth surfaces, relieved to feel they were slightly warmer

"Amanda wasn't running away *from* something," Lander contended, arching a brow. He nodded at the trees. "She was running *to* something. My bet is that she wanted to gain solace from the sacred pines, just like you used to do."

With long, lanky strides, he began to hike down to the ponderosa grove. After several hundred yards, he stopped and glared at the ground. When Nicky caught up with him, she noticed he was studying foot prints alongside cow tracks in a patch of mud.

"Tracks," he said. "They cross under the fence line." Lander leaned forward to examine the fence, carefully running his finger along the barbed wire until he spied the quick repair job where the ends had obviously been crimped together. He pointed to another spot a few yards away on the ridge. "When Dr. Connor came up here and cut through the fence to help Riley, it was over there, not here."

"What are you saying—you had a trespasser?"

"More than trespasser." Lander stared Nicky in the eye. "Cattle rustlers." He tapped his boot beside the fresh tracks. "If Amanda came up here to seek comfort in the trees, and she happened to see them—"

"It must have scared her to death," Nicky blurted, following his train of thought. Searching the ground, her heart began to race. In that instant, Nicky sensed exactly what her student would have done—the same thing *she* would have done if she were frightened that a group of criminals might see her. She would have hidden from them by climbing one of the trees.

"Amanda!" Nicky called out, dashing as fast as she could to the grove. "Amanda, it's okay! We're here! You're safe now—"

When Nicky reached the pines, she glanced up at each one, spying nothing unusual until she drew near the prophecy tree. Gazing beyond the limbs that curled around the trunk like an embrace, Nicky peered at the place where the highest branches conjoined to form a wishbone shape. In the middle was a large burl, big enough for a person to sit on.

And there was Amanda, her face pale, clinging with a white-knuckled grip on the burl.

"Amanda!" Nicky cried, hesitating a few feet from the tree. With everything she had in her, she wanted to scale up those branches to reach her student, but she knew Lander's game net was lying beneath the forest debris. How on earth had Amanda avoided being snared in the net?

At that moment, Lander caught up to Nicky. He gazed up into the tree and gave Amanda a warm smile.

"You must be a lightweight!" he remarked cheerfully. "My net only triggers when something over a hundred pounds steps on it, which is why I keep my cattle in the next pasture. That way I don't have to deal with every fox or fawn that happens to pass by this tree. Luckily, you've got a slight build."

Lander stepped around the net area and untied a cord attached to the back of the trunk to dismantle his trap. Before he could blink, Nicky had already scrambled up the tree to be with her student. She sat down beside Amanda on the large burl and wrapped her arm around her.

"It's okay now," Nicky said softly, stroking her hair. "We're with you—everything's okay."

"I-I was so scared!" Amanda's voice wavered as she leaned into Nicky's embrace. "I came up here about an hour ago, while it was still dark between bed checks. I couldn't sleep any more after what happened to my dad. He's gone—for two more years!" Tears trickled down Amanda's face, her shoulders trembling. "I just wanted to talk to the tree for a little while. I felt like maybe it could understand me, you know? And take my prayers to heaven, like you said."

Amanda studied the large bulge of the burl that jutted out beneath them against the trunk. Her reddened eyes darted back and forth, creased with uncertainty. "But it was really weird, Ms. Box. As soon as I got sleepy and started to nod off on the grass, a voice came through my dreams. When I opened my eyes, it sounded like it was coming from this burl."

"The burl?" Nicky grasped Amanda's cheeks tenderly in her palms. She searched her eyes. "What did the voice say?"

"*Come up here, little one.*" Amanda's breaths became halting, clearly struck by the experience. "*Come up here and be safe. You are loved.*"

Amanda paused, sifting through her thoughts. "For some reason, I trusted the warm feeling I got from that voice. It sounded old and caring—you know, like a grandmother. So I climbed up the branches to this burl. Maybe I was still dreaming a little, but when I first touched the burl it felt like it was…beating. Like a big heart. Then they came."

"They?" Nicky pressed.

"A couple of guys with a truck and a trailer. I saw their headlights down the hill. They walked up to the ridge and cut through the fence, and then they headed into the pasture where the cattle are. When they came back, they were leading three cows. It was so scary! But even when I sneezed, they didn't seem to hear me."

Amanda gently caressed the burl beneath them as if grateful for the tree's protection. She glanced up at Nicky. "When the guys reached their truck and loaded up the cows, I was afraid they might come back later for more, so I stayed put. While they drove off, I noticed that the truck door had a Circle W on it."

"Circle W?" Lander responded from the base of the tree. His eyes narrowed to slits at Nicky and Amanda. "Damn it all!" He shook his head. "I should have known—that's Thorne Wilson's brand."

Crossing his arms, Lander leaned against the trunk of the tree and shifted his gaze to Thorne's mansion in the distance. "That dirty old bastard," he spit out, his hands balling into fists. "I can't believe he sent his goons to take my cattle all along. Guess we'll be looking for a whole lot more than a pictograph at the symposium tonight."

Lander turned and extended his hand to assist Nicky and Amanda down from the tree. "C'mon, you two must be starving," he pointed out. "Let me buy you breakfast at Nell's place. After we let the school know Amanda's safe and sound, of course."

As soon as Lander helped them reach the ground, he gave Amanda a comforting pat on the shoulder. "Thank you, sweetheart," he said, "for solving the rustling mystery. You're gonna make one hell of a rancher someday. Any time you want to help out with my cattle, I guarantee you've got paying job at the Iron Feather Brothers Ranch."

Lander peered into Amanda's face, observing the deep concern that still welled in her eyes. "Don't worry," he assured her, "that goes for your dad, too. If he raised a daughter like you, he sure did something right. I'll have my lawyers look into his case—with their skills, they'll have him out as fast as the law will allow." Lander wrapped an arm around Amanda's shoulder while a relieved smile brimmed on her face. "Because as far as I'm concerned," he darted a confident glance at Nicky, "if your dad genuinely wants to change his life, well, we're living proof that everybody deserves a second chance."

23

As the sun began to set that evening, Lander drove his pickup with Nicky in the passenger's side to the carriage porch in front of Thorne Wilson's white, columned mansion. A man dressed in a black sport coat with a bolo tie and a black cowboy hat approached Lander's window, his face slack in shock.

"Lander Iron Feather?" he muttered, hardly believing his eyes. He stole a glance at the truck behind them, driven by Dillon with Barrett inside. "What on earth brings you folks here?"

"Good evening, Rick!" Lander grinned his wide, pirate smile. "The Rocky Mountain Cattlemen's Symposium is tonight, ain't it?" Lander reached out his window to shake the employee's hand. "If you check the roster, you'll see our names on the list."

Rick scanned his clipboard, running his finger down the index of invited guests. "Well, I'll be jiggered—there you are in black and white. Never thought I'd see the day when the Iron Feather brothers darkened Thorne Wilson's door. You folks starting to get friendly or somethin'?"

"In a manner of speaking," Lander replied. "We're voting for the new Board of Directors in person this year instead of by mail, which means we have to be present. Think old man Wilson will throw a fit?"

Rick shook his head. "Mr. Wilson was supposed to give the opening address this evening, but when I checked on him in his room an hour ago, he was still in his pajamas. Couldn't remember what day it was. It's anybody's guess if he'll make it to the podium tonight—or leave his bedroom, for that matter. They've got a backup speaker, though, just in case. Hank Goodacre's going to talk about refinancing strategies to prevent ranch foreclosure. Speaking of Hank, I heard about you two playing Eight-Ball the other night at the town bar. Sorry about your luck—you've sure been on a losing streak lately."

Nicky's cheeks fluttered with heat, fully aware of Lander's secret on Hank's behalf, which made her fidget in her seat. Nevertheless, she was relieved that Thorne might be too disordered on this particular night to repeat the spectacle he'd created at the bar. Like usual, Lander maintained his poker face.

"Aw, that's all right," he said to Rick. "Guess you can't win 'em all. Should we park our trucks over there by the corrals?" Lander motioned to an open area filled with ranch vehicles of symposium attendees, many from out of state.

"Sure thing—just watch the mud puddles."

"Nothing doin'," responded Lander. "Last time I checked, the dirtiest truck is the sign of the best rancher."

Rick smiled and waved him on through, along with his brothers. When Lander brought his pickup to a stop in front of the corral fence, Dillon's truck soon followed and parked beside him. The three Iron Feather brothers and Nicky stepped out of their vehicles, and Lander pulled his spyglass from his jacket pocket and positioned it against his eye. He slowly scanned the pasture beyond the corrals, then handed the spyglass to Barrett.

"Check out those sleek cows beneath the aspen trees on the left," Lander said. "Recognize 'em? If I'm not mistaken, they've got brand new Circle W brands stamped right on top of our feather brands. You can tell by the blackened fur on the animals' hides that they were done this afternoon."

Barrett gave the cattle a hard look, scrutinizing their hindquarters, and handed the spyglass back to Lander. He ran his fingers through his short, dark hair. "You go inside the symposium while I take a brief walk along the fence line and capture a few pictures. I'll meet you there in a few minutes—after I photograph Thorne's truck and trailer tracks in the mud as well. If they match the tracks I saw near our property this afternoon, we've got quite a case against Thorne for cattle rustling."

Barrett drew a deep breath and turned to Nicky. "Unfortunately, ma'am, court cases can take months. Even though the brands look like they've been altered, I can't seize those cattle without a warrant, and the case would require an agricultural expert to corroborate brand fraud. So any evidence I find tonight probably won't prevent Thorne from shutting down your school or logging the ridge. Our best bet is still to find that pictograph, hopefully inside his house. If we do, we can at least get an injunction to stop Thorne from altering the trees in any way, on the basis that the ridge section might not actually be his land."

A shudder coursed down Nicky's spine. Everything she treasured was on the line right now—the kids, the school, the trees. Swallowing hard, she slid a glance at Lander. "Okay," she insisted, nodding in the direction of the mansion, "let's give this our best shot."

Lander, Dillon and Nicky made their way toward the house, stepping around the mud puddles until they caught up with Rick again at the carriage porch, which spread gracefully over a tall, carved front door. "My brother will be here in a minute," Lander told Rick, inclining his gaze toward Barrett by the pasture. "As soon as he captures that pretty sunset. He's a photography buff, you know."

Rick gave him the go ahead and swung open the door. Once the three of them stepped into the entrance hall, Nicky quickly reached for Lander's hand, her fingers tense.

The entrance hall was stunning by anyone's measure, paneled in ivory wood with gilded accents. It featured a grand staircase with marble columns and a royal blue runner that ascended the stairs, presumably to Thorne's quarters. The floor was tiled in elegant stone, and from the arced windows on either side of the hall that let in the sunset hues, the entire entryway seemed to glow. It was so opulent it made Nicky's breath catch.

Not just because it was beautiful—

But because it was the very same mansion her grandmother had turned down.

Everyone in three counties knew that Thorne had relentlessly pursued Tavachi to marry him, dangling over her head that she could become the grand dame of his spacious home along with his ranching enterprise. With her renowned beauty that was the talk of every town for a hundred miles, she would certainly be considered a notch on Thorne Wilson's belt.

If he could manage to keep her.

Because despite Thorne's wooing tactics and promises of extreme wealth, once Tavachi discovered his brutal nature, she swiftly vanished from his grip. Rumors had swirled for decades that she took Nicky's mother with her and fled to the back country, living according to the old ways where they couldn't be found. Yet others claimed she hid out with distant relatives near the Utah reservation where tribe members kept her whereabouts a secret until Nicky's mother turned eighteen and Thorne could no longer have any legal hold on her. Still others insisted that Tavachi stayed in Colorado all along, and she simply fired a shotgun over Thorne's head every time he dared to come by with his fancy-dancy lawyers, laughing like a demon at his foolishness.

Whichever tale was the truth, Nicky couldn't help being struck by the grandeur surrounding them that had clearly meant nothing to her grandmother—especially if it came attached to a cruel man whose idea of love and affection translated into control and abuse. A man whose iron grip had a corrosive effect on every spirit he'd ever come into contact with.

Nicky shifted her gaze to Lander and Dillon, who were studying the extravagant features of the entrance hall that was crowned by an enormous crystal chandelier. All at once, it hit her that this was the first time *they* had ever witnessed the home of the man who'd once abused them, too. How ironic, Nicky thought, that the Iron Feather brothers are now even richer than Thorne—and like Tavachi, his displays of wealth meant nothing to them.

Another one of Thorne's employees wearing a black coat and a black cowboy hat stepped into the entrance hall and smiled. "Good evening—here for the symposium? Thorne is… uh…under the weather tonight, but Hank Goodacre has kindly obliged to lead the proceedings. If you'll follow me through the gallery, I'll show you to your seats in the auditorium."

Lander raised a brow, targeting a look at Nicky that startled her. It was his fierce, wolfish gaze of protection again, and to her surprise, he linked his arm tightly through hers. His hold was so firm that she got the impression he wasn't attempting to look like a power couple, but rather, positioning himself to be a strong pillar to hold her up.

What's inside Thorne's gallery that has him so guarded? Nicky wondered, curious if Lander had heard some thread of gossip in town that had left him wary.

As Dillon led the way through the gallery, Nicky noticed it was painted a rich, crimson color with velvet-padded benches for viewing the exhibits. The walls were covered with western and Native American artifacts and memorabilia, set off in glass cases by strategically-placed spotlights. By the time they reached the center of the room, however, Nicky stopped and refused to budge. Frozen against Lander's grip, she felt her heartbeat begin to climb.

There, under the designer light fixtures, weren't merely vintage objects—

The entire collection featured everything that had ever mattered to Tavachi Cloud.

A knot twisted in Nicky's chest. Everywhere she gazed were precious items that had once belonged to her grandmother: the traditional Ute dress she'd worn for her puberty ceremony, made of soft, tanned leather and glass beads with fringe on the hem and sleeves. The hand-sewn moccasins and cradleboard she'd used as a baby, which had been handed down by her own grandmother for her and then for her daughter. There were also the first baskets she'd ever made, painstakingly woven out of willow with time-honored tribal designs, as well as her very own set of hand game bones with delicate suns and moons carved into the light and dark pieces.

Nicky swiveled to stare at the opposite wall, spotting the beaded gloves her grandmother had worn when she'd been crowned queen of the Outlaw Days Rodeo, along with her matching beaded belt and the silver belt buckle she'd earned for barrel racing. Beside them in the case were her winning tiara and sash, hung above her championship western saddle. In a large, gold frame was a black and white headshot of Tavachi. She was in her twenties and wearing her tiara, flashing a big smile on her face in the photo like she was the sweetheart of the rodeo.

A prickly feeling clawed at Nicky's stomach, making her

queasy. This peculiar exhibit was far worse than the "Paper Indians" she and her grandmother used to joke about—

Thorne had turned Tavachi into a *Museumized* Indian.

Frozen in time and unable to speak—

And unable to wrench herself free from this man's twisted gaze.

Thorne's whole gallery was devoted to his crazy obsession over possessing Tavachi. Nicky's mind searched for how he could have possibly acquired the items, all so he could display them under the control of his lock and key. Had these pieces been auctioned off after her parents passed away and she'd been sent to reform school? Or even more tragic, donated to local thrift stores where Thorne had gotten them for nearly free?

Nicky closed her eyes for a moment and twisted her fingers together, fighting the urge to break open the glass cases with her bare hands to rescue her grandmother's past. Yet she knew they still needed to search the rest of Thorne's house as clandestinely as possible for the pictograph. Exhaling a frustrated breath, she fluttered her eyes open and spied Dillon stepping toward another case on the wall. He was scrutinizing the old artifacts inside—a ceremonial pipe, a beaded parfleche, a hand-woven saddle blanket, even an amulet made out of bone in the shape of a wolf with turquoise beads for eyes. Though his gaze landed on a slab of stone with an ancient Ute rock carving of a horse and rider, there were no pictographs in the room to be found.

Nicky's heart sank to the floor.

Lander slipped his arm around her, giving her a squeeze. "The day ain't over yet, sweetheart," he whispered in her ear.

"Thorne could have more exhibits in the auditorium or other places. There's no telling how many collections he has."

Nicky nodded, wondering as they headed past the gallery into a hall that led to the auditorium how she could finagle her way into finding other displays. They could be anywhere—perhaps even in Thorne's bedroom. She and Lander and Dillon trailed after Thorne's employee into the brightly lit auditorium filled with several hundred symposium attendees, where the man guided them to a row of seats in the back. Hank Goodacre stood proudly at a podium in the front of the room, giving the Iron Feather brothers a polite smile as they sat down. Then Barrett appeared at the entrance to the auditorium, finished with taking his photos. Hank waited for him to spot his brothers and walk over to join them and take a seat.

Hank cleared his throat to address the audience. "Good evening, everyone," he announced into a microphone. "As you may have heard, Thorne Wilson isn't quite up to doing the opening speech tonight, so I'm filling in for him. We've got a lot to cover, including the latest in veterinary science, market strength for livestock sales, and tips for avoiding financial crisis and foreclosure. Plus, we'll be voting on next year's Board of Directors, so with a pound of my gavel, I'd like to get this session started."

Hank struck the gavel with a sharp knock to begin the proceedings, drawing Nicky's attention to the podium stand. Without warning, she felt her blood rush from her head to her toes.

"B-Burl," she stammered in a low whisper to Lander, who was seated beside her.

"What?" he replied softly, noticing the way her body began to tremble. Nicky's shaking became more pronounced, and Lander curled his arm around her to steady her. "Look, honey, I know this has been really tough on you," he whispered. "Especially with all of the creepy exhibits of your grandmother. But I promise, we're not leaving tonight until we scour this place for that pictograph—"

"No," Nicky managed to utter, cutting him off.

She lifted a finger to point at the podium. Lander felt Nicky brace against his arm with stiff resolve. She leaned in to his ear.

"Burl," Nicky said again like a revelation.

Lander craned his head to scan the podium stand, which was made of a rich, amber wood set off by a well-buffed sheen. In the center of the podium, amidst elegant swirls of aged burl, was a pale stone featuring a pictograph.

And it looked just like Nicky's grandmother.

24

"The stones can *talk*," Nicky declared. "Just like your mother used to say about the heirloom turquoise from Iron Feather—she could hear the stones sing. That pictograph in Thorne's podium was telling me that what we're searching for is inside a *burl*."

"You *heard* the pictograph say all that?" Lander replied with a cocked brow. He'd dismantled his net and was pointing a flashlight at the burl on the old prophecy tree at the top of the ridge, after Nicky had convinced he and his brothers to leave the symposium right away and drive her there. Dillon and Barrett stood with their arms folded beside Lander in the glow of the flashlight, appraising Nicky with stern eyes.

"I didn't hear actual words, if that's what you mean—I don't have your mother's gift. But I felt it in my soul," Nicky defended. "You saw for yourself that the pictograph in Thorne's podium was the spitting image of my grandmother. Remember her black and white photo in Thorne's gallery? I think she buried the pictograph in a tree a long time ago to inspire me to look for a burl on this ridge. Don't you get it?" Nicky's voice cracked with urgency.

When her eyes met the Iron Feather brothers' stares of apprehension, she let out a huff and threw up her hands. "I know it sounds crazy! But I think this is Tavachi's way of speaking to me through time. My grandmother must have known that one day I'd need her guidance. So she hid a pictograph of herself in a tree that she figured Thorne would cut down—you know, to give me the hint to search inside the prophecy tree." Nicky reached out her hand and tenderly stroked the tree's bark with a wistful look in her eyes, as if she were caressing her grandmother's long hair. "In my childhood, Tavachi always told me this tree was special—"

"How could she *possibly* know to do that?" Lander broke in, taken aback. His eyes searched Nicky's. "Okay, I'll admit I noticed an old tree stump along the driveway to Thorne's house, which he probably cut down a few years ago to make room for bigger stock trailers. But what made your grandmother guess he'd keep the old burl with her pictograph? All those years later?"

Nicky squared her shoulders and raised her chin in defiance.

"Because it was his way of *keeping her*," she insisted. "I'm sure it didn't go unnoticed by Thorne that the pictograph was of Tavachi. For Christ's sake, Lander, he built an *entire gallery* devoted to possessing her." Nicky's eyes narrowed as she leaned into his face. "My grandmother was a very deep and mysterious woman. She had a set of hand game bones, too—just like *you*. We saw them in Thorne's gallery, across the room from her picture. My bet is that her hand game bones helped her sense things. You know, things she needed to understand in the future, the same way yours have helped *you*."

Lander's jaw tightened while he silently mulled over Nicky's logic. Despite his resistance to her peculiar line of reasoning, the fact that a pictograph of Nicky's grandmother was in Thorne's possession was far too strange for him to ignore. Inside a burl, no less. The place his father had once taught him was the heart of sacred trees. Lander studied the burl on the old prophecy tree, recalling how his father had told him that the Utes buried spiritual items inside the bark to create the unusual bulging shapes. What he didn't tell Nicky in that moment, however, was that his own hand game bones were ricocheting wildly in his pocket.

Like they'd stumbled onto something.

Lander pitched a glance at his brothers, whose unflinching gazes told him they just might be on the right track.

"What have you got to lose, bro?" Dillon offered in a grave tone, slanting a look at the burl on the prophecy tree. "If Nicky's right, this tree could crack open everything—*and* put Thorne in his place."

Barrett nodded in agreement. "C'mon," he added, pointing to the leather sheath on Lander's belt. "Let's take look into this tree's secrets."

Barrett startled Nicky by reaching for her hand with a strong grip as he grabbed Lander's as well, who in turn clasped Dillon's hand. For a moment, all three of the Iron Feather brothers stood silently and closed their eyes, as though offering up a prayer. Then Dillon began to sing a chant that Nicky didn't recognize, but that was peppered with a few Ute words indicating a call for honor and blessing.

When Dillon was finished, the Iron Feather brothers slowly opened their eyes. They let go of each other's hands, and Dillon gave Lander a solemn nod. Lander pulled an obsidian hunting knife from the sheath on his belt. He handed it to Dillon, who paused to bless the weapon with another prayer before returning it to his brother.

Drawing in a deep breath, Lander plunged the knife with all his might into the burl—into the tree's heart. Chips of wood and bark fell to the forest floor as he stabbed at the burl again and again, until his blade came across something hard. Lander continued to dive his knife into the burl until he managed to carve out an old leather pouch that had been hidden inside. Holding up his flashlight to examine it, he untied the strings at the top and opened the pouch wide.

Nicky peered over his shoulder and gasped.

Inside the weathered pouch was an old pictograph of an owl, etched in deep red hues onto a stone with hematite—and quite possibly the artist's blood.

Nicky released a sharp breath. "It's here—it's really here!" she burst in relief. She slid a glance at the barbed-wire fence they'd crawled through to get to the prophecy tree on Lander's side of the ridge, knowing that this pictograph told a very old story. A story where the Utes had once possessed this ridge and granted Iron Feather the right to use it. Now, she had actual proof that this ridge didn't belong to anyone else—not to Lander *or* Thorne, no matter how much money they'd paid. It belonged to her people.

Lander slipped the pictograph from the pouch and studied

it in his palm for a moment under the beam of his flashlight. The image of the great horned owl was artfully created with flowing strokes, seeming to embody the very spirit of the animal.

"Drop it," a voice commanded from the darkness beyond the tree. "Drop the rock right now, or I'll shoot you to kingdom come."

Lander darted his flashlight in the direction of the voice, only to see the pale and withered figure of Thorne Wilson in his pajamas, aiming a rifle at him. His old cane was by his feet, and in spite of the fact that he was covered by a thin layer of leaves and dirt like he'd taken a bad spill, he let out an amused laugh.

"They tried to lock me up, but I sure showed 'em!" Thorne's lips stretched into a crooked grin. "A couple of knotted bedsheets got me out the bedroom window this time. My staff are so dumb they never dreamed I could walk this far, after believing they had me trapped."

Thorne steered a vicious glare at Lander. "Speaking of traps, I know all about your stupid net, you fool. You're not the only one around here with a scope. I've seen you dismantle that net, so I know exactly how to get close to this tree."

A smug expression lit up Thorne's face, and he pointed a bony finger at the sky. "See them pretty stars? Every spring they shine between the top branches of this old pine. Great Mother Bear, Tavachi used to call 'em. Folks say she shined just like 'em on the day she died."

Thorne's eyes narrowed to dark slits as he inched closer to Lander with his gun. "Some folks even claim they've *seen* her here," he said. He jabbed his finger in the air at the wide space that separated the wishbone limbs. "Right there between them high branches. The ones they call a portal. People say Iron Feather used to slip through there to escape posses in his outlaw days."

Thorne lifted his head high with a proud look on his face. "I'm gonna see her, too," he swore like an oath. "I know it! And that rock you got—it won't mean nothin' once I shoot it to pieces. I always wondered where Iron Feather hid it. Now we all know."

Cocking his rifle, Thorne pointed it directly between Lander's eyes. "So drop that rock, young man. And you—"

His beady eyes shifted to Barrett.

"Don't even think about pulling that gun at your hip. I may be old, but I ain't blind. As long as your jackass brother throws the rock down where I can shoot it, nobody gets hurt. Understand? I ain't about to give up my half of this ridge because of some stupid owl drawn by a mongrel outlaw."

Shaking, Nicky caught the way the Iron Feather brothers traded steel glances. Their fists and biceps were flexed tight, making the men look like they were ready to tackle Thorne at any moment—his rifle be damned. All at once, a silhouette glided past the quarter moon in the sky as the call of owl cut through the night. The raw sound only made Thorne smile.

"Think some stupid owl can distract me, half breeds? Well, think again. Drop the rock or I'll shoot the lot of you. *And* that damn owl."

The owl issued another fierce call, and Thorne fired at it, his rifle blast reverberating over ridge. Though Nicky ducked for a second and choked back a scream, she saw that his bullet had missed the owl. Boldly, the bird landed on the burl of the tree and spread its wings wide like a shield.

Suddenly, the owl began to disappear as peculiar tones threaded through the night air. Nicky slowly rose to her full height. It was *music*, she realized—a low voice singing a tender song, similar to the one she'd heard in the ocean waves in France. But this voice was gentle and distinctly feminine. Although she couldn't quite grasp the words, the deep and compelling notes sounded to her like a summons.

Without warning, the space between the wishbone branches of the prophecy tree became silvery and rippled, reflecting the glow of the crescent moon. Nicky and the Iron Feather brothers squinted at the strange, mirror-like surface, when the air became filled with melodic tones that formed into words.

"You are strong, *pia muguan*," a woman's voice said. "A warrior."

Goosebumps skipped down Nicky's spine—the voice began to utter the same Ute blessing her grandmother had spoken when she'd given her the Lander Blue turquoise. Nicky spotted a look of alarm on Thorne's face, his fingers gripping his rifle until his knuckles creased pale, betraying that he'd heard the voice, too. Even the Iron Feather brothers' eyes where locked in amazement on the glass-like space over the burl where the large owl had vanished.

"Grandma?" Nicky whispered, scanning the area above the burl.

"Tavachi?" Thorne gasped desperately.

Cautiously, Thorne reached out a trembling hand to try

and touch the mirrored surface. The second his fingers made contact, a ripple of concentric circles spread over the burl.

Nicky's grandmother appeared.

"Tavachi!" Thorne cried out. "Is that really you?"

Nicky's grandmother didn't answer.

She remained silent, her long, silver hair reflecting glints of moonlight like the twinkling stars above her head. She was wearing a red Native American blanket wrapped around her body, and her large, brown eyes regarded Thorne with the pitiless gaze of an oracle.

Gradually, however, Tavachi's expression began to harden. Then her image began to fade, and in its place arose an old school building—the Wilson Ranch for Wayward Boys and Girls, back when Nicky and the Iron Feather brothers were adolescents. Beside the school was the suicide shack. Its door slowly creaked open.

And there, inside the shack, was Thorne, whipping Lander when he was a teenager. Dillon and Barrett were in a dark corner of the decrepit outbuilding where they were forced to watch, held back from defending their younger brother by two burly staff members.

Nicky cringed at the welts that formed on Lander's bare skin.

"What is this?" Thorne demanded, waving his rifle in the air. "Those boys were the scourge of the school—everyone knew they were no good half-breeds who did nothing but cause trouble. Somebody had to teach them a lesson! What does it matter, anyway? I'm here for you, Tavachi!" Thorne gazed at Nicky's grandmother with wild, imploring eyes. "Just take my hand and come back," he urged. "All the wealth I ever promised will be yours!"

Tavachi resurfaced over the image of the school, filling the space above the burl. She leveled a dark look at Thorne. "I will *never* be yours," she declared. "Those young men did nothing wrong, and you know it. You'll never be fit for my hand. Look at yourself, Thorne!"

Instantly, Tavachi became hazy, and soon the area above the burl reflected the crescent moon once again. When Thorne anxiously leaned forward to try and find her, an image of himself appeared. Not as an old man in dirty pajamas carrying a rifle, but as the handsome young man with a shock of dark hair that Tavachi had once known, long before his jowls began to sink and his hair had turned white. Right before Thorne's eyes, his image started to grow dark and shriveled, aging into the warped and angry figure he'd become now.

"You sleep with the lights on every night," Tavachi's voice wove through the darkness as she reappeared again. "I've seen you. You live every minute afraid, obsessing over your ranch and your investments. You have no life, Thorne—only your twisted fantasy of control."

"It's because you wronged me!" Thorne shrieked. "We had promise, Tavachi—a future! You're the one who ran away! It's all your fault!"

Tavachi began to laugh.

"No," she replied with an ironic smile. "You wronged you a long time ago. Your idea of love was to put me in a cage. You only ended up caging your own heart." Tavachi turned to Nicky with a protective gaze. "My granddaughter will always find a way. Even if you take away the school, the trees, everything she ever loved, she'll find a way to create another home for the children. *Her children.* Because that home is in her heart, the way I taught her. But you—you'll die alone and full of hate. The same way you lived, old man. The truth is you died a long time ago, and your black heart has just been going through the motions."

Impulsively, Thorne thrust his hand into the space above the burl. Despite grasping wildly at Tavachi, her image began to fade. "No!" Thorne called out. "Don't leave, Tavachi! We can start over again, I promise!" Thorne pawed violently at the space that had now fallen empty. When it became apparent his efforts were futile, he swung his shotgun at Nicky.

"Make your grandmother take me!" he demanded. "Through this portal! I'll let all of you go—"

Before Thorne could finish his words, Lander slid his body in front of Nicky.

"She can't," he replied flatly. "No one can. All your money never impressed Tavachi, Thorne. Just like mine doesn't mean a thing to Nicky."

Thorne fell to his knees, clinging to his old .22 rifle like a lifeline.

"Then what does she want?" he wailed.

Lander stole a glance over his shoulder at Nicky. His eyes met hers, full of a deep level of trust that yanked at her heart.

"Love," Lander said with resolve. "Tavachi already had her people—her home and family. The only thing she was ever in it for was love. And she got that when she gave birth to Nicky's mother."

Drawing in a long breath, Lander shifted his gaze to the lights of Thorne's mansion in the distance. "C'mon," he said, extending his hand to Thorne. "Just hand over the gun, and we'll drive you home. We don't have to mention this ever again. Deal?"

The hand game bones in Lander's pocket turned to ice.

Thorne shook his head and refused to rise. A low moan released from deep within his chest.

"You can still make something of your life, Thorne," Lander urged. "It won't remove the scars from my back, or the scars from the people's souls who you abused." He gazed at the empty space above the burl where Nicky's grandmother had appeared. "But it could be your second chance. Here—"

Lander held out the stone in his palm with the pictograph of the owl.

"Take it. We can trade." Lander shot a glance at his brothers to remind them to stay alert and be ready to spring. "I'll give you this rock *if* you hand me your rifle."

Thorne lifted his head and stared at Lander with a quizzical expression, his watery eyes stained red. For a moment, Nicky wondered if he was fading in and out of dementia, or if he was truly weighing Lander's request.

Lander bravely inched closer to him. Nicky remained stock still, with every muscle in her body frozen in fear, while her heart hammered a mile a minute. She sensed from Lander's intense gaze that if all else failed, he probably intended to rush Thorne and grab the rifle from his feeble hands. And she was pretty damn sure Dillon and Barrett were prepared to wrestle him to the ground.

Thorne carefully studied the rock in Lander's palm like it was a rare diamond. His eyebrows knitted together into a dark line.

"If I give you my rifle," he said in a hoarse voice, shaking his head, "she still won't take me back, will she?"

Lander felt the icy hand game bones in his pocket against his hip. He allowed the silence on the ridge to be his reply.

How could he answer the old man?

Thorne had thoroughly wasted his life. It would probably take an eternity to prove to Tavachi that his dark heart could ever be otherwise.

Thorne nodded at him. He tucked his rifle against his shoulder with his finger on the trigger, then suddenly yanked a pistol from the waistband of his pajamas. Raising the barrel, he pointed the pistol at his head.

"Then neither one of us will ever keep this ridge!" Thorne growled.

"No—no, stop!" Nicky screamed at the top of her lungs at the very same moment she and the Iron Feather brothers dove for Thorne as he fired off his weapons.

In that instant, Thorne dropped to the ground.

And so did Lander.

25

He stood tall in the mist in front of Lander, wearing his flat-brimmed hat with his long, black hair draping over the shoulders of his dark coat. His arms were outstretched like wings.

Iron Feather—

Lander couldn't tell if his outlaw ancestor was protecting him, or welcoming him home.

To his *final* home.

Iron Feather glanced down. Lander was startled to see his body a distance below him on the ground in a forest, circled by mist. Nicky knelt over him in tears while a bright red patch oozed from his abdomen and seeped across the fabric of his shirt.

"Don't you dare die on me! You hear?" Nicky ordered, desperately clutching his hand. Her trembling fingers pressed against his cheek. "I love you, Lander Iron Feather! Dammit, I don't care what your wolf bones say this time—you've gotta live! Hold on!"

Nicky whisked a strand of blonde hair from his eyes as Dillon and Barrett helped Doctor Connor lift his body onto a stretcher.

"We're going stop the bleeding and stabilize him," Doctor Connor declared to Dillon and Barrett as they rushed his body to the waiting Hummer. "Then we're flying him immediately in your helicopter to a top trauma surgeon in Denver. I've already made the calls." Doctor Connor briefly glanced over at Thorne Wilson nearby on the ground, shaking his head while one of his medical staff finished zipping the old man's corpse into a body bag.

At that moment, Lander understood he was still alive —barely.

And Thorne Wilson wasn't.

Lander watched as Nicky ran alongside the men who were carrying his stretcher, her hand still fastened to his with an iron grip. She tried to keep her face stoic, despite the tears that flowed down her cheeks.

Gradually, everything below became obscured by a white mist. Lander lifted his gaze to Iron Feather.

His ancestor's arms remained outstretched, his dark eyes regarding Lander with concern. Lander spotted Nicky's grandmother, Tavachi, slowly approaching from behind Iron Feather. She was covered in her red woven blanket, and she edged in front of Iron Feather, shrouded by the protection of his extended arms.

Tavachi offered Lander a tender smile.

Then she held out her hands with a turquoise pendant cradled in her palms.

The vivid blue stone with a delicate spider matrix was attached to a strand of leather. The turquoise in the pendant was unmistakeable—

Lander Blue.

Lander thought he heard a song begin to rise from the stone. The melody was light and comforting, with sweet notes that seemed to swirl around him in a gentle spiral of air. The hand game bones in his pocket shivered as the song circled to embrace his entire being. With each ebb and flow of the melody, Lander felt his whole body tingle, spreading from his heart to his limbs.

As if the song were bringing him back to life—

Tavachi tilted her head, pleased.

"Welcome home, wolf," she said, raising the pendant higher. "Time to choose."

Lander shuddered. He understood from the gravity in Tavachi's eyes, in spite of her kind expression, that his condition was precarious.

"Will you live for love," she asked, "or will you live for hate?"

Tavachi's words pierced Lander's heart. For the last five years, he'd spent every moment of his existence obsessed over beating Thorne. And now there was no Thorne.

Yet rather than feel hollow, since the rivalry that had fueled his every waking breath was finally over, Lander's heart felt more expansive than ever before.

And it was all because of Nicky.

"I want to live," he stated adamantly, "for her. Nicky is the whole reason I have a life now. I want to love her with everything I've got."

Tavachi nodded, and Lander caught a glimmer in her eyes. "Then you must give this to her, wolf. Your hearts are entwined now, like the pines grown together in the sacred tree. When you find this stone and offer it to her, she will know."

Lander searched Tavachi's eyes. "Will she know because she hears the stone's song?" he asked.

Tavachi's lips curled mischievously.

"Of course not," she replied, amused. "I've lost count of how many times I tried to teach her. It's not her talent. She only hears the trees. You'll have to sing the stone's song for her."

Lander swallowed hard, admiring Tavachi's honesty. "What do the words of the song say?"

"You already know," Iron Feather cut in, lowering his arms. He gently placed his large hands on Tavachi's shoulders and leaned into her. Then he pressed his face against her cheek. "You've known that song since the moment you met her."

For the first time in Lander's life, he felt a blush hasten up his cheeks.

He *did* know that song—it was the song his soul sang every time he was near Nicky. All along, his shimmying wolf bones had merely been reflecting the exhilaration of his heart, like an extension of his own pulse. At this point, he couldn't imagine his life, much less eternity, without her.

Lander studied Iron Feather and Tavachi, the way their bodies seemed connected now like two souls knit together— belonging to each other—the same way he felt about Nicky. In that moment, he dared to weigh possibilities that hadn't crossed his mind before.

Could it be that Iron Feather was the *real* reason Tavachi never returned to Thorne?

Tavachi knew about the prophecy tree and its rumored portal. She'd even used it that night to communicate with Nicky and Thorne. Lander ran his hand through his long hair, his mind caught in a tangle.

What else might Tavachi have used the portal for?

Perhaps the town gossip had more merit than he'd ever realized. And just like Iron Feather, Tavachi had taken her daughter with her and employed the portal to escape her enemies. To escape *Thorne*—

Iron Feather slowly traced his hands down Tavachi's shoulders to her waist and held her close in a tight embrace. She looked happy and secure in his arms.

Protected.

Loved…

Goosebumps alighted on Lander's skin.

Maybe Tavachi had found her one true heart all along. An epic love story that transcended time…

And the notion of time-traveling outlaws, who'd founded Bandits Hollow over a century ago, had actually been *true*.

Lander drew in a deep breath, his chest swelling. He'd give everything he had to secure the same great love story for he and Nicky. But most of all, he'd give his heart.

As if she'd heard his thoughts, Tavachi stepped forward and placed the turquoise pendant in his palm. It felt strangely warm and pulsing in his hands. Soon, it began to throb to a distinct rhythm.

A rhythm that matched his own heart.

Dipping his head out of respect for Iron Feather and Tavachi, Lander paused to study the stone. He lifted his eyes once more to meet their gaze.

"Thank you," he said reverently. "I promise to find this stone and take it where it belongs. Home—to Nicky." A bit nervous, he rubbed his hand lightly over the turquoise like a crystal ball. "When I give it to her," he asked with more urgency than he'd intended to reveal, "will she be mine? I mean, forever?"

Tavachi merely smiled as she gently retrieved the turquoise back from his palm. She cradled it in her hands again as she and Iron Feather began to recede into the mist.

"Find the stone," he heard Iron Feather's voice command from somewhere deep in the mist. "Only the stone knows."

26

Nicky arrived at the Iron Feather Brothers Ranch at seven in the morning, just like she'd been doing for the last two weeks, to deliver breakfast to Lander from Nell's restaurant. When she stepped out of her Jeep, she went around to the passenger's side and picked up a large domed tray of comfort food—pancakes, eggs and homemade sausage, without a hint of the European touches from his chef Francois. This was pure country fare, fashioned by the best home-style cook in the county. But so far, Nicky hadn't been able to witness Lander enjoying a single bite. Lander's ranch physician, Doctor Connor, had kept him on an IV under heavy sedation after his surgery for the bullet that had lodged in his lower abdomen, which required an emergency operation and sutures. The doctor insisted he wanted Lander's vital signs to be stronger before he allowed him to return to full consciousness, because heaven knows Lander wasn't about to linger in bed. "Rest isn't in Lander's vocabulary," Doctor

Connor noted, and Nicky hoped that this morning might be the day when Lander could finally sit up and relish a good meal.

In spite of the severity of his gunshot wound, Lander's prognosis was excellent, and he was expected to make a full recovery. Of course, Nicky had enjoyed the time she'd gotten to spend with Lander's brothers and their wives during visiting hours over the last two weeks, and luckily, Dillon and Barrett were more than happy to finish the meals she'd brought. But on this particular morning, as Nicky walked up to the Iron Feather brothers' mansion and headed to the side entrance of the medical center at the far end of the building, she was surprised to see that the entry door was already ajar.

Hesitantly peering inside, all at once Nicky realized that Lander's recuperation bed was gone.

"Where is he?" she blurted in panic to one of the medical staff who was busy rolling aside the bedside monitors. Her heart faltered as the blood drained from her face. "Did Lander get transferred to another medical center? Has his condition *worsened?*"

The man stopped moving the machinery long enough to shake his head with a wry smile. "Ma'am, I believe you know my boss pretty well by now," he replied. "The doctor finally allowed him to be taken off sedation yesterday afternoon, and the minute he got up this morning, he climbed back onto his horse in a shot."

"You mean he woke up *yesterday afternoon?* Why didn't he call me?" Nicky burst. "I would have visited—"

"I doubt that," the man corrected. "He was on the phone for hours on end making his usual deals till midnight."

"Seriously?" Nicky replied, aghast. "And he didn't bother to let anyone see him?"

"Please don't take it personally, ma'am," the man said kindly. "Not even his brothers were allowed to interrupt his calls. He sticks to his schedule like clockwork—ranch duties in the mornings, then business after that. His doctor said following his routine is therapeutic right now, after everything you folks have been through. As long as he doesn't over extend himself."

Nicky's shoulders sank as she stared down at the breakfast tray in her hands. "I suppose I can see your point," she mumbled, her ego feeling stung from Lander's lack of communication. But she knew she was hardly one to judge, since she *always* put her school and students before anything else. Trying to remain chipper, Nicky forced a smile. "Can you tell me where I might find him then? Before this breakfast gets cold?"

The man moved toward the open door and aimed a finger outside, pointing at the ridge in the distance. "If you look up yonder, you'll see him on his horse. God knows why he had to bolt to the ridge so early, but I imagine it was to check fences. You're welcome to drive your vehicle up there, ma'am, if you want to make a special delivery." He gave Nicky an encouraging pat on the shoulder. "I'm sure he'll be happy to see you."

Nicky nodded, spying Lander's silhouette high on the ridge astride his stallion. "Thanks," she said, letting out a sigh of relief that at least Lander appeared to be back to normal. Just then, her stomach growled, and she gave the man a smirk. "I swear, if Lander doesn't eat this breakfast soon, I'm going to down Nell's cooking all by myself. Here," she said cheerfully, sneaking her hand under the dome, "take a honey-butter biscuit."

"Much obliged," the man replied. He dove in eagerly for a bite.

Nicky turned to walk back toward her Jeep. As soon as she reached the passenger door, she opened it and set down Nell's tray, then gave the door a shove and stepped around to the driver's side to hop in and start the engine.

"I can't believe Lander's *still* a workaholic," she muttered through her teeth, steering her wheels to aim for the ridge. "After getting a bullet in his gut. Guess that's what happens when you love your ranch so much."

Gunning her vehicle to make the steep climb up the ridge, Nicky found herself attempting to swallow a knot that had begun to form in the back of her throat. Though Lander's injuries had certainly been serious, it was even harder to get over the way her grandfather had ended his own life. Not only did his suicide leave Nicky in deep shock, it also forced her to confront the myriad of conflicted emotions that overwhelmed her after his death. By all accounts, Thorne had been a very warped man. And Nicky couldn't help being relieved that she no longer had to worry about him cutting down the sacred trees. Yet a secret, perhaps naive, part of her had actually hoped her grandfather might change. That Thorne might one day acknowledge all the good she'd been doing and encourage her to continue with the school. It was silly, of course. Nicky knew people don't suddenly alter their ways, and a random grandfather who'd never bothered to recognize her as his own flesh and blood was hardly a candidate for offering anyone approval. Although she understood the notion was pure fantasy, Thorne had been the only close relative she'd had left. And now he was gone, too.

As Nicky approached the area where her grandfather had passed, she stubbornly brushed back the tears that tried to roll down her cheeks. She was strong and resilient, just like her grandmother had taught her, and she knew she'd make it through this time in her life the same way she had all of her other trials. "It's okay—it's over now," she whispered, her voice stolen by the breeze as she steadily brought her Jeep to stop. "No one will ever have to face that man and his abuse again."

Nicky cut the engine and gave the parking brake a yank. Then she stepped out and folded her arms, scanning the ridge and the nearby grove of sacred trees. In the early morning, the dew on the tree needles sparkled with sunlight, making even the centuries-old pines seem fresh and new. Nicky's gaze eventually settled on the long fence that divided Thorne's and Lander's properties. For a moment, she imagined all of the barbed wire gone, and the land looking as open and free as it once did in the nineteenth century. With Iron Feather's pictograph now recovered, she was determined to use it as evidence in court so that the ridge land would be returned to her people—along with the sacred trees. It would be up to the Ute tribal council to decide if she could keep running the school on the adjoining parcel, of course. But given the number of Native American students who'd flourished under her care, she had every reason to be optimistic about the future.

A light wind picked up and rifled through Nicky's hair, its gentle warmth caressing her face and shoulders, making her relax a little for the first time in days. Just as she decided to try and locate Lander so she could give him breakfast, a heavy rustle stirred the pine needles and leaves on the forest floor behind her, making her jump. Nicky whipped around—there was Lander on his horse in the tree shadows only a few yards away. His smile stretched as wide as the ridge.

"Damn!" Nicky said, clutching her chest. "You always did know how to sneak up and surprise people."

"It's in my blood," Lander remarked with a twinkle in his eye. "Somebody's gotta carry on the family outlaw tradition."

He hopped off his horse with a sharp wince, and Nicky could tell he was pushing it to be riding so soon. Slowly, with a slight limp on his left side to protect his gut wound, he led his horse Danáskés toward Nicky. Then Lander dropped the reins and halted.

For a moment, he took in the sight of Nicky like she was his whole world—the sun, the moon, the stars—all wrapped together and shining brightly in his heart. A faint call of an owl echoed through the morning air, and he took a bold step forward.

Lander clutched both of Nicky's cheeks for a kiss—

His lips worked over hers with a fierce and all-encompassing need while he wrapped his strong arms around her as if she were his very breath. In that instant, Nicky felt like she'd been cocooned inside his soul, tucked into a secret, safe place where Lander would never let her go. In spite of the many questions Nicky had about the state of his health, his pain, or if he should even ride his horse back down the ridge, all her thoughts fell away in the warm sanctuary of his arms. Lander's heart beat hard against

Nicky's chest like it wanted to leap from his body to join hers, and he ran his hands down her shoulders, pulling her closer as though he could melt them together, never to be parted again.

"God, I've been waiting to do that for days," he gasped after he finally broke free from Nicky's lips. His deep brown eyes drank in her face like he was stealing a glimpse of heaven.

"But you were sedated," Nicky giggled. "How could you—"

"That doesn't mean I wasn't dreaming of you in my sleep," Lander countered with a sly smile.

Nicky dipped her forehead, trying to hide the flattered blush that spread across her cheeks. For once, she wasn't able to argue with Lander, because truth be told, she'd been dying to kiss him like that, too. Reaching up to touch his hard cheekbone, she traced her fingers down to the stubble of his firm jaw, just to make sure she wasn't dreaming. After the initial trauma of the shooting, she hadn't known how badly Lander was hurt at first, or if he would even recover. But now, lifting her gaze to meet his intense brown eyes, Nicky could see for herself Lander's stubborn will to grab life whole for the both of them, and any concerns about their future vanished.

"I've got breakfast for you, you know," she said in a light, teasing tone. "It's in the Jeep, getting cold. I'll have you know I brought a tray of Nell's cooking for you every day this week."

"*You're* the only breakfast I need," Lander replied, leaning in for another kiss. He ran his hands through her long, black hair. "We've got plenty of time for that later—"

"Oh?" she interrupted, her voice sassy. "Apparently, you *didn't* have time to bother calling me last night. After you woke up and spent the whole afternoon and evening on the phone doing business. Your staff ratted you out, Lander."

"Nicky," he breathed in a tone so low it startled her, "there's no business deal on earth that could take me away from you. I was on the phone because...well...I wanted you to have something."

Nicky cocked her head to one side, confused.

"Here," Lander urged, "let me show you."

He kept an arm wrapped around Nicky's waist as he turned to face the prophecy tree in the grove. Lander led Nicky toward the old pine, giving her a wink when they got closer to indicate his game net was dismantled. As they drew near, the sun's rays filtered through the tree's upper branches that formed the wishbone shape and settled on the large burl —the same place they'd witnessed Nicky's grandmother. The glow over the burl gave it an other-worldly sheen, making Nicky tremble at the remembrance of everything that had transpired there. She gazed at the lower branches that circled the tree, where long ago the two pines had been connected to become one. In that moment, Lander entwined his arms around her waist.

"Do you think they knew we'd find each other someday?" Nicky whispered, studying the contours of the fused tree in the enchanted light.

Lander hugged her close. "To be honest, I think they depended on it," he replied softly. Glancing over the ridge, he pressed his cheek against Nicky's. "I believe whoever helped create this tree, all those centuries ago, wanted it to remain sacred in a place where it would be free. I'm giving my part of this ridge back to my father's tribe, Nicky. Back to the Utes. I'll do everything in my power to make sure Thorne's half is returned to them, too."

Nicky nodded, her chest swelling with pride. This tree, this ridge, this wild, wonderful man who'd do anything to help her with her kids and the school—they had all made her life feel full now. No longer was she that empty woman who circled the globe to have her picture taken, yet who'd forgotten who she was. She was *home*, and for a moment Nicky settled her boots firmly in the dirt beneath her. Then she swiveled in Lander's arms and gave him a kiss.

"Thank you," she whispered. "Thank you for believing in me—and for protecting the trees."

At that moment, the low rumble of an engine approached. When Nicky and Lander glanced in the direction of the sound, they spotted Dillon and Barret with their wives in a truck steadily climbing up the ridge. The vehicle stopped and Lander's brothers got out, while Tessa and Lainey took a few more minutes to emerge with a picnic basket, an old quilt, and —of all things—a cake.

Nicky searched Lander's eyes. "They brought you a cake? At seven-thirty in the morning? Guess my breakfast tray just got trumped by dessert."

Lander shrugged, but Nicky caught a glint in his eyes. "Maybe they heard I was here, like you did, and they wanted to throw a recovery party."

"Yoo-hoo! Good morning!" Tessa called out. She carried an ivory, tiered cake on a tray in her arms that matched her pale, blonde hair. "It's never too early for dessert, right? Good thing we found you two."

"I've got plates and forks!" piped up Lainey, catching up to her sister-in-law with the picnic basket and quilt. When they reached Lander and Nicky, Lainey set the basket down and then unraveled the large quilt, spreading it over the ground. As Tessa set down the cake, Lainey curled a couple of loose, honey-brown strands of hair over her ears and shot Dillon and Barrett a sly wink, who'd joined them by the quilt.

"Wait a minute," Lainey mentioned, perching her hands on her hips. "Isn't something missing on this cake?" She tapped her lip. "You know, like writing in frosting that says best wishes or congratulations on your recovery? There's a spot in the middle where the dedication is supposed to go, but it's blank."

Dillon and Barrett struggled to restrain their smirks, shifting their gazes to Lander.

"Well, that's a damn shame," Dillon remarked, maintaining a still face. "Nobody wants undecorated cake for breakfast."

"Think you can do something about that, bro?" Barrett prodded.

To Nicky's surprise, Barrett pulled out a bottle of champagne from behind his back, and Dillon held up a couple of glasses.

"What's going on?" Nicky said, studying the amused look on their faces.

"Well," Lander replied, pointing at the prophecy tree, "if you reach inside the hole I carved into the burl two weeks ago, you just might find out." He gave Nicky a gentle nudge.

Nicky glanced at their knowing faces once more before stepping up to the tree. She reached inside the burl, startled to find something soft and smooth. Pulling back her hand, she discovered it was an old leather pouch, probably the one that had belonged to Iron Feather.

"Oh my gosh, this must have been your ancestor's," she said. Nervously, she held the pouch to Lander.

"No, *you* open it," he smiled.

Nicky unraveled the leather ties at the top and peered into the pouch. Her face blanched—

Inside was her grandmother's turquoise pendant.

"Where on earth did you get this?" she gasped. She heard an owl hoot through the trees in the distance, and it sent shivers down her spine.

"Oh, let's just say a bird whispered to me that I should find it for you. I discovered it online yesterday at a Sotheby's auction site in France, and I arranged for it to be shipped here overnight. The story goes that it was discovered by a fisherman on a beach near Cannes, and local authorities had it appraised by a master jeweler. Due to its rarity," Lander said proudly, "it's considered priceless." He stepped forward and peered into Nicky's eyes. "A lot like someone else I know."

Nicky's body began to tremble all over.

"Th-This belonged to my grandmother," she stuttered. "I thought it was lost forever. She gave it to me when I was child, and it was my favorite piece in the whole world—"

"Oh good," Lander said, slipping his arm around her to bolster her up, "because it perfectly matches this ring."

He dug into his jeans pocket and pulled out a ring, then held it up to the morning light. In the center of the ring was the Lander Blue turquoise left to him by his ancestor. The stone was surrounded by diamonds with two delicate curls of gold crossing over the turquoise—like the entwined arms of the prophecy tree.

"Tessa creates custom jewelry, and she designed this ring especially for you," Lander said, shooting his sister-in-law a smile. To Nicky's astonishment, Lander let her go and slowly lowered himself onto one knee, cringing from his gunshot wound.

"Nicky," he said firmly, "I hope you can see in my eyes how much I've fallen in love with you. You've opened up my heart to a whole new world—a world that makes me and all the kids you care about feel more at home than ever before. And I want your home to be *here*," he patted his heart, "forever—with me." Lander gazed up at Nicky with such raw hope it pierced her deep inside. "Will you marry me, Tavinika Box?"

Nicky stared at the stunning ring in his hand, then at her grandmother's turquoise pendant inside the pouch. She carefully lifted out the pendant and ran her fingers over the beautiful stone.

Without warning, Lander closed his eyes and began to hum.

"What are you doing?" Nicky whispered. Goosebumps trickled down her neck—his hum sounded like the song Iron Feather had sung to her when she nearly drowned in France.

Lander kept his eyes shut for a moment, continuing to hum. Finally, he opened his eyes and gazed at her.

"I'm singing. The turquoise song," he said. "After I was shot, your grandmother and Iron Feather...well, they visited me. They said when you saw this stone," he nodded at her grandmother's pendant, "you'd know. You'd know whether you were going to marry me."

The pendant grew warm in Nicky's hand. Speechless, she struggled to keep from shaking. She was so deeply touched that when she tried to form words, they couldn't spill from her mouth.

"Well, are you?" Tessa asked pointedly.

"You know, going to marry him?" Lainey chimed in.

"Hurry up and answer," Barrett urged, "before the champagne gets warm."

Nicky's heart raced as she turned and scanned the eager faces of Lander's brothers and their wives. She watched Dillon go to the picnic basket and set out several more glasses on the quilt as if waiting impatiently for a toast.

Tessa pulled out a tube of bright yellow frosting from her pocket and held it up. "I'm ready with this icing to write congratulations!"

"Y-YES!" Nicky finally burst, grateful that she managed to spit out the word. She clutched her grandmother's pendant close to her chest and stared down at Lander. "Of course I will! I can't imagine forever without you. I love you, Lander—a thousand times yes!"

Grasping the ring from Lander's hand, she slipped it on her finger and admired the turquoise's vibrant blue. Lander rose to his feet and leaned into her for a kiss, then took the pendant from her palm and tied the string of leather around her neck. He smiled and stroked a wayward strand of dark hair from her forehead.

"Well, thank God," Barrett mentioned as he popped the cork on the champagne bottle, not caring that the liquid bubbled over his hand. "Because I'm starving, and it's time to get this party started."

He waved Lander and Nicky over to the quilt as Tessa was busy scrawling *Congratulations on your engagement* with icing on the cake. Lainey set out the plates and forks, then pulled out a knife from the picnic basket and began to carve slices. Barrett helped her pass the plates around as Lander and Nicky sat down. When Dillon joined them and grabbed a piece of cake, he wriggled a newspaper clipping from his jeans pocket and held it up.

"By the way, future sister-in-law," Dillon said, "do you realize you've become the talk of the town?"

Nicky accepted a slice of cake from Barrett and squinted at Dillon, unsettled. Had the Iron Feather brothers been so confident that they prematurely released the news of her engagement to Lander to the press? Her grandfather's tragic death had been the biggest story in Bandits Hollow for years, and she couldn't imagine anything about her own life that would be deemed as noteworthy.

Lander took the newspaper clipping from Dillon and set it on the quilt between he and Nicky. Unfolding the article, he pressed it flat with his hands and began reading. It was from the front page of the *Bandits Hollow Herald*, with a headline printed in bold letters:

Wealthy Town Eccentric Leaves Assets To A Ghost.

Nicky's mouth fell as she scanned the article, her eyes growing as big as her plate. "What?" She turned to Lander. "Is this for real?"

Lander searched Nicky's eyes, his expression as astonished as hers.

"From the looks of it," Dillon pointed out, "Thorne was still trying to lure Tavachi from beyond the grave. The article says it was revealed in his will at his private funeral a few days ago that he'd given everything to Nicky's grandmother, even though she'd passed away long ago, hoping to somehow impress her. He thought he could still win her over in spirit."

"That's not all the article said," Barrett added, between chewing mouthfuls of cake. "Because Thorne was deemed of sound mind by his psychiatrist before his death, his will is legally binding. But since it's against the law to leave an inheritance to a disembodied person, his estate falls to his next of kin. Which turns out to be you, Nicky."

Nicky dropped her plate, sending her cake tumbling across the quilt.

"A-Are you saying we're actually *neighbors* now…b-because his land is *mine?*" she stuttered, gazing at the Iron Feather brothers. "I mean, except for the acres I intend to give back to the Utes?"

"Reckon so," Dillon confirmed.

Tessa and Lainey eagerly poured the champagne into the glasses.

"This calls for a toast!" Tessa announced, holding up a glass. "Not only are our ranches side by side—we're all going to be family."

"We'll be more than that," Lander noted thoughtfully, clutching Nicky's hand. His gaze settled on his older brothers, who'd always been his models of strength and courage, regardless of how much abuse Thorne had hurled their way. Those days were done—Nicky had helped to ensure that. She'd healed the school not only for her students, but for the adolescent boys the Iron Feather brothers had once been who desperately wanted—no, *needed*—a sense of justice and closure. It really was a new dawn at the Sun Mountain School, like Nicky had promised when she first arrived. Lander picked up a champagne glass and passed it to her, then lifted one for himself. He stared out over the vast land holdings that they would legally share after matrimony.

"We're finally going to be…whole," Lander said.

He turned to Nicky with a fresh look in his eyes that startled her, a kind she'd never quite seen before. In that moment, she realized he meant more than simply joining ranches.

Lander's lips curved into a half smile, and he leaned into her ear. "Think you might need a little advice on managing your fortune?" he whispered. "I've got quite a bit of experience at making deals, you know."

"Only if those deals are authorized by *me*," Nicky chided. "After you let me consult with your wolf bones, of course. You're not the only one you knows how to listen, mister." She playfully bumped her shoulder against his, sloshing his champagne.

"As you wish, " Lander replied, enjoying her usual moxie. With that, he held up his glass.

"To my Nicky," he announced proudly, scanning his brothers and their wives before his gaze returned to her. "I can't think of a finer woman in Colorado to become the next top rancher—especially since I know she'll use every dime to make the world a better place. But most of all, I'm the luckiest guy on earth to get to share my life with her. May our marriage be more than a merger—may it be a true melding of two hearts."

Lander clinked his glass against Nicky's and gave her a kiss. Then he circled his arm through hers, enjoying Nicky's bright smile as they both took sips from their glasses of champagne.

"Welcome home, my love," Lander whispered, pausing to let his eyes linger on her lovely face. "Welcome home."

ALSO BY DIANE J. REED
EXCERPT FROM MY FOREVER COWBOY

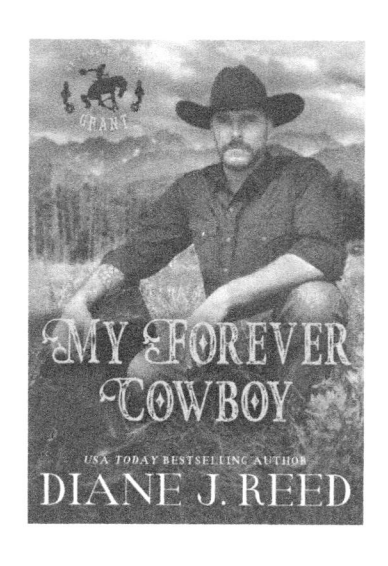

"My Forever Cowboy, can I help you?"

Avery twirled a blue pen between her fingers, customized with her lipstick-red business name and cowboy-hat logo, as she waited for the caller to make a request for her commercial photography studio.

"I'm Dixie Jackson at the Stampede Cards & Gifts headquarters in Denver. Am I speaking to the owner?"

"Yes, this is Avery Smart."

"Well, Ms. Smart, your cowboy calendar last year turned out to be our biggest seller in Colorado. And we'd like to commission you to produce another one for all our stores across the country as well as our website. Naturally, we'd want an exclusive contract. Would that be possible?"

"Exclusive? Can you explain what you mean by that?"

"Certainly. We'd like twelve images of new cowboys for a calendar that's sold nowhere else but Stampede, and we're prepared to pay a premium. I don't know where you find them, Ms. Smart," Dixie gushed, "but those cowboys in your calendar last year are the best-looking men we've ever seen! So rugged yet sincere, like a young John Wayne. Customers tell us they want to throw their arms around these men and ride off into a sunset. Could you find a dozen new cowboys like that for an exclusive Stampede calendar?"

Avery swallowed hard, slipping a lock of her long, copper hair behind her ear. "Of course!" she replied, her acorn-brown eyes narrowing as marbles ricocheted in her stomach. She drew a deep breath to slow her heartbeat.

This was the hard part—

Time to seal the deal.

Avery's anxiety always spiked at moments like this, when she was forced to transform herself into an Ice Queen and demand what she was worth—and then some. She'd worked her butt off for five years to build up this business, and she knew her success depended on two things: raw talent and pure guts. Swiftly, she scribbled her terms on a notepad, adding an extra ten percent just to prove she had moxie. Then she went for it.

"You realize that to produce a calendar with new cowboy images for only Stampede, my rates would have to be…tripled. Up front. And I insist on my studio logo being featured prominently on the calendar as well as receiving…sixty percent…of the profits."

"Deal," Dixie agreed faster than Avery could blink. "Congratulations, Ms. Smart. You've just gone nationwide!"

Avery glanced in shock across the room at her assistant Shae, who was filing her long pink fingernails and applying tiny, black buckaroo stickers to the edges. Startled, Shae met her gaze and punched the speaker button on the office phone at her desk, tilting forward to listen to the conversation.

"Tripled rates and sixty-percent profit on the calendar it is," Dixie confirmed. "My one stipulation is that you supply all images to us within three weeks. We ship calendars to our stores in the fall, and we need the images ahead of time for promo. Will that work for you, Ms. Smart?"

"Absolutely," Avery lied in a silvery tone, staring at Shae with abject panic in her eyes. "I'll send you the contract and invoice right away, and you'll have your images within three weeks."

"Thank you!" Dixie trilled. "It's such a pleasure to feature your cowboys in our product line. It must be wonderful to photograph all those brawny men who were born to forge frontiers and win the hearts of women," she sighed wistfully. "They look so loyal, with that twinkle in their eyes that says they'll be yours *forever*."

Right, forever—as sincere as Satan himself, Avery thought. Because it's all a lie, sold through expert marketing.

The truth was, Avery had never met a "forever cowboy" in her life—without a price. She'd grown up in Bandits Hollow, Colorado, an old western town in the Rocky Mountains historically famous for hiding outlaws. And she'd seen first hand the way most girls from her high school had gotten their hearts shattered by love 'em and leave 'em cowboys. Or worse, thrown away their career aspirations to chase good-looking guys in Stetsons and spurs with big rodeo dreams, only to discover that they'd lost their identities along the way. That was never going to happen to Avery—she was determined to be her own woman. Yet her knack for choosing exactly the right cowboys who appeared as hot and loyal as every woman's fantasy had vaulted her into one of the fastest-growing commercial photography studios in Colorado. It didn't hurt that the cowgirl-gypsy fashion trend was all the rage, and advertising firms as far away as Fort Collins were demanding a constant stable of handsome cowboys as backdrops for their ad campaigns. Avery's timing couldn't have been better.

"Well, Dixie," Avery concluded their conversation, "I'm thrilled you love our unique brand of sexy and sincere cowboys. We'll be in touch soon," she promised. "Have a My Forever Cowboy day!"

Avery hung up the receiver and sank her head into her hands.

"Oh Shae, what have I done?" she moaned. "You heard her! She wants twelve photos of new cowboys in *three weeks*. Who look rugged and loyal to the bone, of course. Do you have any idea how hard that is to find? Even if it is make believe?"

"All the more dates for me!" Shae giggled, fluttering her fingers and admiring the buckaroo decals on her nails. "Besides, MFC will make a *ton* more money now that it's gone national. So tell me, should I wear a black minidress and boots to go with these nails, or more of a neon-pink rodeo ensemble? I love scouting for new cowboys!"

Shae grinned, her smile making her sweet face all the more adorable, framed by blonde, curly hair and sparkly pink eyeshadow that matched her lips. But then her glossy mouth fell into a pout.

"Too bad I never manage to keep any of them."

"Oh Shae, we've been over this," Avery sighed, tapping her pen and glancing out her office window at the downtown buildings of Colorado Springs. "You grew up in a suburb here, not way out on a ranch like me. Take it from a veteran of Bandits Hollow, there are only two types of forever cowboys. One is hot and sexy, rides bulls or broncs, and is great for one-night stands pretty much forever—even if he's married to somebody else. But if you want to see him more than once a year, you'll have to follow him on the rodeo circuit, shine his spurs, and put up with all of his other...shall we say...dalliances? Before he finally breaks a hip or his back and needs a full-time nurse, of course. The second type of forever cowboy is over forty and has a paunch, owns land three hours from *anywhere*, and will be loyal to you to kingdom come if you move to *his* ranch, attend *his* grandma's church and punt out at least three of *his* kids—with no time off for good behavior."

"Can't you find one that's *both*?" Shae asked, looking dejected. "You know, sexy and loyal?"

"There's no such thing!" Avery shook her head, knowing that hot-to-trot Shae had blistered through nearly all of the cowboys in her studio arsenal, and she was running out of inventory.

"Why not?" Shae protested, appearing miffed. "Maybe we just need to try harder. You know, beat the sagebrush a little more."

Avery leaned forward on her elbows and stared intently at Shae to make her point. "Repeat after me: hot, sexy cowboys don't abandon their thrill-seeking ways to move to the suburbs to be cabana boys, mix fruity drinks, and service young women's needs. Alpha, Shae—they're all alpha! Sure, you may dress like the sweetheart of the rodeo, but unless you feel like giving up your family and friends and that shopping mall you're addicted to, you're dreaming. This is more than country-line dancing at the Saddle Swap Bar and then going back to your old life. Cowboys always want you to give up everything," she paused with a fragile crack in her voice, "and then they *leave*. Got it? So I suggest you have as good a time as you can until the right kind of forever comes along. Which won't be a cowboy."

"But I hate paunchy! I'm too young for a guy who isn't fit. By the way, today's nail base color is hot pink," she insisted, holding up her bottle of polish. "It wouldn't kill you to spend a little more time on upkeep. As in, look approachable for a change? I have enough polish to do all of your nails—both hands and feet."

Avery glanced down at her neutral-beige nails that coordinated with her crisply-tailored, ivory blazer and skirt, specifically designed to keep rough and ready cowboys *away*, not attract them. She rolled her eyes.

"Cowboys are the drug, and I'm the pusher."

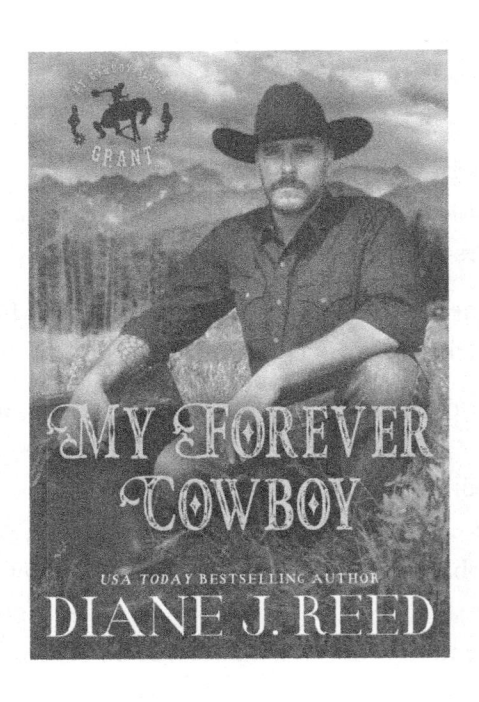

Just when you least expect it, love finds you forever...

Buy now!

UTE LANGUAGE GLOSSARY

The fictional characters in *Lander Ridge* are not fluent speakers of the Ute language, nor did they grow up on a Ute reservation. In the story, however, Tavinika Box acquired a few Ute words in childhood, primarily from her grandmother who had a more traditional upbringing. The following Ute words featured in the novel are listed in alphabetical order with translations and approximate phonetic pronunciations in English. Please bear in mind that many Ute sounds are either highly complex or do not exist in English. As a result, pronunciation accuracy can only be given justice by listening to a native Ute speaker. All Ute terms in *Lander Ridge* were derived from either native speakers or from the *Ute Dictionary* by T. Givón with Pearl Casias, Vida Peabody, and Maria Inez Cloud, John Benjamin Publishing Company, Southern Ute Tribe, Ignacio, Colorado, 2016 or from the *Ute Language Dictionary* by Evin P. Holle, Robert Gallegos, and John Green, Southwest Public Services, Durango, Colorado, May 1976.

danáskés: (dah + nah + skehz) **new moon.** The accent marks indicate stressing those vowels during speech.

kagu-chi̱: (kah + gooch [+ ee]) **maternal grandmother.** The underline beneath the last vowel indicates it is either whispered or silent, depending on the tradition of the speaker.

káni̱: (kahn [+ ee]) **home, dwelling.** The accent mark indicates stressing the first vowel, while the underline beneath the last vowel indicates it is either whispered or silent, depending on the tradition of the speaker.

múu-pu-chi̱: (moo + oo + pooch [+ ee]) **owl.** The accent mark indicates stressing the first vowel, while the underline beneath that last vowel indicates it is either whispered or silent, depending on the tradition of the speaker.

náyu̱-kwa-pu̱: (nah + y[uh] + kwahp [+ oo]) **hand game.** The accent mark indicates stressing the first vowel, while the underlines beneath vowels indicate they are either whispered or silent, depending on the tradition of the speaker.

pia-kwiya-chi̱: (pee + yah + kwee + yahch [+ ee]) **mother bear.** The underline beneath that last vowel indicates it is either whispered or silent, depending on the tradition of the speaker.

pia-muguan: (pee + yah + moo + gwan) **my sweetheart.**

sakwakar: (sah + kwah + kahr) **turquoise.**

sinae-vi̱: (see + nah + ev [+ ee]) **wolf.** The underline beneath the last vowel indicates it is either whispered or silent, depending on the tradition of the speaker.

Tava: (tah + vah) **Sun Mountain or Pikes Peak.**

tavachi̱: (tah + vahch [+ ee]) **sun.** The underline

beneath the last vowel indicates it is either whispered or silent, depending on the tradition of the speaker. However, when used as an individual's name, the last vowel is often pronounced.

tavinika: (tah + vee + nee + kah) **sunshine.**

yogho-vu-chi: (yo + go + vooch + [ee]) **coyote.** The underline beneath the last vowel indicates it is either whispered or silent, depending on the tradition of the speaker.

ADDITIONAL TERMS

Ute: (yoot) The origin of the word Ute is unknown, but *Yuta* was first used to denote the Ute tribe in Spanish colonial documents. The Utes refer to themselves as *núu-chi*, meaning "the people." Members of the Ute tribe speak a southern Numic branch of the Uto-Aztecan language group, and according to tribal members, have lived in the region of present-day Utah and Colorado for thousands of years where they hunted, fished, and gathered food. The Utes consider themselves to be the first Native American tribe to acquire the horse in the early seventeenth century after the Spanish imported horses to the New World, and subsequently they became a revered horse warrior culture that also engaged in raiding and fierce warfare. In addition to their home regions in Colorado and Utah, their hunting grounds extended into Wyoming, Oklahoma, and New Mexico, and their baskets, tanned hides, and exquisitely crafted clothing were highly prized at trading posts and fairs.

AUTHOR'S NOTE ABOUT SACRED TREES

In 2016, I went on a hike by my home in Colorado near Pikes Peak and took a photo of an unusually beautiful tree. It was a tall ponderosa pine with high branches, bent at distinct right angles, that formed a wishbone shape in the sky. Because there was a lovely sunset at the time that shined through the tree's branches, I posted an inspiring image of this tree on social media (which I later took down). To my surprise, an enrolled member of the Ute tribe soon contacted me regarding this specific tree. He told me the tree was very sacred to his people, and that members of his tribe had been lovingly fashioning the tree into the shape I saw now over a period of centuries. Ponderosa pines can live up to eight-hundred years, and this tree was approximately four-hundred-years old, based on its identifying features, so I knew the man's timeline was credible. Then the Ute man asked me if I would mind doing a ceremony to "refresh" the spirit and medicine inherent in the tree, which involved following a certain ritual developed generations ago by the Ute tribe. This ritual, he believed, would heal the chronic pain that had been plaguing his back, and because he lived a great distance from the tree, he sent me several sacred items through the mail to accomplish this task. He also had to get permission from the Ute tribal council to share the correct prayer with a non-Ute individual, as well as to inform me of the specific steps that the ritual required. In addition, I was to vow not to tell anyone of the sacred Ute terms employed in the ritual, nor was I allowed to share the ritual's exact steps and meanings. After he later sent me a thorough instruction packet for the entire ceremony, I agreed to do the private ritual for him.

A month later, the man was healed.

I was deeply humbled and honored to participate in this age-old Native American ceremony, and out of respect for the Ute tribe, I am not at liberty to share details about this experience except in the most general of terms. It is historically well-documented that for centuries the Utes modified many trees into different sacred shapes, particularly on their yearly pilgrimages to Pikes Peak (or *Tava*), which served their tribe's needs for ceremony, medicine, directions, memorials, spiritual development, and even prophecy. Several Utes have gone on record to discuss the doorway or portal quality to certain trees as well, which enabled them to speak with their ancestors and the holy people of their tribe to receive instruction and blessing. Though I can't divulge how these spiritual traditions were employed, I can say that the venerated knowledge about the sacred trees among the Ute is *vast*, and what appears in this

AUTHOR'S NOTE ABOUT SACRED TREES

novel is only the tip of the iceberg and can be found in many public documents and texts regarding the Ute's traditions. It is not my intention to impinge on the Ute's privacy about their rituals, but rather, to simply demonstrate in fictional form how blessed we are to have these sacred trees still in existence. It is my hope that, due to the diligence of many professionals who endeavor to identify and document the remaining Ute sacred trees, every effort will be made to preserve these ancient works of beauty and wonder. It is also my fondest wish for readers to find special trees in their own lives to bond with, pray with, and share the magic of love and healing.

ABOUT THE AUTHOR

USA TODAY bestselling author Diane J. Reed writes happily ever afters with a touch of magic that make you believe in the power of love. Her stories feed the soul with outlaws, mavericks, and dreamers who have big hearts under big skies and dare to risk all for those they cherish. Because love is more than a feeling—it's the magic that changes everything.

To get the latest on new releases, sign up for Diane J. Reed's newsletter at dianejreed.com.

Made in the USA
Las Vegas, NV
24 May 2022

49301324R00173